ALSO BY BRADLEY SOMER

Imperfections

Fishbowl

Extinction

WE ARE ALL OF US LEFT BEHIND

WE ARE
US LEFT
BRADLEY

A

ALL OF

BEHIND

SOMER

NOVEL

Freehand Books gratefully acknowledges the financial support for its publishing program provided by the Canada Council for the Arts and the Alberta Media Fund, and by the Government of Canada through the Canada Book Fund.

This book is available in print and Global Certified Accessible™ EPUB formats.

Freehand Books is located in Moh'kinsstis, Calgary, Alberta, within Treaty 7 territory, and on the traditional territories of the Siksika, the Kainai, and the Piikani, as well as the Iyarhe Nakoda and Tsuut'ina nations.

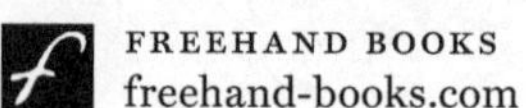

LIBRARY AND ARCHIVES CANADA CATALOGUING IN PUBLICATION
Title: We are all of us left behind : a novel / Bradley Somer.
Names: Somer, Bradley, author.
Identifiers:
Canadiana (print) 20250229749
Canadiana (ebook) 20250229765
ISBN 9781990601927 (softcover)
ISBN 9781990601934 (EPUB)
ISBN 9781990601941 (PDF)
Subjects: LCGFT: Novels.
LCGFT: Queer fiction.
Classification: LCC PS8637.O4479 W4 2025 | DDC C813/.6—dc23

Edited by Deborah Willis
Design by Natalie Olsen
Cover photos:
Sky © WhataWin/Shutterstock
Rome © Artokoloro/Alamy
Club © Boris Jovanovic/Stocksy
Blossoms from *The Tree Book* by Julia Ellen Rogers, 1920
Author photo by Phil Crozier
Printed and bound in Canada

FIRST PRINTING

for anyone stuck in a three a.m. airport.

2005

BOOK I

1

My name is Molly.

I'm fourteen years old.

I'm glad to meet you.

Only one of these things is true, which is okay. I type them and click the button to send them to a guy in this chat room who asks me a bunch of questions. I don't feel bad about these lies for a lot of reasons. I think I use them only when I have to. I've told so many and can see when they help out. They're all I have at the moment and they're a tool I'm used to now and get better at using the more I need money.

And money's needed really pretty badly right now.

Lies don't run out like money or time or people do. Lies don't go missing, like parents and friends can, no matter what their reasons. There're always more. So, right now, I tell them to whoever sits, lit up in their own computer screen glow.

The computer chimes like a bell. It does every time someone writes something. He asks me into a private chat and I click through into it with him. It always gets bad in the private chats, but that has to be part of it. He asks me a bunch of questions, one bell sound after the other, and I answer them in turn.

I'm wearing a dress my mom gave me.

There're flowers printed on it.

It's green, my favourite colour.

Only one of these is true, which is okay.

I don't know this guy or even where he is in the world. That's the best part, he doesn't know me or where I am in the world either. Whoever's on the other end is going to full-on deserve what's coming. I'm going to deserve what I get, too. I know it. It always just seems to work out that way. Can't much escape it, so best to accept it's on the way and deal with it when it knocks.

To strangers, lies go easy from me. They don't matter. To friends, they're harder because it's like each one twists up a bit of the real me into something else, but I don't have any friends. Not here. Not anymore. No matter to who, the more the lies fill up my past, the harder it is to keep them straight and from piling into one another. One told today crashes into one told last week or yesterday or an hour ago. But, right now, it's easy because there's nobody here but me, sitting in the sound of the air conditioner running hard under the window. It's late-afternoon hot outside. I can't put on more clothes without sweating, that's why I'm just sitting in boxers. It's been like this for days.

The curtains are drawn. There's nothing much to be missing out there but the view of a parking lot. Past that's the highway, the strip of shops on the other side, then a few rows of rooftops. The river's hidden between them and the far hill, on the other side of the valley. That river cuts dinosaur bones out of the dust, enough for the university to take notice and come digging. The hills behind give oil, enough to see one nodding donkey from the next. There're some up on the ridge. I remember when you could only see one, all spinning parts, unceasing. Now, there are seven. I can't remember when the others showed up.

Aren't more than a thousand people in this town. It's where I grew up for eighteen years. I went out to see the trailer, still sat an hour's gravel-road walk past the town line and down a bit of dirt track from there. It was pretty broken up. My room was wrecked, broken bottles and beer-can bongs with burnt craters in the aluminum dents. The bookshelf was broken and all my posters torn off. Someone shit in the corner. Some animal had made a home in a kitchen cabinet. No one there though, didn't think there'd be, but something made me go check that my dad wasn't around again.

Eighteen years, this town. That's a lie though. I haven't been back here since four years ago, when I had to leave. I came back because there's nowhere else familiar and these small places don't change much. Of course, a lot of people who lived here knew me, but not too many do now. The kids I knew from back then, most are gone somewhere else. Most here grow up with the sole purpose to leave. Also, a kid changes a lot in four years, becomes a stranger at a passing glance. I haven't left this motel room much, anyhow.

The guy at the pawnshop, he didn't know me, but he knew I had money enough to buy this old laptop he was probably happy to get rid of, judging from the skin of dust on it. I'm not too good at computers, but for what I need it for, I'm good enough. The guy knew my money was as good as the next's and that's all.

This place exists between better ones, at the right distance to stop and rest before moving on in the morning. There're enough people passing through for there to be two motels, basic rooms telling on this geography, a good-enough bed, a toilet, a shower.

Of the two motels, this one has free internet. This one, with the curtains drawn and the hot sunlight creeping in yellow around the edges like some stain on the wall, is where I set up my pawnshop computer. This one, with the constant rattle of the air conditioner underneath the window that drowns the highway noise, is where I type the words, Sure, I can send you a picture.

Then I type, If you send me one first.

The cursor flashes on and off and on.

I've done this a bunch of times over the week and I'm never sure what the next chime will bring. I pull a leg up and rest my chin on my knee, run light fingers over the scars there, knee to ankle and back up again, feeling the smooth bumps but not really paying attention.

I stare at the screen and wait, wait, wait.

I've figured out a lot of ways to get by. None are good. Most of them are done because they have to be done. I'm getting good at this one. It's paid out three times and it's a lot easier than some other ways I've earned enough to eat. I'm still waiting for the computer to ring, to see what he sends me back. I get up and stretch my legs. My armpits are sweaty, and even though it's trying hard, the air conditioner can't get the room cool.

At least here, I get to sit and watch teevee. There's a bed if I want to lie down, though I can't sleep. My dad told me I didn't sleep much since I was born and that holds true through now. There's a shower when I need it and food from the vending machine over near the office. I like the dill pickle flavoured chips. Second favourite is jalapeño and cheddar. They're good, too.

Sometimes at night, with the curtains drawn back, I just watch out the window for the cars coming and going on the highway. The rigs, I can't help always squinting to see the driver, to see if that silhouette is my dad. No matter if I close my eyes, no matter the time, I can hear them coming and have to look.

Those late hours are my favourite because they're quiet. Sometimes, there's no car for half an hour, more. Sometimes, I'll open the door and sit a chair on the parking spot in front of my room. It'll still be hot outside. It's late in the year for it. Breeze or still air don't matter, it comes up in waves from the pavement, but it'll be quiet under the street lights along the highway. I can sit alone and listen to the air conditioners running in the other rooms around me, until later, when the last one shuts off and all that's left is the distant metal rattle of them pumpjacks up on the ridge.

And there's the free internet, which is what I really needed.

I go back to the computer and type the words, Are you there?

And I send them.

I wait, wait.

Sometimes they don't send anything back, just disappear like they were never there, nothing left of them except some typed words to scroll back through to see if there's anything I can use. There never is. I'm always curious about who's on the other end, but I'll never know.

Everyone's looking for someone here, all looking for different things, and I'm whatever they want. It's easy to figure out. If you pay a little attention, they'll tell you. To strangers, my name is Molly or Mary or Martin or whoever. I'm blonde or chubby or small or whatever. I'm a schoolgirl or choirgirl or an after-practice-locker-room boy, whatever. I'm lots of things but none of them. I'm onto something good.

I wait.

I know he's still there because the computer hasn't told me he's gone. Maybe he's scared or nervous; maybe he's just trying to take the perfect picture to send. Maybe his wife or girlfriend walked in or maybe he's pulling the blinds closed, hiding the outside world from what he's doing. Maybe it's going to get that bad. Maybe he's thinking of what else to say or maybe he's just trying to figure out the point of all this.

The computer bell rings and he's typed, Yes, I'm still here.

Then he sends, Where are you? Alone?

To strangers, I'm whatever they want even if they don't really believe me. Even if they're suspicious that I'm a lie, they still fool themselves that I'm truth, every one of them. They believe me because they want to so bad and it's easy to be blind when their dreams are right in front of them.

I type, Yes, I'm alone.

I type, I'm at home and my parents went off to a friend's party and won't be back until real late.

The cursor blinks.

The air conditioner rattles.

The computer chimes and the message asks, Where's home?

I type that I'm not stupid, that I'm not telling.

The computer chimes, I'm in Ontario.

I type, So weird, I'm in Ontario, too. Kingston.

I type, What should we talk about?

The cursor blinks.

The computer chimes.

His words there read, What I want to do to you.

This was the only way this conversation would go. From the very start, it had to end up here. In the short time I've spent doing this, there've been one or two of these conversations every day. At first it was hard because, whenever a guy walked by the motel or when I went out to get food, I couldn't stop thinking everyone

I saw was the guy on the other end of this conversation. Then, I figured out to think like it's a job and I'm talking to a computer, a pervert computer sure, but thinking of it like this makes it easier. Sometimes it pays out and sometimes it don't, but it's cheap to do and the numbers are here to play at this for as long as I want.

The computer chimes and chimes with line after line of things that shouldn't be thought. I prompt with a few shy questions, like Molly might ask if she was alone and behaving like her parent's worst nightmare.

I type, What's that?

I type, How big?

I type, I don't know, maybe.

That's all it takes for fuel. The stream of chimes mostly runs itself. The nasty rolling in all on its own.

I type, What's your name?

The computer chimes, Mr. Langman.

The computer chimes, Or Daddy.

I type, What do you look like?

The computer chimes and images flash onto the screen. A bit out of focus, a shelf with books and a few photos on it, blurry in the background, quick pictures for me to look at his body, his face, and those're the last pieces of the puzzle.

I type, Email a thousand dollars or I'll send these pictures and our chat to the cops. Then I type an email address and click the button to send it.

My heart pounds from waiting. Doesn't make much sense, sitting here safe but still being so scared. But it happens like this every time.

I tell lies because some people deserve to be told them. Some people can't sort them from the truth, and most don't deserve to have the truth told. Some people want them. I like to think I only lie to people who need it and I'm honest with everyone else, but sometimes I catch myself doing it just because I can.

The idea is simple enough, there are dark corners online where the Mr. Langmans live. I read it in the news and thought out how

I could get Mr. Langman from Atlanta or London or Toronto to give up something that I could find him with, or at least something that makes him think I could find him. Then Mr. Langman tells me a bunch of the nasty and sends me a picture or two he probably wouldn't want anyone else to see. There's his face and there's his dick and then we're done. I got one of those free email accounts you can get without giving anything of your information in return, the kind that's perfect for this. I tell him to email some money and I'll wipe everything and we both can move on. I never need to do anything about it, just the threat is enough to run him scared.

No matter what, he's not telling me where he wants to stick his dick anymore. He's shy now. He's small. Even if I can't find him or even try to, he's no longer in charge. He realizes what he's done and he'll do anything to keep it hid. Most Mr. Langmans just disappear, the chat room tells me so with a line of text on the screen. I imagine their coming months, wondering if his wife will get an email from me or if it's the cops whenever someone knocks on his door. Some Mr. Langmans get angry and say things like I'm going to kill you and rip your head off and far worse stuff than that. And some Mr. Langmans act all quiet and meek, beg just please don't tell, I'll do anything, just don't tell. Those Mr. Langmans transfer some money, a thousand, two thousand dollars, whatever, depending on what I think Molly or Mary or Martin can get away with. Then it goes to my bank account.

I wait to see what this Mr. Langman will do.

The cursor blinks.

I bet he'll disappear, just a feeling. This one probably won't stay and pay. He doesn't seem like one of the ones to get mad and threaten either, but you never can tell what a person will do when there's nothing left but the wall at their back.

I stand up from the bed and stretch my arms over my head. My shoulders crackle and my elbows pop, and it feels like I've been at this forever. The clock on the bedside table glows red numbers, early evening, but that doesn't mean much because I can't remember when I sat down in front of the computer to start with.

The cursor blinks.

He hasn't left the chat, still sitting there somewhere in the hotel room next door or in a dark bedroom two thousand kilometres gone, staring at his own computer screen glow. Maybe he's thinking on which of the three things he's going to do, disappear, pay, or rage.

I cross the room to the window. The air conditioner blows cool air across my stomach and I pull the edge of the curtain back. I squint because it's bright, even though the sun's setting on this side of the valley, up on the flat land behind my room. The far ridge is still in full light, but the base of the hill, the valley bottom where this motel sits, it's shadow now. The parking lot light comes on even though the sky's still blue.

It's a weekday and there's only one car in the parking lot. More will come in over the next few hours, when the sun is set and the night is full and people decide they've done enough driving for a day. Most nights it's like that, the dull clap of a car door over the air conditioning rattle, and then the teevee noises seep through the walls. Sometimes I hear voices outside, not words, just noises, as they smoke a cigarette or get bags out of the trunk or just move around, stretching the road out of their legs.

The computer chimes and I blink because I had faded away, staring at the dry hill on the far side of the valley. I wasn't thinking how the dirt is ashes-grey there or how the dried-up plants look like sun-bleached paint in the twilight or how they're a colour I don't think I've seen anywhere else. I wasn't thinking how I've lived mostly here in this valley, eighteen years with a kilometre-wide horizon. I wasn't thinking how I've gotten used to the airlessness or how these valley walls feel as much like safety as they do a cage.

I wasn't thinking any of this, just staring.

In my time spent in this room, I don't think I've slept, only drifted like this sometimes.

The other night I sat in the motel's laundry, behind the office, the cinderblock walls, glossy, cream-coloured paint reflecting pitted green lines of wet fluorescent light. The door propped open with a grey-water janitor's bucket, I watched the dryer spin my clothes for forty minutes. I don't remember any of it, just the buzz when the machine stopped. When I hugged my clothes from the machine, I noticed the moths and night-bugs tracing lines in the air as they battered up against the light. I'm thinking of all this now though, when the computer chimes again.

Another message from Mr. Langman.

The curtain slips from my fingers.

I cross the room back to sit on the bed. The screen has gone dark, but it comes on when I touch a key. There're two messages.

I'm not in Ontario, one reads.

Neither are you, one reads.

I stare. The words fuzz out, the blinking cursor, on and off and on. I rub my eye with a fist. I pull my ankles up under me to sit cross-legged on the rumpled sheets.

This is new, not mad or pleading or disappearing, but fighting. I haven't run into this before, so I have to think on what to do. Maybe I now have the same options that all the Mr. Langmans did. I can get mad, get scared, or disappear myself as easy as clicking the chat room closed.

I choose mad.

I type, Doesn't matter where you say you are because the cops are still going to be keen on you.

I type, Send money and it all goes away.

My heart's pounding hard again and I didn't know it until now. My hands shake a bit because I wonder if he really figured out I'm not where I say, and from that, can he know where I actually am? He can't . . . probably. I'm not totally sure.

I wait, tracing a slow hand up and down my leg, but don't really think of it, the scars like river-smooth pebbles rippling under my fingers. The air conditioner rattles heavier. The light creeping around the curtain isn't as bright anymore, tinted deeper orange than it was before.

The clock on the computer tells that it's past suppertime and the sun will be all the way gone soon. I think of what I want to eat. Maybe the dill pickle chips or maybe I'll cross the highway and get a burger and fries and a soda. I'm so hungry I could eat all that, so decide that's what I'll do, whenever Mr. Langman's sorted.

The computer screen goes off, again.

I sit until the feeling goes out of my leg, leaving it all fizzy.

Now I'm curious about what he'll do, not chicken like I was a few minutes ago. He can't know me or anything about me. All he knows is I'm not Molly, and the funny part is, he only knows me as Molly. He knows nothing.

The computer chimes and I click the screen to come on.

The message reads, Be here tomorrow. Same time.

I start to type a message back, but only get a few letters in before a line of text comes telling me Mr. Langman has logged off. I look at his last note and read it a few times. I'm pretty sure he can't know where I am, but don't know enough about it to be certain. This is the middle of nowhere in the real world, so it's probably even more nowhere in the computer world.

The air conditioner shudders to a stop now the sun's been off the building for long enough. The silence is complete, as it can only be after steady noise for hours ends.

The computer screen goes dark.

I blink.

After a while, through the walls and shut-tight window, I realize I'm listening for the shush of the occasional car passing on the highway. It's a unique sound, a sticky one that passes from one end of the room to the other, quickly even though the speed limit is slower through town. The light creeping around the curtain is milky blue and the walls are close and the ceiling is close and it's hard to breathe, like the air was all used up a while ago.

I've been sitting in this room for so long that the sunrise and sunset only happen in that gap around the curtains. I'm thinking about stuff too much and know I won't sleep, not a chance of it now. I pull on my jeans and put my teeshirt on. I grab my notebook and pen from the nightstand.

The computer chimes as I step out the door, but I don't go back to see who's checking into the chat room. I'm done for now, tired of working with lies and my brain feels dull and I need a burger or something. I close the door and rattle the handle to check it's locked.

The numbers one-eleven were painted black on the red door, but are now sun-faded grey on pink. There's always too much sun here. The whole town is washed out and tired by it.

2

The "Vacancy" sign draws twitchy neon outlines of the two cars parked in the deep blue evening. The pavement throws back a bunch of heat it stole from the day, ripples the air like ghosts, if you believe such things. My armpits sweat rings. I stop at the highway and look both ways. A set of traffic lights a few blocks up drops green onto the road, but there're no cars right now, just someone standing by the side, near the gas station, the silhouette of a woman in front of the red and white awning light. She paces a few steps up, a few back. I start across and it's good to move the blood, my legs have been closed up in that room too long.

Across the highway, over a stripe of sunburnt grass and past a chip-paint concrete stegosaurus, I walk through the electric doorbell of the burger place. The air smells fried and the light is sharp grey compared to the thick dark piled up outside. The place is clean, but worn out. The tiles on the floor are from decades ago and the posters on the wall are from decades ago, when they still advertised big burgers and piles of fries, before the place got so ingrained in this town they didn't need ads anymore.

Laminated newspaper clippings are on the walls. Serving girls on roller skates used to bring trays of food to your car window. They don't anymore, but there's a bunch of pictures from when they did. Sodas used to come in glass bottles. They don't anymore. The place used to have a giant highway sign with a smiling dinosaur on it. It's gone, too. Now, they don't stay open too late on weeknights, but there's still half an hour before they close tonight, so still enough time to eat.

The guy behind the counter is a bit younger than me maybe and I know I've seen him around, just can't place where. He's thinking the same thing and jerks his chin at me, says, "Hey."

I nod and tell him a burger and fries and a large orange soda. I pay and he counts me back some change, then he's gone to the back. The fryer bubbles and I like that the fries will be fresh. I sit at a table by the window.

I write in the notebook I brought with me. I want to write a book so I spend lots of time working on bits of it that don't seem to come together properly. It seems easy when I read books, looking at how stories are made, how they make sense and paint a picture in my imagination, but I think it's harder to put one together. I'm just starting though, just learning about it. It's something that helps pass the nights.

Waiting for my food, I write about the traffic lights going green-yellow-red, again and again, where they hang over the near-abandoned highway that cuts this place in half. Looking now, the silhouette woman is gone, just the stegosaur's left.

I want to write the motel vacancy sign into words, how I can hear it glowing when it's so quiet near sunrise because the town is sleeping and the air conditioners aren't working like they do all day. I try to write how the power lines are swoops hung from one star to the next and how the pumpjacks are creeping closer to town all the time, circling right up to the edge. I try to write the feeling of this town being sunk deep into the earth, like underwater, like pulled down, and the feeling that everyone who passes through looks at how pretty these valley walls are, and then they keep moving.

I write down how bright the lights of the burger place seem right before closing time and how me and the cook are the only two guys in it, in the middle of it all.

Then he calls out that my burger's ready and puts my tray of food on the counter. I get it and go back to my table.

It feels like forever since I ate anything that didn't fall out of a vending machine, feels flash to spend a few bucks on a full meal. I don't have much cash left, but don't want to get what I earned from the Langmans out of the bank just yet, don't want to part with the money I have that easy. There's still enough for another couple days at the motel and then it'll be time to go. Good things only last a short while and never longer.

The burger is good and the fries are hot and salty. I didn't know how hungry I was until I started eating. The parking lot, it stays empty and I eat looking out, but there isn't much to look out at.

The burger guy moves in the window reflection, checks the clock on the wall. I like to look at him when he doesn't know, like now, his wooly double reflected in the night glass. I like the colour of his eyes and the line of his jaw. I like the square of his shoulders and how his voice is, stupid of me though because he only ever says a few words. It's easy to be here, not like most places.

He looks over and I look down, but he can't know I'd been watching, more like he would see me staring into the dark parking lot, thinking or something. When I look again, he's back at his comic on the counter.

I think about Mr. Langman, about how he didn't get chicken, how he told me what to do and ignored me telling him. He knew I wasn't in Kingston, then reckon it was a guess, because of all the places in the world I could be, why would it be there? I worry a bit more about getting caught out, but then reckon I'm not the one trying to get on with little kids. I'm just the one taking his money because he is.

I eat some fries and figure that tomorrow, if Mr. Langman's logged in, I'm going to tell him again that it's all getting sent to the cops. If he mouths back, maybe I really will send it this time. I don't know if the cops would do anything, but they probably would.

I eat and read some of the stuff I wrote. None of it really came out like it was in my head, so I stop and think on it a while, but Mr. Langman keeps getting in the way. He didn't seem fussed by me and he seemed to know what he's going to do. He's messed in the head and he's got a plan. I don't have a plan beyond right now and that puts him the better of me, which is a place I don't like to be. I think of not being there when he signs in tomorrow, but I'm too curious and figure there's nothing he can do to me over the computer.

My soda's empty. The straw makes static when I suck it, and I ask the burger guy if I can have a refill. He looks up from his comic, shrugs, and says, "Sure." His eyes are dark brown.

I write a little more and try to make a story of this place, but can't keep it only fiction. Maybe it'll be a short story when it's done, maybe not enough for a whole novel. It's about a guy my age who steals a car and sells it in an alley for money because he's got none. He doesn't get caught by the cops or anyone, he doesn't get scammed or beat up, and he gets to keep the money. That's it. He leaves the keys in the hand of some guy and counts the money as he walks away, turning the corner from the alley onto the street. Then he skips out, catches a Greyhound back to his hometown.

I can't keep it only fiction and I can't make a point of the story. The guy who stole the car should get caught because then there's a lesson in it. But he doesn't get caught and after he sells the car, he has enough money for food, a pawnshop computer, and a motel room for a while. Things are better than they usually are for him and what's the lesson in that?

I fold my pen into the crease of the notebook and pin the book firm between my hand and the table.

The guy behind the counter closes his comic and clears his throat and tells me that it's time to lock up.

I say, "Okay."

I shake my cup. There's a little soda left in it, but it's mostly just the rolling gravel of ice. I get up, dump all my wrappers in the garbage and nod again as the guy follows me to the door, tumbling the lock from the inside when it's shut behind me.

I stand under the parking lot light for a bit because there's nowhere to go, kick a stone, look into the night. Up the highway, most of the stores are dark with only their signs left lit, tracing shadowed jags of parking lot cracks until the morning comes back. A car drives by, white headlights into red taillights. Country music comes through the window, quiet then loud then quiet, and then gone.

There're a few honey squares, lights on behind the curtains in the motel. On the sign, under the name, it reads "Free Internet" and still, "Vacancy." There's the heavy wall behind it, the valley back rising high, big and black. Above, a skunk's stripe of stars in the clear sky. I know what it is, that it's the galaxy spinning out, but can't think on it too long or too deeply without going crazy from how small it makes everything else.

Behind me and behind the glass, the restaurant lights go off and all that's left is a dim glow from somewhere far back in the kitchen. The burger guy's shadow comes through and out. He locks the door again. There's a skateboard under his arm and he sees me with a quick shock, like he didn't before.

He tells me to have a good night and I say it back. I really hope he'll say something else, ask me to hang out while he skates, but he just throws the board on the pavement, jumps on it and is gone. Fading wheels rattle the dark. The silence that follows makes me feel like the last person in an empty town.

I cross the highway and don't even look because there're no cars. I think about going back to my room, but it's too small and I've been in there too much and for too long, so I decide to walk the highway edge instead.

Anywhere but there. Anywhere but here.

A warm breeze nudges my sweat-damp teeshirt, but doesn't cool me any. I take my shirt off and hang it from the waist of my jeans like a tail. I feel better because I'm not as hot. It'll cool down by morning. It's still a while until then.

The motel is behind me. The traffic lights, the gas station, they're back there, too. The highway is beside me and the dry grass, what little of it there is, clumps like crumpled paper under my sneakers. The dirt the plants root in is fine sand. There's no sidewalk, but there is a black billboard with bright yellow letters, all lit up by lights hooked over the top, reading "Ready for Friday night? Cash advances for pay cheques. Turn right at the lights."

The highway edge seen from a moving car looks smooth, but it's a jaggy line from up close and at walking speed. I cross the driveway to the mechanic's shop, a rusty Toyota, a pickup truck with a tow hook, oil smell, and then I cross the one for the hardware store. There're a few houses set a short ways back, dark windows, tacked to the highway by dirt driveways. The breeze comes back, smelling like nothing and feeling good all over my skin at once.

I stand under the last street light. The highway keeps going on into the dark, or it doesn't because maybe it stops. I can't see it and that's what I'm trying to scratch down in my notebook, the last light throwing the world out another hundred feet, then gone. There, nothing is waiting to be anything. It's like how I can't remember the future and can't ever leave the past. And on the edge of light stands a man, head bowed and hands tucked behind, curved like black wings. I can't see him and don't know anything about him, but he's there, stood on the bone-coloured dirt in between scrubby tufts of grass, just off the pavement, Mr. Langman.

I can't remember the future, so I don't know what happens next.

That's what I write anyway, because he's in my head tonight.

Of course, I'm going to be there to see what he'll do. Maybe it'll be good, like he'll send me money. Maybe he won't show up or maybe something completely different will happen. Even if it's bad, I have to know it. I put my pen away and I put my notebook in my back pocket. I walk out to the edge of the light and then into the darkness on the other side.

My eyes are on the highway edge and my heart beats hard because it's chicken in the night. There's no moon out for light, not yet anyhow, later though. The occasional breeze slithers through the grass. Something fast darts from a bush. My heart splits and I try to reason that the rabbit's more scared than me. It was probably sitting there watching, getting more scared with each step closer, waiting to see if it'd get eaten, and then instinct overtook thought when the danger got too big. Better to run for it than hide tight and get eaten. No wolves to run from anymore though. Ranchers hunted them out a hundred years ago. But a rabbit doesn't know that danger's been shot dead because the ranchers hunt them, too. There're still coyotes, though I don't hear any of them right now.

I'm listening for other noises, for anything saying there's danger out here, but there's nothing.

Following the highway line, my eyes get used to the dark as much as they can and I see a bit better, but still not too much. After a while, I let the highway line go off in another direction, and then all around are clumps of dry grass and low shrubs and bone dirt that seems to glow cataract blue, as if by its own milkwater light. It can't be true, but seems it.

The breeze tugs on the shirt hanging from my jeans, runs gentle fingers across my chest, my back.

When I'm a long way gone from the last street light, when I'm a long time gone from where the highway left me to get lost, when there's no more breeze crossing my skin in one way or another, when all of that's done, I stop.

The valley is wide here, the land a little higher than the rest. Bone dirt goes out in every direction. Far back is the town, just half an orange bubble in the black. A truck, nothing but a string of red and white running lights, moves out there, quiet and barely heard when I hold my breath. It's then I look up. There's still no moon, but the stars are everywhere and clear and forever.

I sit in the dirt, looking up.

I lie on my back, looking up, barely blinking.

I'm in space.

There's a lot I don't know, sure, but this is certain, when history ends, the last person ever alive will feel alone this way. There may as well be just me left here tonight, dirt sticking to the sweat on my back, the breeze rolling whispers through the grass, a breath across my skin, and an everywhere depth of stars, all around, so deep that I keep falling up into it.

I put my arms out to the side, dust making mud of my sweat. A beetle crawls a tickle-line across my stomach and is gone, and with that feeling, everything goes. There's no more Mr. Langman on the dark side of the street lamp, no more fighting for money all the time, and no more worry without it. There's no burger place and no air conditioner rattling out the cool air from under the motel window.

There's nothing, and somewhere in this feeling of forever falling up, I finally find sleep. My dreams are black, like being awake out here, so I can't tell when it happens, but it does.

3

There's a lot I don't know, sure, but I know there're no ghosts in this valley, just a billion rabbits hiding scared in the brush. A coyote didn't eat me in the night and I hope most of the rabbits survived the same. I blink at the bruised sunrise creeping over the valley rim. The black edge turns purple to red.

I feel pretty good from sleeping, better than I have since staying in the motel. I shiver and sit up. The dirt doesn't glow anymore, not like it did when I came out here. It's forced to be orange instead. The highway is there, a black thread a mile away, stitching the town in place a ways back up the valley. A pumpjack works those faraway flats.

I used to do this sometimes when I was a kid, when Dad was working the rigs and not around for stretches. He would sometimes call around bedtime, to hear if I needed him to send money. He called me "Champ," which I liked. He'd be on a pay phone in some truck-stop parking lot with diesel engines idling loud behind his voice. He always sounded far away. He didn't mind being a dad whenever he was on the road, but the longer he was gone, the fewer times he'd call. After Mom was put away, he was barely around. I knew there'd come a time he wouldn't come back, could feel it, could hear it in his voice. He knew it, too. Here was too hard, so he was gone.

Sometimes I get it.

Sometimes I'm not even mad about it.

Some nights, after he called to hear that I was okay and I was going to bed on time and I was eating enough, after I was tired of reading my books and staring at the posters on my bedroom wall, I'd come out here. I'd walk out in any direction from the trailer's light and find a place in the valley to sleep. The first time I did it, might have been seven or eight years old, I remember being so chicken about it, like ghosts really exist out here or like a coyote was going to eat me or worse, just eat bits of me and I'd have to be alive through it.

All my bits are still here this morning and I stand and my muscles are stiff, but pretty good for having slept on the ground. I rub my hands over me, brushing dirt off my skin and my jeans best as I can. The air got cold and there're goosebumps on me, so I pull my teeshirt on and then work my palms together to get the dirt off them, too. I have to piss, so I do. No one's out here to see, so I'm not shy about it. Then I walk a distance back toward town, toward the highway, and have to trust that I'm getting closer even though it doesn't seem so.

Mr. Langman is in my head, even if I try to keep him from it.

The sun comes over the valley rim and starts heating my neck.

I'm hungry as my feet work the highway back, but I have only some coins left in my pocket and not much more in the room. I'll have to go for the money in my bank account soon, which is okay because I'm done. Playing at being Molly or Mary or Martin is taking more of me than I realized. It's all in my head now, how some people are. I can't be in that chat room much more.

The sky's come washed-out blue, almost white, and it will stay that way for the rest of the day. I reach the first street light. Just a painted metal post with the light at the top. Like most everything, it's less in the daylight than it had been in the dark.

The diner, past the set of traffic lights and on the other side of the highway from the gas station, it's been there since before I was born. It's got pretty good coffee and there's enough money in my pocket for that and probably some toast. There's usually a newspaper left behind to read and that's a good-enough way to wait out the morning.

I walk past the motel, room one-eleven with the air conditioner already running under the window. I can't even go back in there to get the rest of my money right now. It's like Mr. Langman's in there, waiting for me behind the door when I open it, waiting under the bed, no face just a shape, just a hazy bogeyman, a ghost. Anywhere but there.

Past the traffic lights and across the highway and through a door with a cardboard "Welcome" sign hung by a string. The waitress is Elise by her name tag. She looks at me a bit skewed, which is probably fair because I slept on the ground all night and probably look it. By the time I think she's going to kick me out, she waves me to a seat at the counter, in the corner and out of the way.

I push my coins around on the counter. Elise pours me a mug and asks what I want to eat. I'd love to tell her bacon and eggs and biscuits with white gravy on top. Instead, I fidget with my mug, look at my change, try to hide dirty fingernails, and tell her, "Toast."

She nods and scratches my order on her dog-eared notepad, tears the sheet off, and slides it over the counter to the kitchen. I rip open a few packets of sugar and dump them into my coffee. I pull the tops back from a few little containers of cream, pour them in, too. Stir it with a spoon. Drink it a bit.

I get bored of staring at the wall. There's a newspaper on the counter so I flip through the sections and pull out a few. They're a day old, but it doesn't matter much because this place is a day late in the world, too. I drink coffee and read the comics until Elise sets my toast on the counter and puts a napkin full of cutlery next to it.

I say, "Can I have some peanut butter and jam?" And she pulls a wire rack of little plastic packets from under the counter, tops up my coffee and says for me to enjoy the food, and I tell her thanks. She just nods and walks away. I spread peanut butter and blueberry jam as thick as the toast can hold.

The comic section isn't big and none of them are funny. I flip through the rest of the paper, fill out some more of a crossword that somebody's left half-done, while I eat toast and drink the coffee that Elise keeps topping up. I catch her once, out of the corner of my eye, watching, but she looks quick away.

When I'm done, she doesn't give me a bill and tells me not to worry about it. I leave my change next to my plate on the counter anyway. It's already hot outside.

4

There're no cars in the motel parking lot. The few who stayed are gone, always passing through. Car radio goes quiet when they kill the engine at night. Radio goes on the next morning, same station, different song. Blinker at the highway, and then gone.

All the air conditioners are quiet except for mine. The manager shuts them off when people check out, to save on the power bill. He doesn't much care if the room is hot when a guest checks in because it's not the kind of motel where anyone would expect better.

I fish my pocket for the key and open the door. The air's cool and the room's dark. I check behind the door because I thought earlier about Mr. Langman hiding there. It's impossible, but I look anyhow before sliding the chain-lock into place. I kick my sneakers off and poke the computer, but it doesn't come on. It's shut itself down. I relax a little because the room feels more private without the computer looking in.

The clock on the nightstand tells me it's a bit before lunch. I pull the notebook from my back pocket and toss it there, don't turn any lights on because there's enough sneaking in around the curtains. I stink and my clothes stink and Elise's coffee is working its way through me so I take my clothes off and leave them where they fall.

The air is cool and feels good on me, so I run a hand over myself before going to the bathroom to hang a piss. The little window set over the toilet looks out back the motel, a bright wash-out because my eyes got used to the dark in my room. Four wore-out tires are stacked out there, a few wooden pallets with rusty nails hooking out of them. A rusty roll of chicken wire leans against a tangle of scrub brush, an empty oil jug on its side, a plastic bag hung on a branch. The valley back isn't far behind those things, twenty feet, if even that. In the coulee cutting up the ravine there, are the closest things to trees that'll grow around here, hardwire scrub with small dust leaves.

When I'm done my piss I turn the shower on and get in. The water's cool on the back of my neck, over my shoulders, and I keep it that way. I shiver and watch pale grey dust track from my body, down my legs, and spin a milky circle around the drain between my feet. After a span, the water runs clear so I wipe soap over me, rinse it off, and then shut down the tap. I shiver but don't dry myself. It feels good to be cold, cheating the heat instead of sweating all the time.

At the bed, computer on, I check the screen. There're still a few hours to wait for Mr. Langman, so I lie down and turn on the teevee. It's car-racing noise with kitchen gadget commercials. I don't listen much and just drift in the sounds of the air conditioner, the teevee, its pictures flicking on and off and on.

After a bit, I grab my paperback from my backpack on the chair by the window. The book is falling apart, the spine long since broken, now chunks of pages held together with a rubber band. There's a yellowed newspaper clipping, folded over once and used as a bookmark. It's always been a part of the book, something my dad put in there the day he gave it to me, a second-hand birthday present from long ago and the last one I ever got from him. Only saw him a few times after that, and then gone.

I read the book though, learned all the words by heart. It's a book I'd read most often before walking away from the trailer light as a kid. The story's by a writer named Miloš Milić, about a guy who's dying from too many years living and he's trying to finish the last manuscript of his life. He never does finish.

He's writing in English, taught school in England when a civil war took his country away. He's won a bunch of prizes and his books are my favourites, though they're hard to find. I had them all on that now-busted bookcase in my old room, the ones that were translated or in English anyhow. Now, I only have this one and it's tatters.

I've got big plans to go meet him. Maybe he'll teach me because I want to learn, but maybe also because he's my granddad. My dad never talked much about him, always got this look on his face and walked away if I asked, maybe once saying something like, "He's no good." Maybe I'm just remembering what I made up, don't know anymore.

Good or bad, he doesn't know me, knows of me maybe, but I'm not sure. Such are things. And I want that, a granddad, a family where I'm safe and not alone all the time, some kind of family to help me, that I can help, something to be part of.

I've tried to find him, anything about him, but he returned home and there's nothing more about him. His name was in an article a few years back, but in an alphabet I don't know and a language I don't understand.

There's no one else.

He's all I know of.

I know it's weak, but blind hope is better than none at all. So, that's what it'll be. Besides, people in this valley were born for only two reasons: to leave or to get stuck. I won't get stuck.

I read the book until I don't want to anymore, then put it back into my pack. I've read it a hundred times through to the back cover, only to start at the front one again right away. The way he writes gets in my head and I can't let it go. The things he says make sense and sometimes they're the only things that really do.

I log into the chat room and wait. I go and pull the curtain back a bit and look outside. No cars, nobody here but me and the guy who owns the place. His silhouette moves like a ghost behind the parking lot reflected in the office window. I let the curtain drop. The teevee flickers its pictures and I can't hear it because the volume is turned low and the air conditioner is running loud. The computer screen goes off.

The room flashes like the light from the teevee, on then off then on, and it's putting me on edge because it's never still. I turn it off and go dig around my pack for a granola bar, but I must have eaten the last one. I find some cash in there, not much, enough for another night here and maybe another burger. Then I'll either have to cash out on my Mr. Langmans or sleep outside again, doesn't much matter which one. The way I reckon, I was born with a number of nights with a roof overhead and the rest without. That's what it's been so far and there's no reason to believe it'll change, since nothing else has.

I pull some clean clothes from my pack, put on boxers and jeans, pull on a shirt and my shoes. I step out into a wall of heat, wedge the door open a crack with my backpack because I don't take the room key. I walk across the parking lot to the vending machines in front of the office. Hollow coins into the slot and a bag of dill pickle chips falls out the bottom. The soda machine sounds like it's going to blast off. It's in full sun and trying to keep its belly full of cans cold. Behind the office window, the guy at the desk watches me. I watch him back. He doesn't do anything and I don't either. We just look at each other.

I go back to my room. The door clicks locked behind me and I eat the chips and wait.

5

The clock shows it's been more than a day since my chat with Mr. Langman. This feels wrong, the opposite of what it should be, me waiting on him and him playing at control, not the other way around. But I wait anyhow. I poke a key and check I'm still logged in. The chat room's there, waiting behind the dark screen. There's a scroll of text moving from bottom to top, silent words stacking up, everyone typing and talking, hidden from each other, knowing nothing except for those lines on the screen. Liberated to be whoever they want or unhindered to be whoever they are. Terrifying for the same reason, to see what they truly are. I don't think too long on who I'm being on there, or what it means of me. It's not real, the words on the screen, but somehow, it's become so.

When the screen goes black, I realize I've been staring at the lines going by as movement, not meaning. I look around my real world, my motel room space-pod with its air conditioner engine. The light creeping in around the curtains doesn't seem as bright as it did a while ago, but maybe I'm just wanting to see it that way. Willing time to pass is hard because it only seems to go on however it wants to. I grab the notebook from the nightstand and scowl at what's inside: nighttime traffic lights, ghosts and coyotes invisible in the valley.

I turn the page.

The next one is blank white.

The computer chimes.

A prickle climbs the back of my neck, a bug on spike legs. I blink and my heart skips a bit faster. I put the notebook down, put the pen down. The computer sounds again and I press a key and the screen comes on.

Molly, Mr. Langman has typed. Next line asks, Are you there?

I think for a moment of not sending anything back, not doing anything and maybe he'll just move along and away for good. I don't like the way he acts, bold, like he's the one with something on me.

The computer chimes, I know you're there, Molly.

He knows that's not my name, uses it now as a taunt. I wonder if I should correct him and tell him my real name. Big brave thoughts, sure, but I don't do it. I stare at the screen, chew a fingernail, and wait to see what happens next, like I still have a choice not to be a part of this.

He types, Come on, I'm tired. Been up all night and I know you're there.

Of course he knows, the chat room would have told him otherwise. I know it, too, but don't know what to say. The motel room is gone from around me. There's just the screen and I'm with Mr. Langman, seems like being sat right in front of him, seems like being inside his brain. It's uncomfortable how close he is.

I type and click the button to send, I'm here.

That's it and I wait. I figure the less I say, the less he can get into me.

The computer chimes, Still want your money?

The cursor flashes on and off and on.

This feels tricky, like the edge of something already going wrong, except I just don't know how wrong yet.

I type, Yes.

And the computer chimes, You're not going to get it.

And it chimes, You're going to give me your computer.

And it chimes, You've been enough trouble.

I don't know what's in me but I type, Send me the money now. Last chance.

I type, I'll send everything to the cops.

The cursor sits at the end of the words between us, on and off and on. And that's it, as far as this can go. No more words, no more manoeuvring. What's left is for waiting.

The clock tells me a few minutes pass. The colour of the light around the curtains is inching bluer. Over the sound of the air conditioner, I hear the bass thud of a car door, the murmur of someone talking, the sounds of people getting off the highway, end of a long day and starting to think of sleep, and here I am watching the cursor go on and off and on.

The computer chimes, Do you want to see another picture?

It chimes, I'm going to send you another picture.

I don't reply and don't have to because the image follows the words pretty quick. It's a picture of the sun-faded door to room one-eleven, the numbers washed to grey from black. The light is the bluing of early evening, same light that stains the wall around the curtains.

I can't even breathe.

I look at the door.

He's here, two inches of wood between us.

I didn't put the chain in place when I got back from the vending machine, just let the door handle click locked. It'd be easy enough to force. A shoulder could shake it from its hinges, so really, there's nothing between me and Mr. Langman.

I get up and move to the door. The spy hole gives a bent view of the world, a white pickup truck parked and a guy standing next to it, far enough away that he's just a blur in a baseball cap. I think he's looking at the door, but can't tell for sure because of the distortion. I quietly slide the chain into its track. It scrapes the loudest noise on Earth and I can't help wincing at it. Through the spy hole the figure moves, and for a moment, I can't tell which way. Then he's coming at my door.

Everything in me says to run, to get to anywhere but here, right quick and now, sprint through town and up the bone dust valley until my legs can't move anymore and my lungs can't keep up, just go. It's a great plan to think about, and there's only this door in the way, and through it, I watch Mr. Langman walking closer.

Everything in me is panic. My skin prickles and my heart thrums hard in my ears and I can't unhitch my breath. Even though there's no way he can hear me, I try to hold quiet what little breath comes out of me. My hands are flat to the door. The paint's warm and my palms are slick-sweaty against it. My brain races to catch up and starts to poke bits of reason into me like, how could he figure it was this motel, in this town? Reason like, he can't be certain which room I'm in. As I think that, through the spy hole, Mr. Langman stops at the far end of the parking stall in front of my door and seems to survey the building, like maybe he's not as sure as he first seemed.

It's hard to tell what he's doing because he's small and curved over in the spy hole. He wears a ball cap and sunglasses, like a state trooper, like the aviator kind. My brain pokes some more reason into me, like how he doesn't know what I look like or even anything about me? Like, how I could open the door, walk out, and he wouldn't know me from Molly or anyone else in the world.

My hand drifts to the chain-lock and slides it out of the bracket again. The slow scrape doesn't scare me as much now, he probably can't hear it over the air conditioner anyhow. My hand drops to the doorknob, and as I wrap my fingers around the handle, I think, I will just step out and walk right past him and say "hi" and go across the highway for a burger. He'll have nothing on me.

My eye's still at the spy hole, but my fingers are frozen on the handle. I can't make them open the door. My brain is bold but my body is chicken of this guy, frozen no matter how I think different. Out there, the shadows have settled across the parking lot and snugged up to the base of the valley on the opposite side of town. I watch his outline, the bill of his ball cap, the gap of light between his knees. He holds his hand in front of him, looks at it and types, his phone. And as my breath comes back to me, the computer chimes.

I don't want to, but I drag my eye from the spy hole and go to the computer.

The cursor blinks at the end of a line of text that reads, Got it right?

My scared comes back hard.

The computer chimes and reads, That's you in there.

My fingers hover over the keyboard. They don't move but for shaking a bit and I can't control that. I can't think of what to type, my words have left me. I want to type, Go away or Wrong place. I want to type, Not here or Nice try, guess again.

I type, Don't know what you're talking about, and click send.

It's the best I can do.

I leave the computer on the bed and go back to the door, palms flat to paint again and eye close at the spy hole. The white truck sits on the other end of the parking lot, too far away to see the license plate numbers, but the colours aren't from here, they're from some other province, maybe a state. Now, it's just the truck out there, the empty lot, the heat and the sun ending at the top of the far canyon wall. I can't see Mr. Langman now. Worse is knowing he's out there somewhere.

The computer chimes and I flinch.

The computer chimes and I close my eyes.

The computer chimes and I step back from the door, go to the bed, and stare at the words on the screen.

Three lines. It reads, The IP address brings me here. Two motels, one has free internet. Only room with AC running.

The cursor on and off and on.

My eye is drawn to a shadow tracking the light creeping in around the curtain. It blacks a line, moving from the far corner toward the door. It's gone and then there's a knock.

The air conditioner rattles, loud and stupid and obvious under the window.

Mr. Langman knocks again, three sharp.

I don't want to, but I have to carry my lie until it either sticks as truth or crumbles to nothing. It's the only thing on my side. I have to work with it and just hope hard it won't fail.

I type, Don't know what you're talking about.

I type, Sending your stuff to the cops now.

It's a bluff though. It smells like one too, even to me. No cops will come here, not anytime soon. I'm alone.

Mr. Langman knocks again, three times again, louder and slower, like in case I didn't hear him the first time. I throw the bed sheet over the computer to hide it and take a few steps toward the door.

"Who is it?" is what I call out.

The air conditioner quits, absolute quiet after all the noise it's been making. The late-afternoon shadows have settled over the motel. My heartbeat's so loud in the silence.

A voice outside says, "Just open the door."

To act true, I think how someone who isn't me would play this, what someone who has no idea what's going on would do. It's hard to think like that, knowing what I do, knowing who's on the other side of the door and why he's here.

Mr. Langman hammers hard, like with his fist.

I can tell he's sure it's me in here. In his mind, there's no chance that this is the wrong room or that I'm not the person on the other end of the chat.

At the door again, my hands flat to the paint, but this time, it's more to keep them from shaking than to look out the spy hole. The view is dark, blotted with a hand or something else over it.

He says, "Open the door, Molly. We have to talk."

He hammers again. It jumps under my palms and shocks up my arms to make my pulse run even faster.

I say, "What the hell, man?"

I say, "Do I sound like a Molly?"

I slide the chain-lock back in place and it scrapes loud, and this time, I hope Mr. Langman hears it. I'm going to open the door. This has to happen. The longer I don't, the madder he gets and the smaller the chance my failing thread of make-believe will hold.

Everything in me says not to turn the handle, but I do. I'm trying to make my face match my story, trying to make it look confused instead of chicken, but it feels like the harder I try, the more I fail. The problem with this level of lie is that I'm thinking about it too much, which never happens with truth. Truth never needs a thought because it just is. If Mr. Langman sees me for the lie, there's nothing left to keep this from going really bad, really quick. He has to believe my face as much as he does my words.

I'm screwed.

I won't be able to do this.

Everything in me says not to open the door, but it's not a choice.

The door swings open a gap. Mr. Langman is pushing and it bounces at the end of the chain and holds there. The chain vibrates tight and I look at it, judging my safety net as weak.

Mr. Langman is taller than me, bigger than me. I glimpse him in the gap and then step so he can't see more of me than the side of my face, my eye. In my glimpse, he's a ball cap, sunglasses, black stubble chin and white teeth. He's not old like I thought he'd be, maybe late twenties, early thirties most. He holds his cell clenched in one hand, like a hammer.

He says, "Give me your computer, Molly, your backups."

"The hell are you talking about?" I say. My voice shakes a little. Though he can only see a bit of me through the gap, I must look as true as I sound because he pauses, seeming uncertain for the first time.

I tell him a story. I'm travelling to meet my girlfriend. Before he can ask where my car is, I tell him I got off my bus this morning and my connection doesn't go out until tomorrow morning. I tell him she's gone to university on the coast and I couldn't follow. I tell him I've saved my money to go to her and maybe I'll stay, if she wants that.

It's lies, which is okay as long as he takes it. His silence tells me he's weighing. His face, it tells on him, that he may be starting to believe me. He glances at the phone in his hand, like it might be the one lying to him. He's not so sure now that I'm Molly.

I reckon I can remind him why he's here, put the doubt deeper in him.

I say, "Whoever you're looking for, I ain't him."

I reckon now he can give me his pity.

I say, "But I'm not surprised you're here, bad always seems to come at me, always follows."

I say, "I didn't have the money to go to school with her, my girlfriend. Probably not smart enough to get in either, but I think she loves me anyhow and that's good enough for me, for the rest of my life."

I feel like crying but figure that would be too much, so I don't let myself.

Mr. Langman is nodding, his eye on the phone, thumb poking it like it can show him where he went wrong.

Voice calm, he says, "Okay. Okay, kid."

I don't want to, but now it's been spun, I have to call in what he buys of my story. I look him once over, say, "I don't know you and I don't know this town. I've got to be on a bus at quarter to six tomorrow morning, and that's it."

Mr. Langman nods like he's heard all he needs, and again says, "Okay. Okay, kid."

He takes off his sunglasses. Through the gap, one tired eye goes from his phone to look in my eye.

He says, "Look, I get it. I've got a girlfriend too and I'm probably lucky to have her, just like you and your girl."

He says, "That's a hard story you're telling me. I feel it. I really do."

He shifts on his feet and looks down at them, seems embarrassed a bit.

He says, "Sorry to bug you."

He says, "I'm going to go."

With that, he turns and starts away. He's three steps gone and I blink like I can't believe it. At that moment, I'm glad to have his back to me because there's a truth on my face that would betray, right quick.

As I'm closing the door, he turns again and says, "Just one more thing."

He pushes a button on his phone. A second later my computer chimes and it's done, recognition on his face like the recognition on mine. There's nothing left for cunning and there's nothing left for lies. Now there's a fight. Now there's running.

He rushes the door and forces it back hard against the chain. It bounces against my head. The chain strains tight and holds, but the blow strikes me stupid. I fall back. There's another bang as Mr. Langman tests the chain again, and again it holds. It buys me time enough to work through my daze, the instant stabbing headache. I wobble to my feet and charge the door, intent to force it closed and set the deadbolt. Mr. Langman shoulders the door a fraction of a second before I meet it. It's enough for him to push through, the chain snaps at the links. I hit the door full-on and it stops dead with Mr. Langman running into the other side. I'm pushed to the ground again, but he is too. There's a scrabble of him falling to the pavement outside.

I can't fight him because he's bigger than me. Everything in me says to run, but there's nowhere to go. I grab my pack from the chair on my sprint to the back of the room. His boots are loud on pavement and then soft on carpet. The door slams hard against the wall when he comes through. His breath sounds close on me.

I spin into the bathroom and slam the door shut. I fumble with the lock, my fingers shake so much. It's just a handle lock meant to keep someone from accidentally walking in on your private. It won't hold. I put my back to the door and wedge my feet in front of me, like I can brace it shut. The door is hollow and flexes, all weak under my weight. It won't hold.

I hear him move in the room then quick at the door, which shakes in its frame, jumps against my back. I'm staring at the little sliding window above the toilet. The opening's too small for me to fit through, but if I could push it out of its frame I might be able.

Mr. Langman says, "Open the door, Molly."

His voice is in my ear, close and clear from the other side.

I take a deep breath and say, "My computer's on the bed. Take it and go."

He shuffles around in the room, likely going for the computer. It buys me time. I push off the door and go at the window. I use my backpack like a battering ram at the end of my arms and with three hits, the window breaks and I push through the flimsy aluminum frame. The noise it makes brings Mr. Langman back to the bathroom door. It jumps hard and crackles in its frame.

I shove my backpack out the window, climb up on the toilet seat and squeeze out the frame headfirst as the bathroom door flies open. I'm through and tumble to the dirt. Mr. Langman, his face twisted to hate, is framed in the window for a second before it disappears. He can't fit through, so he's going back out front to come around the building at me.

In a swirl of dust, I snatch my pack from the dirt and I'm sprinting as fast as I can. I bodycheck the stack of old tires as my feet get under me, find the coulee, and use it to work my way up the valley side.

A rabbit shoots out of the underbrush and my heart shoots with it. I shout in surprise, can't help it because I didn't see the thing there, a mangy, skinny prairie hare, frozen still and looking just like a rock until it bolted.

I stop halfway up the valley side. The coulee makes an easier slope to climb, but I still have to work for breath. Here's the only place some trees grow, and though they aren't much taller than me, they're thick and gnarled and dense. They hide me better than anything else around. When I turn to look back, my backpack catches on a branch and it snaps like a gunshot. I flinch at its giveaway.

In the gaps between the spindles and in the spaces between the grey-green leaves is the backside of the motel, painted white and peels curling to show the cinderblock underneath. Everything's in shadow. I'm in a shadow on the side of this hill. I don't see Mr. Langman, but I can't see much down there. He could be close and I wouldn't know it. I hold my breath, quiet in favour of hearing something, anything else, but there's nothing so I suck some more air into me.

I hope Mr. Langman won't give me a chase because he's already got all my stuff, except for my backpack. While there's not a lot left in the hotel room but some dirty clothes, there's the computer, which should be all he wants.

He'll just take my stuff and go, I think.

He only ever wanted the computer, I think, not me.

My breathing gets easier but my heart still hammers hard. I'm out of the worst it, I think, because I start to feel stuff again, and what I feel is like steady water down my left arm and a solid drip, drip, drip sucking at my fingertips. I look and my forearm is slick with blood. There's too much red to see where it comes from. I give a quiet cuss and slip my backpack off, pull out one of my clean teeshirts, and use it to wipe my arm down.

I lose a bit of my calm when I find the cut. It's long, from the inside of my elbow and up halfway to my armpit. It's a clean line splitting my skin, not wide but deep. It wells up with blood real fast whenever I swipe it clear, like it's got a mind not to heal up anytime soon.

A cold sweat sprouts on my skin because it's serious and I shiver with a chill even though it's still hot out. The flesh moves like butcher meat and looks bad enough that I feel like puking. I don't, even though the taste is in the back of my mouth. I've never bled so much. Seeing it come out so quick gives me panic because I don't know what to do with it. It's spilled on my jeans and my shoes and on the scrub brush around, glazing dusty green leaves with a glossy maroon. My trembling hand pushes my bloody shirt against the cut and holds it there, apply pressure, my brain trips. I raise my arm, elevate it above my heart, my brain trips.

I'm pushing as hard as I can, like trying to keep the rest of my blood inside me. I grit my teeth because the pain of it comes inching back now my run's done and my body's not blind to itself anymore. It's a strange pain, strong pins and needles, but it's also good because it brings focus. I can't tell whether I'm really getting faint or whether I just think I should feel that way because of the cut. I didn't notice when it happened, but it must have been when

I scrambled through the window, manic and careless like an idiot. There was all the broken glass and the snapped aluminum frame. Any of that stuff would have been sharp enough to gash me good.

Should've been more careful, I tell myself. It'd be stupid to die here in the bush, a couple hundred metres from where I got free. It's just I wanted to get away so bad.

I lose every last bit of my calm when Mr. Langman calls out from below.

"You okay, Molly?"

He says that I left a lot of red behind, that it looks pretty bad, that he's worried for me.

Last bit's a lie, can tell from his voice. I can't see him, only hear him, and that's worse because the coulee walls make every noise sound close, like he's standing in the bushes right beside me, like he's talking in my ear.

I grimace and lower my arm. The scrub brush goes watery because I'm crying, all quiet and tears down my cheeks. I want to say it's for the pain of my arm, but it's mostly for being chicken. I pin my elbow to my hip, the wad of fabric held tight against my side. I find two loose ends to wrap around and pull as tight as I can before knotting them. It's as good as it's going to be, but there's already a line of blood leaking from under it and running down my forearm.

I freeze when Mr. Langman calls again.

He says, "I think I better come up to you, help you out."

He says, "Stay there. Right where you are."

From that, I think he can see me when I can't see him, and it scares me. He's crazy if he thinks I'm not going to run. My good arm hooks the backpack strap and slings it over my shoulder. The spindles grow so close, I can't move without making noise.

I wipe my eyes with the back of my hand and suck the snot up my nose and get tough on myself for wasting time being a baby when I should have been moving. I suck a deep breath and then continue up toward the valley rim. I'm moving as close to running as the steep slope and crowded brush let me, but it still feels too slow.

The tree line breaks near the valley rim and I glance back. There's no Mr. Langman and the sunlight's all gone from the valley below. These bright plains will lose their light soon, too. There'll be no moon, not until later anyhow, only starlight reflected by bone dust to illuminate the night.

I know the plains.

If Mr. Langman follows, I can slip him in the dark and be far away when the light comes back in the morning.

I stop and wait, but for only a moment, holding my breath to listen for him. He's down in the coulee, a big cow crashing around in the brush. For the first time since going through the window, I know where he is and that gives me a bit of peace. I keep my arm pressed to my side and the shirt's getting soaked through, but I can't do anything about it right now but keep moving.

I'm walking as the valley slope smooths to flat, chest heaving for breath from the climb. The setting sun is a blinding giant sitting there, more'n half-sunk into the horizon and gone. It'll probably only be another fifteen minutes of light and an hour of twilight before the night's true pitch. I glance behind me and still don't see Mr. Langman, meaning he's either given up his chase or he's still stuck in the trees somewhere.

I start to run toward the sun.

I don't go as fast as I can because I have to last until full dark. If Mr. Langman comes up top here and looks around, he'll be blind to me if the angle's right. If I'm straight-line between him and the sun, I'll be disappeared and he'll give up on the chase. The pack bounces on my back, only over one shoulder, annoying but there's no way I'm slipping my cut arm through the other strap. The longer I keep it still against my side, the better it'll slow my leak. I look back every few strides to see if there's cause for me to pick up the pace.

I'm a few minutes gone from the edge and have made a good distance. The sun's still a few finger-widths from setting, but it's almost gone, turned into a tangerine smear. I drop my eyes to near my feet, because looking at the horizon makes them hurt and leaves dark sunspots behind. Another rabbit gets scared up from the brush and bolts a zigzag line out from me. Dust puffs in little clouds from where it's been.

Behind, it looks like the valley is disappeared, angled so the close edge of it connects to the far, with no gap in between. I lose a bit of my calm when a figure seemingly climbs up from inside the flat land. Of course, I know it's not like that, I know it's Mr. Langman coming over the valley edge, but just as the sun's setting, he's a demon on fire, rising from the bone dust as we spin around to the dark side of the world.

I kick into a shrub and stumble through a cloud of dust because I've been staring back. I fall to my knees and throw my hands out to catch my fall. I cry out. I don't go all the way down, only to hands and knees, but it's enough to pull a fresh thread of blood from under the bandage and down my forearm into the dirt. It soaks into the thirsty ground and is gone from me forever. If anything was starting to heal up, it's open again. My bandage is bled through and I wonder how much a body's got in it to lose. I stay there, on fours like a dog, the ground sticking to my palms, a million grains of dust billowing up between my fingers.

Deep breath and push upright again.

Sling the backpack over my shoulder and get going forward again.

I steal another look back. Mr. Langman holds his hand up to block out the last sunlight. He spots me pretty quick and starts a straight line after me. I cuss him under my breath, for following me, for not giving up, for even showing up here in the first place. It scares me that he doesn't call out or yell anything at me.

I move faster even though I just want to lie down. I keep my eye on him in glances, frequent enough to judge a steady distance between us. I'll try to keep it that way until the sun is all gone and the grey light it leaves behind turns to black. My legs burn and I'm exhausted and short on breath, but Mr. Langman is still there, a twilit silhouette chasing, barely visible except for a hazy movement in the gathering dark.

A flare stack glows on the distant, dark flat. It wouldn't be seen in the burning day, but now it's a stuck shooting star. Looking deeper, there are more, farther, burning gas spread out like the fallen sky pinned to the bone dust until morning.

I lose a bit of my calm when the flare blurs and I start feeling weird, wobbly. My legs are heavy and tired and instead of dodging around the bushes or stepping over them, I'm plowing through. At first I think it's because it's now almost full dark and I can't see, or I've just been running for too long. But it's not these things, it's more. There're cold sweats on my forehead and under my hair and tickling down my neck. It's still hot out and I'm running, so I shouldn't shiver like I do. The side of my leg is slick with the blood spilled on it. My jeans stick to my skin and are heavy on that side when I move. I pull breath far down into my lungs and force it out again, but it doesn't feel like enough.

I drag one foot and then the other, both of them so much heavier than even ten minutes ago. This new state scares me worse than the shadowed figure drawing closer across the scrubland from somewhere behind. His raggedy breaths are clear, in and out and again, his feet grinding the dust, and the rustle of brush as he goes through it. It's so quiet and flat and empty out here that sound travels, like he could be at my heel or a kilometre away.

Maybe he's right behind me.

I glance back and can still see him a little, but not much. He's a trick of the eye moving in the darkness, not a half-kilometre back. It will be near pitch soon, and I have to have more space between him and me for my dodge to work. The farther out I am, the easier it'll be to go silent, go sideways, and double back without him knowing it. But I don't think I can get the space between us bigger. I'm flat out and almost done.

I stop and wait and catch my breath and let my head steady a bit. I know it's the cut on my arm that makes me feel sick and my heart flap faster than it should, like a sprinter, like a bird trying to get away from a wire around its leg. For the first time, I worry if maybe I won't get away and if maybe I won't even make it to sun up. This scares me sick because, in the world of an hour ago, I had never in my life had such thoughts. I'm different now because of this doubt.

My head doesn't steady and I have to sit down, but it's more like my legs falling out from under me and my ass hitting the ground. My backpack slips to the side.

It's night now.

It's near complete black, except for the starlight's soft glow in the dust, and yellow flares marking the distance.

I hope it's enough to hide me because I'm not moving from here. Mr. Langman scrambles around in the pitch, his grind and rustle sound close in the dark. I try to still my breath, but I'm afraid to for too long, in case it doesn't come back.

My head spins and a rolling nausea washes over me. I taste puke and clench in a heave, but nothing comes out. I slouch onto my back, strapped to the ground by gravity and facing skyward. I shift and pull an orange-sized rock from under me and push it aside.

The sky spills out black and forever deep, and the thin smear of stars set in it is nothing by comparison. I think of the quiet, complete stillness of floating through the stars. I think myself back to last night, think of sleep and the silent truck lights moving slow and smooth on the highway, far away.

Mr. Langman's out there, his noises in my left ear. He cusses, stumbling in the black, but I can't make out his words. He's close because I hear his small noises, the creak of his boots and the little rasp at the end of each breath, the whisper of his clothes. I stare up into forever and then close my eyes. I don't care if he finds me. His noises fill me now, so much that he must be right over top of me, but my eyes keep closed. Then, I hear him out there in my right ear, on the other side. With each step, his small noises fade and then only his big ones come, like he's gone past.

I call out to him, which seems stupid, but my heart is moving weaker than it should and there's a black coming toward me like I've never felt before. My voice tremors when I don't mean it to. I'm more scared of being alone now than of anything he could do.

I think, I need help more than I need fear.

I think, either he helps me or he doesn't; there's nothing more to lose and I might just gain.

I catch my breath to hear him better. He's stopped walking because there aren't any sounds from him. Or else he's too far away. The silence is near absolute, not a breeze, and the rabbits are hiding still and quiet in the scrub. Somewhere, far out, come noises that were hidden before: the rhythmic metallic whisper of a pumpjack, the quiet, ceaseless tear of the flare burn.

Mr. Langman says, "Say it again. Speak, so I can find you."

He sounds close, but out here sound travels distances, and deceives. But there's his voice, offering me a second chance to make the same mistake.

"I'm here," I say.

"I'm here," I say louder.

"I'm scared," I whisper to myself.

He's moving again. A growing noise in my right ear.

A few steps at me and he asks, "You pulling some trick?"

And I say, "No."

I say, "I'm cut and I'm bleeding out pretty bad."

He keeps walking toward me and I'm looking up and listening, the sound of him growing against the still everything around.

"I saw it," he says, but I can't tell what he means because he says it flat, just a statement with nothing else.

I can't help but laugh, quiet and to myself, because of how stupid I'm made to be, to have to ask for help from the guy who has the chase on me. His voice is beside me and his walking has stopped.

"What's funny?" he asks, cautious.

"Me begging help from you."

He nods, but I can't tell much else from his face in the dark, can't see anything on it, just the outline of him. He's looking down on me and I see the mess I am, in him.

"Oh, Molly," he says. "You don't look so good."

He surveys my body, top down and back up again. Then he sits on his heels beside me, hugs his shins, and says, like to himself, "What to do? What to do?" which makes me laugh again.

It's stunning, this feeling of drifting back a bit from myself.

Mr. Langman looks at me, a tortoise turned on its back, thinking whether to let things take their course or to flip it over again. We watch each other from a few feet apart, our thoughts probably along the same line, except from opposite ends. I'm his problem and he's mine, and because of that, we're stuck together.

I'm thinking, he could leave me here and his problem would likely get solved on its own. He wouldn't even have to raise a finger. He might be thinking that maybe I could get myself back to town and get help, then I'd still be around. To cover that base, he could stay with me and watch me fade out, but that would be as good as killing me himself. I have to believe he's not a killer. Otherwise, he could just pick up the rock I pulled from under me and bust my head in. Not likely I could do anything about that. Of course I'd try, a weak arm working to deflect the hit, but he's bigger than me and I'm not doing so good.

And these are our thoughts.

Mr. Langman picks up the rock and weighs it with a bounce.

"You," he says, "have been a pain in my ass."

He says, "I've been awake for two days now, searching you out, driving out to you, chasing you up a hill. Now here we are, and I really don't know what to do."

I glance at the rock. He sees me do it and cocks his head to the side.

I say, "You have the computer. I'm a bluff anyway."

"You can look," I say and struggle the backpack across my body to him. "Never downloaded nothing."

He glances at my pack in the dirt between us.

He sighs and sways back and forth a bit on his heels, crosses his arms in a hug around his knees again, and looks out sideways, like at the horizon, like at the answer to what he should do. There's nothing to see but dark, so he must be thinking this out some more.

It's amazing, the feeling in me, the terror of it, but also the pride that I won't let myself cry to him or beg anything of him.

He could be anyone, but I'm betting on the base of him, that he'll help, and if not help, at least he won't do more harm. Either way, he won't be a problem any longer.

I don't say anything more, just float on and look up at the sky going out so deep-infinite that I can feel myself spinning off into it. There's no ground under me anymore, no gravity, no burn from my tired legs and no more dull pulse from the cut on my arm. It's all numb and tired now. The air's warm and dry, but I've still got a clammy chill in me.

I'm pulled out of my thoughts when Mr. Langman says to himself again, "What to do? What to do."

I get bold and answer him, "Help me back to town's what you do."

He weighs the rock in his hand again and says, "After the trouble you caused me? Don't see why I should."

I've got nothing to lose, so say, "Because you're a pervert, not a killer."

And Mr. Langman freezes all his swaying toe-to-heel and his fidgeting and he stares at me, his eyes unreadable, sunk as they are in black pits.

I say, "If you're sore about the gas money getting here, I'll spot you for it."

He doesn't laugh or anything, just stands up and holds the rock out at arm's length, over my face. I reach up frantic, grab at it. He pushes my arm away with a boot, with his toe in my armpit, pins it, and I can't fight that. He stands over me, a boot on each side, like he's on an invisible horse. He holds the rock out over my face.

My perspective, he's holding a new moon against the sky, a black hole sucking light, and it's pretty in his hand. I stop straining against him because there's no point of it anymore.

I say, "I ain't going to fight you. That's done."

I say, "Do what you do."

I shout when he tilts his wrist and lets the rock roll from his hand. It lands with a muted thud, a few inches from my ear. The ground tremors beside my head. The impact kicks dirt in my eye. I close it and a tear runs a line out the corner.

Mr. Langman steps his boot off me and asks, “Anyone going to come looking for you?”

I don’t answer, just blink a few times, trying to get the grit out of my eye. I roll to one side and rub it with the back of my hand, but that’s dirty too, so it doesn’t help much.

“I asked you something, kid.” He pokes at my side with the toe of his boot, says again, “Anyone going to come?”

I say, “Probably not.” My voice cracks. “Probably nobody’ll be missing me.”

His silhouette nods and he takes a few steps back. He stands there, quiet for a bit, before saying, “Look at you, Molly. You’re a mess.”

And then he’s walking away, back the way we came from. His noises growing smaller and his voice getting farther in the black.

“Lonely, that’s a hard place to be. It’s probably time you find a new line of work,” he says. “And somebody who’ll miss you, who’ll come looking when you’re lost out here alone.”

“I ain’t lost,” I say back. My throat’s a dry croak. “I know where I am, just don’t like it much.”

He doesn’t respond and I’m speaking to the night. After a while I don’t hear him anymore, only the spinning rasp of the distant pumpjack. It’s amazing the feeling of exhaustion that pins me to the ground, like Mr. Langman’s boot is still on me, heavy, and I’m not going to fight it. Just me and the rabbits left behind, just us hidden in the scrub brush, hoping hard that nothing more comes by to spook us tonight.

I don’t know what it’s like to bleed out, never done it before, but I’m cold and sweating and don’t have energy except to lay for a while and sink back into the dirt as I float through the sky. It’s opposite, being strapped to the ground, feeling so still, but watching the stars spin off to the side, sliding by as I’m pushed through, the last man ever alive. It doesn’t stop, nothing does, even when it seems to. Even when I work hard on being still, I’m always moving until I’m dead and still carrying on even after that. This place doesn’t care because it’s got nothing but all the time ever invented, so much it’s meaningless, and I’ve only got such a little bit.

A coyote calls, far away. Maybe it was waiting to hear what me and Mr. Langman did, or maybe it was making noise the whole time, but I was too focused on being prey to notice.

I'm not dead and I maybe won't be tonight, not if I don't want to be. I can't see my arm, but a dull throb still pulls at me gently there. It feels more tacky than wet, like it's drying up, like the ground has soaked it all up, and my blood is part of the dirt now.

Mr. Langman was right, probably time for a new line of work, time to find somebody who'll miss me and come looking.

I don't know when I fall asleep, but I do. I dream the sky is dark water and the stars are jellyfish and I'm floating by them as I sink upward. Their tentacles string past me for a bit and then gone.

6

It's amazing, this feeling of pure white everywhere when I open my eyes, and I want to stare into it, but it hurts so I shut them tight again.

Something tickles my arm and I squint sideways through an eyelash haze. Red ants swarm across my skin. They aren't biting, just thousands of jittery legs crawling all over and I watch them for the time it takes my eyes to adjust to daylight. The blood there is caked and cracked, dried up like clay, like lizard scales. I watch the ants and think that might be what they're after. Or maybe they're mad that I'm lying on their nest, blocking the door. Same-same and I watch them still.

After a while, I sit up. Raising my head makes it pound hard and I have to wait for the stars to get out of my eyes before looking around. All washed out and over-exposed, straw yellow and grey scrubland, bone dust stretches out to a denim sky. The sun is right above so it's around midday, but there're no shadows to tell on what direction's what. The town, the valley, they're hidden, somewhere sunk below the ground.

I stand up, wait for more stars to go. My head hurts worse and that won't go. There's a good goose egg over my eye where Mr. Langman bounced the door off me, and my mouth is pasty dry.

When I brush the ants from my arm, dried blood comes off too, I'm already turned to dust. It marks my palm with rust in the creases and lines. The shirt I used as a bandage is crusty and it pulls my skin when I try to peel it off to look at the cut, my blood soaked through making it part of the scab that seals me shut. I don't want to open it again, so I don't play with it much.

A trickle of sweat runs from my armpit to the bandage and I test my arm. It hurts, but it's also numb, opposite sensations I can't figure out too clear. I'm thirsty and hungry, like I haven't been in a long time.

In the distance, a speck miles away, a quick flicker of light catches my eye. A truck on the highway, from where it comes up out of the valley and sets south across the plains. I track it for a while, trying to get its line. Distance pulls the sound of the engine from the air and it stays complete silence. The windscreen flickers one more signal though, giving me a direction to get back.

I snag my pack from the ants and shake it out before slinging it over my shoulder.

I walk.

I call out while I walk, like Mr. Langman is still nearby. I yell like I'm mad at him, like he can hear me and will be chicken of me.

I rage at him with a dry, raw voice and call him all the things I was too scared to last night, when he was so close on my tail.

The rustle and bolt of a rabbit comes from the scrub. It sets my heart fast and I laugh loud because if anyone was out here, they'd think I'm crazy and try to get away from me. But there's nobody here except the rabbits to see the last man on Earth lose it.

Then I get quiet a while and think. I can't be here anymore, the prairie, this town, any of it. And I can't come back again once I get out. This place is too small even though it goes on forever, to every horizon. I need to get my arm looked at, probably stitched up. There's a clinic in town. The numbness in my fingers worries me. I think of how I need a shower. I can smell the sweat and armpit funk of me. The cleanest thing on me is probably the dust caught in my hair and stuck on my skin.

I need to lie down but I keep walking, a headache pulsing like crazy, my body dumb, groggy and weak. I don't know how long has passed before there're the first hints of the valley, a couple hours maybe. It starts as a thin dark line across the ground and gets broader as I get closer. Mr. Langman and I went out pretty far last night, farther than it seemed in the dark and panic.

When I reach the valley rim, I look down and I'm just outside of town.

Stumbling down the slope, the loose dirt breaking in waves, it doesn't take long until there's pavement underfoot and then buildings on either side.

The town I knew is different now. Overnight, it's become new, less familiar and more threatening. I'm a staggering mess, but the town doesn't seem to notice. Cars drive by on the highway, all tacky-sounding tires on the hot asphalt. I'm watching close for white pickup trucks, in case Mr. Langman is still around and isn't done with me yet.

A woman walks her fat dog on the other side of the highway. She wears bug-eye sunglasses, a white sundress, and she stops to let the dog piss. She watches it unload and I walk by. Maybe she looks back at me when I'm past, but she doesn't let on that I exist while I can still know it.

There're people going through the sliding door of the grocery store, pushing empty carts in and rattling them back out full again. I scan the parking lot for a white pickup but there isn't one. It doesn't feel that last night was real, not with the regular motions still going on today. Surely, there should be some disruption here.

The clinic is past the grocery store and a block more toward the river, away from the highway. I turn to it and there's a house with the sprinkler raining onto a sunburnt square of grass. I watch the water a minute, the individual droplets invisible for the haze they make together. There's no one around, so I walk over and take the sprinkler. It sprays me but it feels good. I go to the shade beside the house, unscrew it from the hose and drink big gulps because I think the last time I drank anything was the coffee at the diner yesterday afternoon. The water splashes from my chin and onto my shirt. It's warm and tastes like plastic, but I drink until I feel a bit sick from it.

I take my shirt off over my head, carefully over my arm, and wash the dry blood and dirt from my skin the best I can. It's hard to control the water and my jeans take a soaking, too. I curve over forward and hang my head upside down. My headache pulses harder flipped over, and I run the water over my hair, watch it rain into a muddy sky at my feet.

A voice asks what I'm doing.

I stand up straight and stagger back a dizzy step. The stars go from my eyes and the voice is from a grey-haired lady wearing a shirt with big, bright flowers printed on it. She stands at the corner of the house, watching, and I can't read her expression. A sun visor rests on her brow and casts a green rectangle on her face.

I'm embarrassed by her eyes on me so I drop the hose and clumsily work my shirt back over my arm and head. It takes too long, just bringing attention to how awkward I am. I hope the heat in my cheeks doesn't show through much.

She asks, "Are you okay?" in the span that I don't answer.

I tell her I am and her face calls me a liar.

"Well," she says. "Why don't you put my sprinkler back and I'll bring you a proper glass of water."

I want to apologize, but she's already gone, so I have nothing but to screw the sprinkler on and put the hose out on the lawn again. Once it's set up and watering, I go to the sidewalk to leave. Not two steps gone and the lady calls at me. I stop and look. The screen door bangs shut and she's coming with a glass of water in hand. I don't go to her, but I take the glass and drink it while she watches. Her eyes keep going to the ratty bandage around my arm.

I say, "Thank you."

I say, "Sorry." And gesture with a shrug at the sprinkler.

"It's okay," she says. "Your arm, do you want me to call someone?"

She puts a hand on my shoulder and I flinch away even though I don't mean to. She draws off quick again. Her face softens.

"It's okay," I say. I nod up the street, "I'm going to get it looked at."

There's not much left to say for us so I thank her again for the water, and as I'm going up the street I hear her say, "You're Matt and Stacey's boy, aren't you?"

I stop because no one's said my parents' names in years. It's like ghosts to me. I miss them so much and all at once, just from hearing their names after so long. It's like I've forgotten about them on purpose, forced them from my head, and every day that I did piles up at once. It's them I miss, the idea of family, the idea of safety in a person. I remember my bookcase in my room and the feel of Mom's arms around me because I'm sitting on her lap, the smell of Dad's cigarette. Dad leans back, talking. I remember his voice, clear as today, like he's talking here, now. There's a yellow plastic lamp hanging over the table, dropping yellow plastic light onto some after-supper dirty dishes, tater tots and ketchup smears, some scattered cards from playing crazy eights on the silver flecks in the blue top. I remember dark kitchen windows and being safe. We're laughing. I don't remember why, but it's a true sound. Family's a feeling I miss so much.

I turn and nod, not trusting my voice to talk.

The lady says, "My name's Evelyn. I worked with your mom for a while." She looks down at her hands. "A long time ago."

I nod again, looking at the ground between us.

I want to go.

Evelyn says, "If you ever need a door to knock on." And then she points to her house.

I say, "Thanks for the water."

And I go.

7

A tired voice tells me to take a seat and fill out this form as I walk through the door. Then the lady behind the counter looks up. Her eyes fall to my arm and she holds up a wait-a-minute finger, sets the clipboard down, and gets on the phone.

She says, "Barry, you're needed in room one." And then hangs up.

She comes around the counter, says, "Follow me."

There's a guy in a long white coat coming up the hall and he holds an arm out to the side to direct me into an examination room. He tells me to sit on the crumple-paper table and asks what happened.

As he cuts my shirt off with scissors, I say, "Dirt biking up a coulee out of town."

He nods and tugs at my bandage. I wince because it pulls on the cut too, all of it a clotted mess of fabric and blood and dirt.

He asks, "And when was this?"

He runs some water and then uses a cloth to clean my arm.

I say, "Yesterday."

I say, "I landed on some scrap metal and it took me all this time to walk back to town. So mad, my bike's totaled."

He starts hacking at the bandage with some scissors. It hurts, but I don't say anything else. Dr. Barry doesn't either for a while, because he's either satisfied by my answer or concentrating on my arm or it doesn't matter much. He cuts away as much material as he can and then wraps what's left in a warm, wet cloth to soak it.

We wait. I look at Dr. Barry, then away because he's staring at me.

Dr. Barry asks, "You allergic to anything? Medications, penicillin?" and I say, "No."

Dr. Barry asks, "You currently on anything, prescription or otherwise?" and I say "No."

I tell him they have my file, that I lived here a while back, that I've been to this clinic before, but a long time ago.

He asks my name and I tell him.

He leaves the room and I stare at the clock, then the poster next to it, a sad-looking kitten hanging onto a rope with its front paws. The poster reads, *Hang in there.*

The clock ticks seconds by, then minutes. More than five pass before Dr. Barry comes back in with a folder and some other stuff. He sits in the chair across from me, leans forward, elbows to knees, leafing through the file.

"You had your tetanus shot a while back," he says. "You should have a booster just in case."

I nod and he peels a needle from plastic, swabs and pinches my shoulder. I turn my head away. He lets the pinch go once the needle's in me.

When he's done with that, he peeks at my arm under the towel and says, "This may hurt a little." And it does. I don't watch him do it, but can feel the bandage pulling apart. Afterward, the cut is open again. It's bleeding again, though not as much as it did last night.

He tells me it needs stitches and has another needle that he sticks right into the meat of my cut at few places and pushes the plunger. He says, "We'll wait a few minutes until that kicks in."

Then he leaves and I'm there watching the clock again. Hang in there, kitten.

Dr. Barry comes back with another plastic container he peels open. There's a U-shaped needle and thread and I watch as he sews my skin back up. It doesn't hurt much, just a dull pull on it, like it's someone tugging on my shirt. He talks a bit while he works.

"You out there alone?" he asks and I tell him, "Yes."

He steals a look at me, as if to judge me dumb or naive, true or a liar.

He says, "You're pretty lucky. It's a deep cut."

I don't feel lucky but also don't say anything, only nod.

He finishes up and puts a gauze on it and tapes it down. Then he gives me some extra and tells me to keep it clean and not to keep it covered up all the time. "It needs to breathe," he says. He scrawls on a prescription pad and says, "Antibiotics twice a day for two weeks. You'll live. Those stitches should dissolve in a week, then you can pull the ends out."

He says, "You should be fine, but if it turns pink, hot, or if there's lots of discharge, come back."

On his way out the door, Dr. Barry stops and says, "And next time, wear a helmet."

I'm confused until he points at the goose egg on my forehead from when the motel door hit me.

I say, "Thank you."

I'm left alone with the tick-tick of the second hand. There's a sink and a soap pump, so I use them to wash up the best I can. I throw my shirt out and use paper towels to get as much blood off my sneakers as I can, but it mostly just smears it around and makes a more even stain, which I guess is less noticeable than it was. I get a fresh shirt and my shorts from my backpack, push my hair around until it's less messy, and then go.

8

I walk the few blocks to the motel, going the back streets. The shadows stretch long, and even the heat seems tired of itself. I watch for Mr. Langman's white truck. The door to one-eleven has been patched with a strip of plywood and a bunch of screws run through. I don't want to go closer in case the manager sees me, so I give up on the stuff left behind and head back toward the grocery store. There's a pharmacy in there.

A voice calls for some kids riding bikes around in the road. It sounds like it's from the next street, over rooftops and a bit away. The kids say bye to each other with their little kid voices and they make plans to ride bikes again tomorrow. It's suppertime and the spalling asphalt crackles under bike tires as they ride away. The sun is setting. Most of the shadows are gone from this side of the street. I hear the kids laughing far away.

When I get to the grocery store, I freeze because there's a white pickup parked near the door. It has local plates though, so I settle a bit. The doors slide open and I'm hit by fluorescent lights and air conditioning. And I stop just inside. The past twenty-four hours being done makes me feel like I could lie down on the cool linoleum and sleep for a week, lost in the rattle of shopping cart dreams.

At the pharmacy counter, waiting for them to fill the prescription, I sit with my elbows on my knees and my head hung, held in hands. No matter how tired I am, I can't stop thinking about what I'm going to do next. It's always there, one of the two thoughts pecking at me all the time, one about what I've done, and the other about what I'm going to do next.

The pharmacist calls my name a few times before I hear it, I can tell by his face. I grab the pills and am gone. The automatic doors slide closed and I'm in the late-afternoon light again. I find myself scanning for Mr. Langman's truck all the time now. I've got to get gone. His truck's not here, only the usual come and go.

It strikes me again, how normal life is, people popping into the grocery store to grab diapers or milk. A kid on a skateboard at the end of the parking lot, his buddy on a BMX bike, they take turns egging tricks from each other. It's weird how, up above, the plains of scrub brush and hidden rabbits stretch on, absolutely alone and big and seemingly forgotten. It's weird how, last night, I left blood in the dust, while people down here were buying teevee dinners and candy bars.

I walk to the side of the building. Evelyn's house is halfway up the block. Her sprinkler's gone from her lawn, but she sits on the step. Her sun visor's gone from her head, but her hair still sticks up funny from it. She sees me, but I don't think she recognizes me. I could walk away, but I don't.

I stand there thinking about Mr. Langman's shadow leaning over me. I could only see him from where the stars weren't, like there was only me and his gap in the night. I think of the thing in me that broke when the rock fell from his fingers, the thing that broke in the tremor of it landing beside my head.

That's how I could have ended.

I could still be there, now, with red ants crawling over me. In a way, I am.

The automatic doors here would still slide open and closed. People buying diapers. People buying milk. The rattle of the kid's skateboard wheels on the pavement. Evelyn sitting on her step in the twilight, just me missing, everything carrying on otherwise.

I go to her.

When I get closer, she recognizes me. I see it by how her face changes.

I ask if I can sit with her for a bit and she nods. "Of course." She shifts over to make room on the steps. I tuck my backpack on one side and sit next to her, one step down.

Evelyn speaks after a bit of quiet, tells me it's too hot to sit in the house, so that's why she's here. "It's a good evening for sitting out and watching the day end," she says.

I nod and we slip back to an easy quiet. The air's blue between us, but the sky's still turning as the sun sets where we can't see it. The bright orange trail of a jet plane, cutting the blue sky from one valley edge to the other, reminds me that things can still be pretty if you look.

We watch a couple walking a dog toward us, toward the river park. They're in shorts and teeshirts and sandals. The dog's a hairy thing, no leash, so it runs up to us, tail wagging and pink tongue out. I pat it until the couple passes and the guy calls it back and gives us a wave.

I don't know what to say to Evelyn and after a while she saves me from wondering and says, "I didn't think I'd know the young man having a bird bath in my sprinkler this afternoon."

I can't tell if she's ruffled or joking.

"Sorry," I say. "I was out of town dirt biking and crashed and wrecked my bike. I had to spend the night up on the plains."

Her face turns all concern and worry.

"It's okay," I say. "Just some stitches and a bump on my head."

I show her my arm, point at the lump, like none of it's obvious.

I hate that my first words are lies.

She shakes her head, her tongue ticks against the roof of her mouth a few times. Then says, absently, fondly, like almost to herself, "I remember being your age, making decisions that barely made sense. I remember when everything was still new."

She doesn't say anything more, just looks back up the street to the highway traffic lights.

I ask, "You knew my mom?"

She smiles sad and says, "We worked together at the post office for a few months."

She says, "That was a while ago though. I remember you, too, but as a little boy, not . . ." Her eyes look me over, like she's trying to match the two together.

I say, "I don't remember that."

"That's okay. You were small. You came in with your dad a few times."

The cars down the block, the ones going by on the highway and the ones coming out of the grocery store parking lot, they all have their headlights on now. The gas station flickers on there, red and white. Evelyn looks at her hands, her fingers knitted, her brow, too.

She says, "I didn't get to know your mom all that well. Was only a few months and all. I wish I knew her better for me to tell you more."

"Me too," I say. "I don't remember much about her, from before."

Evelyn sighs and smiles and says, "Well, what I did know of her, I liked. She was kind to me and we laughed a lot when our shifts overlapped. I feel bad for her now, forgetting a whole life would be hard."

Evelyn pauses and I want to tell her that being forgotten is hard, too. Probably harder, because my mom can't be sad about what she doesn't remember. But I stay quiet.

Evelyn puts a hand on my shoulder and I flinch, but she doesn't move it, says, "I'm happy you're here. There's a pizza in the oven you can help me eat."

She uses the hand on my shoulder to help her stand. The weight of her pushing on me makes me less lonely. Being even that little bit useful, to help her stand, feels good. Even if our talk is a bit of work, it's good work and she's willing.

"Nothing fancy," she says. "Just a frozen pizza. Pepperoni and mushroom."

Her hand's gone and the screen door thumps. She's noisy, moving around inside, a cupboard door banging closed, cutlery on the counter. I think for a second to not be on the porch when she returns, but I like pizza and I like her, so I stay sat.

She's got two plates when she comes out. She hands them both to me. Goes back inside and comes back with a couple sodas. She settles next to me, our knees bumping a couple of times.

I don't want to ask her much because it feels like prying, and she's still a stranger to me. If I could, I'd ask her if she has any kids, if she has a husband, what else did she do besides work at the post office, like if she painted paintings, like if she did gardening, grew things. I look at the sunburnt grass and think it's probably not that one.

I'd ask her more about Mom, but find I don't really want to know. It's easier to shut those memories down like they're not even there and never were. If I was braver, I'd try and find out if Evelyn's had a good life or a hard one. I'd ask if she had fun times at night, dancing in a bar when she was younger, or whether she stayed at home reading books, or liked going to movies with her friends instead.

I watch her when she's looking down the street. I hope she has someone because that's what I think makes people happy. It would make me happy. I hope she has kids to check in on her, or a sister that calls from the city every once in a while, to hear she's okay. I think of Evelyn alone and want to ask if there is someone for her.

Instead of all of this, I say, "Thanks for the pizza. It's good."

Evelyn nods and doesn't say anything because she's chewing a mouthful. When she's done and swallowed, she tells me she's glad I popped by and that having real company is always better than the teevee playing for noise. She asks if I want more pizza and I tell her no thanks, because I don't want to be rude. She smiles when she sees my lie and goes to get more. The screen door bangs against the frame, once when she goes, once when she comes back.

She looks up. "We're supposed to be able to see the space station tonight."

I look a question at her and she nods that it's true, tells me she watches for these things, comets and meteor showers and everything.

She says, "The man on the news said it would be just a pinprick the size of a star, but moving faster than everything else up there.

The man on the news said it goes more than seventeen thousand miles an hour."

I can't imagine that beyond the fact that it's fast. I finish my pizza and lick my fingers and wipe them on the cuff of my shorts.

Evelyn tells me about a partial eclipse of the moon she saw from her front step last year. "Imagine," she says. "The whole Earth blocking out part of the sun. An entire planet casting its shadow through space and blacking out the surface of the moon."

Evelyn stares toward the valley rim, quiet for a minute. Then she says, "There it is."

She points like it makes a difference, but she's somewhere else, her mind is out past the tip of her finger. It has taken her into space to look back down, or to stare out into nothing the other way.

I squint to make things clearer. I think I see a speck of light moving faster than the others, sunlight from behind the world bouncing off a bunch of metal canisters going seventeen thousand miles an hour. I don't know if it's a space station or a star, but either way, Evelyn and I stare. It's us, people, made it out in space.

Evelyn says, "There're two astronauts on it right now." Her voice is low like she's still out there. "A Russian and an American."

My brain goes to how it would be to share that canister with one other person, looking out a little circle-window, cold to touch, looking down at us on Evelyn's front step. I wonder if they flew over me last night, if they could see me with infrared sensors, a tiny dot in the dark, lying on the edge of a black gouge in the Earth. A pixel of heat seen by them riding a grain of sunlight through space, both wonders, that there can be something in so much nothing.

I blink and lose it.

It's not there when I say, "I have to get going. It's getting late."

I have nowhere to be, but don't want to outstay my welcome. I think Evelyn probably wants to go to bed even though she's still staring at the sky with distant eyes.

She tells me the couch is a pull-out bed if I need somewhere to sleep tonight.

It gets to me, that she's so nice, that I can't accept her kindness.

I'm not her problem. I concentrate on making my voice steady and tell her I have a place and I'm all good and thanks for the pizza, it was really good. Only one of these is true, which is okay.

She asks me to help her take the dishes inside and I do. Her house is hot and amber lit and it smells like pizza. I kick my shoes off at the door and hope she won't notice how dirty they are. She doesn't because she goes straight to the kitchen. She's talking about her house, apologizing about the mess, but I don't think it's all that messy.

When I leave, she tells me to come back anytime. "Door's always open," she says.

"Won't be around long," I say and tell her I'm going to the city soon.

She stares at me for a liar, then smiles. She rummages a scratchpad from a drawer and writes something.

"Here's my daughter's number," she says and hands me the page. "She's in Calgary, now. We talk on Sundays. I'll tell her you might call, that you might be coming her way."

I look down at the number, tidy writing above a smiling real estate agent who's *Bringing you home*. I tell her I'll call.

Evelyn sees I might not, so tells me, again, "If you head to Calgary, call that number. My girl's always happy to have an ear to fill."

The screen door bumps shut behind me and I sling my backpack over my good arm and walk back to the grocery store. It's late enough to be dark behind the automatic doors, except for a few security lights making long shadows down the aisles. The parking lot lights are on too, will be all night.

I sit on the curb beside a dark phone booth and watch the traffic on the highway drip slower and slower, fewer cars and longer between them as the hours go. I think about what to do next. I fish through my backpack, some clothes, a few granola-bar wrappers, my paperback with the newspaper-clipping bookmark.

I pull out a journal and this one's all blank pages. The one I was working in got left behind at the motel. I picture the old man from the office fixing the door to one-eleven this afternoon, ticked off because the room is trashed. I picture him going through whatever of my stuff Mr. Langman didn't take, sitting on the edge of my unmade bed and flipping through my notebook's scribblings. I'm embarrassed to think about what he reads because there's some private stuff, things I don't want to tell anyone, but wanted to get out of my head.

I write for a while under the parking lot light, write about Evelyn watching the sky and her being an astronaut in the space station. It seems both funny and sad and I write a story about an old space lady, making a frozen pizza for the other astronaut. And she talks to him all the time and she takes care of him like he's her own kid, all the while they're in orbit together. The astronaut is polite back, because she does all this stuff for him, but they're not really friends. It's sad because I think Evelyn watches the sky for dreams, so she doesn't feel so lonely when she's by herself in her house, just the teevee playing for company. Sometimes people need people around like they need air.

I write down what Evelyn said about my mom, not that I'll forget it, but I just want to think about her some more, now that I'm by myself. There're no cars on the highway. There're no people walking dogs. There's just me and a few moths bumping against the lights. Their wings catch the light, so quick they flicker like an old movie, almost invisible they move so fast. In their trails, I see where they've been, but never know where they are.

The other motel is across from the curb where I sit, beside the gas station. The "Vacancy" sign shivers with failing neon and I think I'll have to go there. I need somewhere to get cleaned up and some time to get my arm healed, to think about what comes next. I'm not going back online, so I have to think of something else. I've bought time though, with the money from running the Mr. Langmans for what they're worth.

I hold the page from the scratchpad that Evelyn wrote on, a name and a number, then pack up my stuff and cross the highway. This motel is painted white and the building is laid out in the shape of the letter cee, with the parking lot set in the middle.

I say, "I'll have a room." And the big lady behind the counter nods and pulls out some paperwork.

She wears a tank top and there's a fan blowing warm air around the office. The back of her arm wiggles as she writes. I wait and answer a few questions when she asks them. There's a small teevee on her desk, its reflection pink and blue in the window behind her. It bleats and flashes and she pauses to watch what's happening.

I don't listen to it. It's only noise.

When she asks how I'll pay, I root through my backpack for some cash. She takes most of it and asks me to sign the papers, says, "Room two oh seven."

I ask the time. She shrugs at the wall clock behind me and it's just past midnight.

Her eyes go back to the teevee show right away and the office door has bells that jangle on my way out. My room is on the second floor, so I go up the stairs and walk along the balcony until I find it. It's dark inside, but I don't turn on the lights. A bed, a little table, a nightstand, a chair, and a teevee, all the shadows arc in different places, but feel the same as every motel I've stayed in. I pull the curtains open and there's enough light coming in from the flickering motel sign, from the highway street lights. Someone stands on the corner near the street lights, the silhouette of a woman.

I drop my backpack and kick my shoes off. I strip off my clothes, leave them in a pile, and go lie on the bed. I'm too tired to shower and too hot for covers, so I lie on top of them. There's no way I'm turning the air conditioner on.

I watch the sky outside until it starts to get brighter.

Sometime after that, I fall asleep.

9

I have money now, for now. Ten thousand dollars is a bus ticket out of here and maybe enough to go find Miloš, maybe get a family again. It's a new pair of jeans. Ones that don't have holes in them, or frays at the ankles, or blood on them. It's a bed to sleep in and a roof over top of it. It's bacon and eggs and biscuits with white gravy on them, not just toast and not just counting coins out on the counter and then taking a penny from the penny bin near the till. It's the kind of money that gives the feeling that, for the next little while, everything will be just fine. It's everything.

I spend a week with the money sitting safe in my bank account, a week grateful for the rented roof over my head. I couldn't have it here with me, the money, not in this rundown, highway-side motel next to the gas station. I would go nuts thinking the door would get busted in and it would get stolen.

Across the highway, there's the supermarket. There's a sign on it that says it's "Big T" and some guy climbed up there one night and spray painted it so it says "Big Tits." It's only there for a morning, until it's painted over again.

Deep at night, through a gap in the curtains, sometimes there's a car parked out there and sometimes there's not. Around three o'clock, a garbage truck engine roars and bangs the garbage bins empty. The noise is okay. I don't need sleep anyhow and my injured arm alternates between aching and a steady pain-pulse. Sometimes my littlest two fingers go numb and disappear from me. When that happens, I have to open and close my hand again and again, like priming them to feel something again.

I spend a week living in that motel room, watching for the white pickup with out-of-province license plates in the motel parking lot, passing by on the highway, in the Big Tits' lot. Mostly it's just a big rig sometimes parked there, diesel idling a few hours of air conditioning into the sleeper. Then the lot's empty again a few hours later.

I saw the white pickup one night. I'm sure of it. Maybe Mr. Langman was waiting around for word of my body being found. Maybe he changed his mind on leaving me out there and was wanting to find me again, to finish up what he didn't do in the scrub brush. Maybe it wasn't him at all. Maybe I'm paranoid and maybe I've been in this town too long and have to be gone for no better reason but to be gone.

The motel room's nothing fancy. There're faded pastel paintings hanging in frames, prints of forest scenes and deers drinking from a creek run through the trees, a few others that don't have anything recognizable, just smears of colour. A stripe has formed along a seam of wallpaper in the bathroom. The glue let go and the paper started to curl to show that over time, things just come apart.

There're boot prints stuck in the carpet. I find a long, blonde hair under the pillow. My hair is brown, almost black, and cut short. I wonder what piece of me'll be left behind, missed by housekeeping to join the thousands of other ghosts in this room. The thought of this history, these hauntings, makes it hard to settle, and I don't sleep too good because of it neither.

I spend a week lying on the bed, the teevee burbling. I don't watch it, but it's always on, always flickering in the corner of my vision, no matter where I look. Instead of watching, I spend my time lying on the bed, scribbling in my notebook, trying to see through the world to what's behind it. Sometimes, what I write is good. Sometimes, when the good words aren't coming, I watch the semi-trailers sleep in the dark of Big Tits' parking lot.

Sometimes I read the paperback. I read it to the back cover and then start from the front one again, using the old newspaper article to mark the spots I stop.

Some mornings, looking out over the motel parking lot, I watch families pack their campers, or couples shuffle their belongings around in the trunk, and I cry that it's not me there. And it's okay, no one's around to see these times.

A week in this rented room. I take my pills and I keep my arm clean. I don't go to Evelyn again. I'm not her problem and should keep it that way. I look at her handwriting sometimes, on the scratchpad above the real estate agent's face, bringing you home.

If I'm here when housekeeping knocks, I ask them to come back tomorrow, no I don't need anything right now, thank you, well, maybe one of those little bottles of mouthwash and another little bar of soap.

I go to the diner near the traffic lights a few times, but don't see Elise waitressing again. There's always someone else and she charges me for every coffee, never giving it for free, not like Elise did.

I have a coffee and they make good chocolate chip cookies, so I keep going back for those. I read the day-late newspapers on the counter, working my way through the sections for a few hours, wasting bits of the day. There's usually nothing much interesting in the pages, but I like the comics and do the crossword as much as I can. Mostly get stuck, but once I get all the words.

10

I have money now, for now, and late in the week I turn stir-crazy, just animal-driven by something I can't help. I walk out the room and across the street and look back at the nighttime gas station, the pumps lit up in red and fluorescent white. A semi-truck pulls into Big Tits behind me and sits there idle. I keep still and watch the shadowed cab for a bit, then figure the driver's clambered in the back and gone sleeping for a few hours, won't be looking for me none.

I turn back to the gas station. The teller moves behind the window, lit up by the lotto sign's million-dollar red, and I watch from the shadows, the woman I've seen standing out here, down by the lights, sometimes one, sometimes two of them at the edge of the highway, every night, the night after, and again. Once, the RCMP pulled by, but the women were gone before he saw and were back quick enough to be lit by the cruiser's taillight glow.

I'm curious, what they're about, how much they cost, what they do, how they feel about it. And cast green by the traffic light, Cheryl, that's the name she gives me, she looks me up and down, says, "Nothing but a lanky damn kid, ain't you?"

I shrug because there's nothing can be done about that. We talk.

Cheryl is addicted to something, but won't tell me what. For twenty dollars, she says she'll give me head. She says she doesn't feel much about it one way or the other, thinks it's weird that I ask, says, "Nobody ever asks more'n a few questions of me."

I have more questions and she answers by asking one back.

"Want a smoke?"

"Don't, thanks."

She fumbles the pack back into her bra while watching, sidelong, a pickup pull into the gas station across the road. She flares bright in the lighter flame and then drops dark again, the bead lights off her eyes when they turn to me, like a small glow from inside her.

"Hey, I gotta work some. If you do too, s'fine." She points the tweezered cherry at the semi that pulled in a while back, says over its idling diesel, tone tired but not mean, "That's a good man. He's your kind."

I burn red and turn to hide it and wind up facing the truck. The cab's dark; the engine mutters. By the time I turn back to Cheryl, she's become a waft of cigarette smoke. I catch her crossing against the red to the gas station. She gets in the pickup, then's gone. I don't burn anymore because she was nothing but beat-down honest.

The sleeper hatch cracks open when I tap, tap, tap, then comes a bit wider to show a bearded guy, bleary, who looks me up and down, confused a moment, then he motions for me in. I stretch a few seconds out, then look at him again, then walk away.

I put my hands in my pocket to keep them still. I look back once and he's not moved. I keep walking.

The sleeper hatch claps shut and I check back again to see him follow. In that glance, I caught not much, a guy, bigger than me and older than me, jeans and broad shoulders in a teeshirt, brown work boots.

My heart flies inside, caught-bird crazy, battering itself stupid against my ribs, trying to bust out. I cross the highway and look back to see he's stopped, staring at me. I stop, too, look up the length of red-lit highway, him a shape in the corner of my eye. He's got a beard and a ball cap on, a bit of a belly.

When he decides this is real, he starts to cross and I lead him back to my room, kick off a shoe to prop the door, and he's through seconds later. The door clicks shut behind. He's a rush off with my clothes and there's only us breathing hard. He stops, stares at me by the highway light, looking everywhere but my eyes. Then he's a rush off with his. I try to see him in the faint light and he's thick and muscle pushing under flesh, then he shoves me to the bed and holds me down, hot skin and strong gravity. I wince at a shock from my cut arm.

In my ear, he says, "Okay?"

I strain back but get nothing, he's twice me. My skin feels tight and tender touch gone. My head is thick and cloudy and diluted.

I nod and say, "Anything." Then say it again, so he's got no doubt.

His mouth tastes like cigarettes and his beard is rough. His skin tastes salty. His chest is coarse hair and I want to touch, but he pins my arms harder. The smell of him is sweat and earth and a hundred of miles of highway.

He doesn't waste much time on my lips or neck before he pushes back, clamps my ankles to twist me over facedown, and goes down. He becomes heat and pressure, more important, that, than anybody specific. It's only one part of him I want anyway and he holds my hips in a strong gripped promise.

And even wet with spit and tongue-teased first, it hurts.

And I want it to because it's the only thing I want to focus on.

It's been a long time and not often before, but comes as a release, the total demand of these smells and sensations that makes everything else telescope back, pulled far away and made small to hide in the corner of the room for these minutes. It's quiet here, focused, so filled there's not room for anything else. It's a feeling I want to never get used to, so that it can be this hiding place every time.

It's like that for a bit, before it isn't anymore.

I come first and too quick and it takes him longer. It's okay, because the end was never the point, the time between was, and that can drag on for as long as it needs. And finally, he grunts and curves forward onto my back. We stay there a while, then fall side by side, quiet for a while.

Then he thanks me, the two words delivered by warm cigarette breath. I wish he didn't say it, like I wasn't the one who knocked on the side of his trailer, the assumption wasn't that he'd served me, that he wasn't the one to submit. I don't say any of it, though.

Let him think whatever because it doesn't change how we each got what we needed. Doesn't matter because there's no more here.

Headlights slide across the ceiling and he asks if he can use the shower.

I say, "Sure."

He clicks on the lamp and looks at me good for the first time, in good light, slow and top to bottom. I don't feel shy about it and look at him, too. He smiles and I don't feel like doing it back, so I don't.

From the shower, over the sound of the running water, he asks, "What happened to your arm?"

I say, "Fell off my bike."

"Looks bad," and he doesn't say anything else, just shuts off the water after a while. Then all that's left is steam and a slowing drip from the shower head.

After he dries himself, he asks if he can use the mouthwash.

"Sure," I say, then add, "but not the toothbrush."

I watch him from the bed. He comes out naked and gathers his clothes from the floor and sits on the end on the bed to dress.

He says, "I can stay for a bit, if you want."

I say, "Don't."

He nods, putting his boots on, then stops. Just for a second, he looks back at me, says, "You got a family here?" Then quickly shakes his head, ties his laces. "Shouldn't have asked."

A few minutes after, I'm alone again and staring at a fifty he'd dropped on the nightstand. I don't care he did it because it wasn't about that. But maybe it was for him. I didn't notice it before the door clicked shut on the end of us.

At the window about ten minutes later, his truck is already gone.

I shower and use the towel he'd left on the bathroom floor, hold it to my nose and hunt for a hint of him in the damp cotton, trying to get back to where we'd been, but there's nothing there. In the mirror, the skin at my hipbones is still red from his grip. I don't look at the fifty on the nightstand when I come back out.

I spend the rest of the night trying to get this feeling on paper, the chicken I'd felt just before tapping, the uncertainty when he followed me, the feel of him pulsing down after he'd done, and those fifty bucks left back. And I wake in the morning with my cheek on the table. And I read what I wrote and it didn't work out how I wanted.

I put the fifty in my pack because I don't want to look at it, because that's now past, something done and over, to carry to tomorrow and tomorrow again. I think last night just had to be, no choice in it, just don't think of it again, the clear mind judges the animal one differently, but not always correctly.

If nothing, slept better than I remember in forever.

I pick at my stitches, but none let go. I take my pills and my arm doesn't get infected like Barry said it might. I put some cream on it and stretch it gently because the skin is scarring and feels tight. I flex my fingers to get the feeling back and wonder if it will always be like this now.

I can't think on living in the boredom of this rented room for longer than a week. When my arm feels good enough, when I feel safe enough from Mr. Langman, I'm ready to go. I get more granola bars from Big Tits because I'm leaving and want some food to take with me. I stuff my backpack with my underwear, my extra pair of jeans, my teeshirts, my notebook and paperback, and sling it over my shoulder.

Bells on a string bang against the office door and the air inside is warm laundry and cigarette smoke. It's hot and loud, the sun coming through and the laundry machines running hard in the back room. The woman behind the counter doesn't know me from when I checked in and doesn't seem to care much about anything either. She doesn't look away from the little teevee, sticks to watching it when I drop the key on the counter.

She just says, "Checking out," like it's a question or a statement, either way doesn't matter. She reaches for a cigarette that's burning down in the notch of an ashtray that has the motel's name and phone number printed in gold letters flaking from the black plastic.

I don't say anything, just leave. The bank's about a ten-minute walk beside the highway. The heat comes back off the pavement and it gathers thick, even though it's only early morning.

The bank is the same one my dad took me to ten years ago, when I was a little kid opening an account to start saving my money. I remember being excited to get taken around the teller's counter, to sit at a desk in the back. My dad had to sign all the papers too, to start the account, and whenever I wanted to take money out of it. I remember my first attempt at a signature and how it looked like what an eight-year-old thought a signature should look like. It looked bad next to my dad's, which was smoother, more effortlessly tangled from a life's worth of use.

I tried saving up for a computer, but after a few weeks, I couldn't figure the difference between what I had and what one cost, so I took out my money and bought comic books instead. I couldn't wait because I couldn't figure the passing of time too easy, had no perspective of what it was. I have more now. Ten years and your brain firms up a bit and you know what's important and how much a computer costs, and how to better judge of the gap between what you have and what you want. More important, you can better figure out if you can even ever make the two meet.

I get to the bank early. The doors are locked and the sticker on the glass says it doesn't open for another half hour. So, I sit on the curb and pick at my stitches more. I want them out, but they just pull up my skin like meat with hooks through it.

11

When it's morning and you don't know what day it is, it can be any day. When you live a good part of your life in the same place and then have ten thousand dollars in your backpack, you can go anywhere. Why any of this matters is because I stand at the gas station beside the highway, looking at the bus schedule. I have to ask the guy at the counter what day it is.

He tells me Tuesday.

And what time it is.

He tells me almost noon.

I ask for a ticket for the bus to Calgary and he tells me seventy-seven dollars and fifty cents, which I pay from one of the two envelopes the bank teller put my cash money in.

I think I see him raise an eyebrow at the envelope, so before the bus comes, I go to the washroom round the side and lock myself in. I take out a few hundred dollars and put it in my pocket, so I won't have to show off all the money every time I need just a bit of it. The rest I try hiding in my jeans pockets, then tucked in my belt line, but it looks funny wherever it's stashed, so in the end it goes back into the backpack.

The bus comes a while later, me sitting the whole time on a bench, squinting in the sun at people filling their gas tanks and moving on after. It pulls up under the awning alongside the station and brings a cloud of dust and diesel fumes. I squint and stand behind the only other guy getting on. The driver lady, she asks for my ticket and waves me by when I show it, her eyes looking distant, past the bugs stuck on the windscreen.

There's the smell and the noise of the bus engine churning. The air conditioning is on, but only does a little work against the heat. The guy who sold me the ticket comes out and throws a duffle bag into the cargo space under the bus. He bangs the compartment closed then walks by the door, slaps it twice with a flat hand. The bus driver lady nods and waves at him, before putting us into gear and getting us rolling.

The bus is quieter when it's moving compared to when it's stopped, now a purring thrum through my feet on the floor and on my cheek against the warm window. My backpack's in my lap, hugged against my chest with arms crossed over tight. I don't want to put it in the overhead compartment, and I don't want it out of sight under the seat in front of me.

The bus trip's going to be something like five hours. That's what the guy who sold me the ticket said. On the map he had pinned under cloudy plastic on the counter, the actual distance from start to end, across the land drawn in a straight line, was not that far. But with the bends in the roads and all the stops in tiny towns, all of them smaller than this one we're pulling out of, with all that, the trip's longer.

The bus doesn't bother me, the hours sitting don't either. I have this thing where I can fall asleep on a bus and not wake up until the engine stops. Nothing can bug me and it's the best sleep a body could want. It happens in cars and trains and airplanes too, though I've never been on an airplane or a train before, so just guessing on those. The doctor called it motion-induced narcolepsy, which I guess is true because I even fell asleep on my dirt bike once. While the doctor was picking gravel out of my leg, he told me I couldn't have a driver's license anymore. That's why I never drive anywhere now and why I don't have a dirt bike anymore. It's also why my leg's scarred up with marks that'll last as long as I do.

We rumble down Main Street, the morning highway, past the diner and past the bank, past a pink concrete triceratops near a fire hydrant, and in a few blocks, past the motel I spent a week at. I don't expect to see Cheryl, swaying foot to foot by the highway, because her life is at night. She's somewhere else, now, maybe sleeping away daylight. On the opposite side of the highway, the Big Tits parking lot is half-full with parked cars and one that's driving toward the exit. We roll past room one-eleven with the sun-faded numbers and the sheet of plywood still holding the door shut.

Then the engine gets louder and it's the last time I'll see these buildings. The bus climbs the hill, up and out of the valley. After that, there's just flat land and pumpjacks nodding and pale blue sky and the straight road ahead.

The horizon is so wide and I wonder if the ants have eaten all my blood out of the dust, or if it'll just stay there forever in the sand.

Then I fall asleep, arms hugged tight around my backpack.

BOOK II

1

The bus is quiet and still, and when I open my eyes, it sits in a giant, grey-lit parking garage. There are ten other buses in a line, or something close to that. The driver's shaking my shoulder and telling me we're here and if I have to transfer, to do it because her bus isn't going anywhere else. She looks tired and smells like her musty polyester vest, the bus line's name patch sewn on the pocket.

I thank her, confused from just waking up, hug my backpack to me and get off the bus, through a door, and into the terminal. It's a wide space with low ceilings and a fluorescent-light hum. There're lockers and plastic benches and a diner to one side, one guy there, curved over a coffee, and the server stares at the weather forecast on the teevee sat at the end of the counter.

Outside, I'm blocks past the tallest office towers. It's night, but no stars make it through the city glow. It's dark from here to there and I walk across some grass and along an empty road. All the buildings have their lights on, boom-time hotels and oil companies, and it's hot and the streets are wide black asphalt between the sidewalks. I guess it's not too late yet because there're still restaurants and bars with lit-up open signs. Then again, this is the city, and things don't close much or for long, so I'm really not sure how late it is. Cars drive by a guy, him pushing a heaped-up shopping cart through the darkness between headlights.

There's a bank of pay phones, one has gum stuck on the mouthpiece, one just makes static, and the last one works fine. I pull the number Evelyn gave me and call it. I don't know what else to do. A girl answers, Evelyn's daughter Angela, and she's confused for a moment until I explain how I got her number.

She says, "Oh right, Mom said you might call. Didn't think you would though. People always promise stuff they never do."

She gives me an address, says it's a laundromat, and we plan to meet. She says she's happy I called and it sounds true that she is.

I walk one street and turn down the next, through a shadowy underpass that booms thunder from a train passing overhead, and find myself surrounded by the shop lights and noise, just few blocks from downtown. I follow street numbers to the place Angela said to go. There're people, more than I've seen, and the car headlights and the street lamps fake daytime. It's hardly night without looking up to the barely dark sky beyond the washout.

An electric sign in a convenience store window scrolls that it's ten thirty-five and it's open twenty-four hours a day and the lottery is worth twenty-three million, if you can win it. It doesn't scroll the temperature, but my teeshirt's sweaty-wet where it's pinned between my back and my backpack. The air smells like exhaust and dust, sometimes a whiff of vomit or garbage when I go by an alley.

There're people walking. A guy bumps into me and looks at me like it's my fault. He's had drinks, the smell of it's sweet on him, so I mumble an apology and look away because I don't need a fight right now. I feel in my pocket for the money I put there earlier, scared the drunk guy pickpocketed me. In the movies, that's what happens when someone bumps into you. The bills are still there. I hold my backpack straps inside fists and walk tall, trying to make myself seem bigger because I can't make myself disappear.

A motorbike blasts by and the riot from its tailpipe kills every other noise, wrestling it from the air for a split second and smacking it against the walls all around. I'm not used to things this busy. There's too much noise and it's weird there're not any stars when the sky's night. I'm glad to step into the laundromat next to the convenience store. I need to stop for a moment. There's still time to when I meet Angela and I should wash my clothes because alls I have is dirty.

There's a lady on a stool reading a magazine behind a scratched-up counter. I give her a twenty and she gives me two small boxes of detergent and fifteen bucks worth of coins from a metal box. I thank her, but her eyes stay fixed on the magazine like I'm not even there.

I look at the machines, the washers and the dryers. Two washers are full and spinning, but no one else's here but me and the lady.

I'm not used to this, being so out of place and awkward. I'm over-thinking everything I do, even how I move, trying to look like I belong. I'm just off a bus, in a city I don't know, and pretty much all I own is what I put into the washing machine. The detergent smells like how a chemist thinks lemons smell, but it's not close. The dust that comes up from dumping the powder into the machine makes me cough. The lady doesn't look up from her magazine, doesn't say, "Bless you," which is fine because I wouldn't know what to do with that.

"Regular" and "Cold" click and the machine hisses loud when water flows into it.

The bench I sit on has the word "skeezy" scratched into the plastic with lightning-shaped letters. I don't know that word. I pick at the dark gunk that fills the scratches and it's greasy and gets stuck under my fingernail. I flip through the pile of magazines on a nearby chair, but there's nothing there for me, only pages full of beauty secrets and love quizzes and dieting tips.

I pull the newspaper clipping from my backpack and look at it. It's suddenly the only thing that keeps me from getting lost; it's an endpoint, a purpose. I'm not used to this, having a plan and a place to go. Even though I've barely started, and have so much farther to go, I don't rush. There's time. I fold the page over, between my thumb and forefinger, the paper feels like dust and it makes a shiver crawl my spine.

Someone asks, "Interesting article?"

And there's a girl there. I didn't see her come in and I didn't see her sit next to me, but there's so much movement here that it's not a surprise. I tuck the page back into the paperback in my pack.

I'm not used to this, a pretty girl talking to me in the too-bright lights of a city laundromat at night. She realizes this right away, because I don't answer her.

She says, "Sorry," but then looks at me a little pissed off.

She says, "You know, you can talk to me. There's no reason not to."

I still don't know what to say. She's around my age, probably a few years older. She wears makeup and a tank top and jeans that fit her right. I can't stop looking at her. Her hair is thick brown spirals to her chin and looks soft. Her lips look wet and they ask, "Are you simple or something?" She doesn't say it mean, just asks it because I still haven't said anything back.

I say, "I'm not." And then ask her why she has to get in my face like that, just because I didn't answer her right away.

She doesn't apologize, says, "It's rude not to reply when someone talks to you."

She's right and I tell her that I'm sorry. She smiles and it's nice. I guess it's not too late to make this better. The machine that's sloshing my clothes around says twenty-three minutes left.

She grins big like she's been joking me the whole time, says, "I'm Angela."

And I'm relieved in those two words.

Angela laughs because it's so clear on my face. Then serious. "Thanks for stopping in to see my mom, really. Evelyn needs people."

I nod and there's quiet between us a bit. Awkward because I don't know what happens now, I ask her what she's doing here, and she smiles again, says, "Waiting for my laundry."

Then she sees that I'm trying and that she's hurt my efforts, so she asks me about what I'm doing and I tell her I just got into the city. She nods like it's obvious.

She points at my arm, at the stitches and asks, "What happened?"

I say, "I fell off my dirt bike."

She says, "Did it hurt?"

"Not at first." I scowl at the cut, remembering. "It was weird. I didn't notice for a while. Now, I can't stop the tingling in my little fingers."

"It's probably nerve damage," she says matter-of-fact, like she's a doctor. I ask how she knows, and she shrugs and tells me she doesn't really, says, "Just a guess. Makes sense though, doesn't it?" She watches people go by outside for a moment, then asks me where I'm staying tonight and I tell her I don't know.

She says, "You can crash at my place, if you've got nowhere else." She looks at me, says, "You remind me of someone."

She reads my face and says, "I see you're not a threat because you're a bit simple." She smiles, like at a joke. "You don't scare me. I have a football player roommate and I sleep with a gun under my pillow. I'll shoot your face off if you try anything." She laughs. "Anyway, Mom would kill me if I left you on the street."

I can't tell if she's joking about the gun, but I'm raw about her calling me simple twice so I tell her again I'm not.

I say, "I just don't have much practice talking to pretty girls."

And she says, "So, you think I'm pretty."

Heat rises in my face.

She says, "You can sleep on our couch, as long as you promise not to steal anything."

I promise her I won't.

2

My dryer-warm clothes are stuffed into my backpack and Angela leads me up four flights of worn-carpet stairs in her building, a creaking walk-up a few blocks from the laundromat. The air smells old, but not bad, like it's been breathed a few times before. I'm carrying her duffle of clean clothes, too. She didn't want me to at first, but I thought it was right and she let me. She called me a dork, but looked at me kindly when she said it, so I got it as her joking around.

There's a mismatched pair of letters on her apartment door, yellow plastic "4", small brass "C". It's unlocked, a one-bedroom place, and she wasn't lying about the football player roommate. He's there and as big as she said he was. She was lying about the roommate part though, that's clear in the way they kiss each other. So, she has told a truth and made up a fiction, which still leaves me wondering if she has a gun under her pillow.

"What's that?" her boyfriend says and points at me.

Angela tells him that I'm the guy Evelyn mentioned and he mumbles something about her charity cases. Angela tells him that

I don't have a place and that I remind her of her little brother. She asks, "If Jake was new in a city and didn't have anywhere to stay, wouldn't you want someone to give him a couch to crash on?"

Her boyfriend mutters that I better not steal anything and I tell him I won't.

I'm not used to this, kind strangers in a small, hot apartment. We sit around a messy coffee table, candy wrappers and magazines and a plate with a peanut butter smear. Angela and her boyfriend are on the couch and I'm kneeling, across the table from them, sitting on my ankles until my legs go numb. Then I sit cross-legged, my hands on my knees. We talk and we laugh and we listen to music coming from an iPod hooked into some small speakers.

They're all right, Angela and her boyfriend. He's not such a dick like he seemed at first. He rolls a joint and we pass it around. I've smoked pot before and it just made me dizzy and sleepy. I tell them this and they laugh when I slide sideways to the floor and curl up. I push my pack under the coffee table because I think it'll be safe there for the night. I close my eyes. Angela and her boyfriend talk some more. I watch the red light coming through my eyelids, the ghost shapes floating inside my eyes, listening to them and to the music.

After a while, Angela lifts my head and puts a pillow under it, puts a crocheted blanket over me. When I hear them go to the bedroom, I throw the blanket back. It's too hot, but it's nice to have her think of covering me up. I lie on the floor and take off everything except my boxers and I still sweat.

After a while, I hear the gasp and creak of them having sex and I try not to imagine them together, but I can't help it, picturing their skin pressed together and moving. My hard-on keeps me awake because I can't stop thinking about them like that, so close in the next room. After a while, all I hear is the occasional car go by on the early-hours street. The sound comes through the open window, and at some point I don't hear it anymore either, because the buzz brings sleep.

3

It's light out again. Windows show blue sky. I blink a few times to clear my sight. Angela's sitting on the couch across from me. She points the back of her cell phone at me and it makes an old-time camera noise, even though there are no parts that would make the noise. I can't think if it's weird or not, her having my picture. I just woke up and can't think quick enough. I pull the blanket over me because I'm only wearing boxers and lying on their floor. Her boyfriend's in the kitchen, cutlery and dishes making noise.

From under the blanket, I ask Angela what she's doing and she tells me that she's sending my picture to her little brother.

"I think Jake would like you," she says.

I nod. "Is he gay or something?" I ask and she tells me she doesn't think so, but maybe he is and just hasn't said.

She says, "You look and talk just like him, so I think you would get along."

I ask about where he is and she says he went to the coast for university.

I sit up for a moment, drowsy, and can't think the last time I slept so much. It makes me want to lie down and try to go back to sleep, so I do. As I'm pulling the crocheted blanket over my head again, Angela takes another picture of me and then puts her phone on the coffee table.

A few minutes pass and I wake up some more, listening to Angela and her boyfriend talking, moving around. From beneath the blanket, through a gap near the floor, I see dust under the coffee table. I think about it for a moment before throwing the blanket back. My backpack isn't there. I bolt up and look around, frantic, my heart pounding.

I say, "Where's my pack?"

Angela and her boyfriend sit on the couch eating cereal out of mismatched bowls they hold under their chins. They freeze, mouths open a bit and spoons halfway there.

"Right there," Angela says, pointing her spoon at where it sits beside them, at the end of the couch.

"Don't touch my stuff," I say instinctively, but then regret it.

"Sorry," she says. "I just moved it off the floor."

"A little grace, maybe?" Angela's boyfriend says to me and folds his leg under.

"I'm sorry," I say. "It's just all I have."

Angela's boyfriend gathers the cereal bowls when they're done and takes them to the kitchen. Angela watches me get dressed in the same clothes I was wearing last night.

Her boyfriend comes back, looks at me, then kisses her, and says, "Almost ten. Got to get to work."

It's then I realize I don't know these people. I don't know where they work or what they do when they aren't at work. He leaves me and Angela alone.

There's some quiet between us and then I point to the iPod and ask how much they cost.

She tells me a new one is a few hundred bucks and I ask if she'll sell me hers for that price and then she can get a brand new one.

She looks at me funny before agreeing. She disconnects it from the speaker and gives it to me. I root in my backpack and take three hundred dollars from an envelope, trying not to let her see the rest.

"That's too much," she says and I tell her it's okay. She looks at the cash, gets up and then comes back with some earphones and the charger cord and hands them to me.

I say, "I should go."

Angela asks how long I'm in the city for and I tell her I'm going to try to leave today. She points at me, all serious, and says, "If you need any help, like directions or anything, you call me."

I tell her I will, and at the door say, "Thanks for letting me crash."

"You're welcome," she says and hugs me.

I sling my backpack and leave.

The stairwell is dim, seemed brighter last night. There're stains on the carpet and some muted thumping coming through the wall.

The small lobby smells like piss now, when it didn't last night, and I push my way through the door and onto the street.

Everything's different in daylight. The bars are quiet and buildings hunker down there, behind them, not glittering anymore, and the company signs at the top are now just washed out, not even real colours. It's only a city today, where last night it was something more, more alien, and more intense.

I didn't have breakfast and I'm really hungry. I go to the convenience store that I saw last night near the laundromat and buy a shiny hot dog off the roller and a cold soda from the fridge. Back on the street, I give my leftover coins to a guy in tatters who asks for them. I eat the hot dog and drink the soda. There're not many taxis but I wave at each until one finally pulls out of the traffic going by.

I ask the guy to take me to the airport and he pokes the meter to start it.

4

At the counter I ask for a ticket to Belgrade.

The lady pecks at the computer and says, "All connecting flights are full until early next week. You could always fly standby, but of course, you wouldn't be guaranteed a seat."

I ask for a ticket to London and she examines me for a second before pecking at her computer again and telling me two days.

I ask where in Europe she can get me sooner than that, and she says, "There're some seats on an early flight to Schiphol."

I ask her where that is and she says, "Netherlands." And I tell her that's fine.

She says, "It's a six a.m. departure." And I say, "That's fine."

She asks for my passport and I give it to her. She asks for thirteen hundred dollars and when I pull one of my envelopes out of my backpack, she asks me to wait and calls her manager over. She explains to the manager lady that I'm purchasing a ticket and then she watches me finish counting out cash from the envelope. The manager lady, Lydia by the printing on her name tag, waits until I stop. Then we all look at each other for a moment. I tell her

I'm going to Europe, have a big trip planned, meeting some friends. Only one of which is true, but that's okay.

Lydia looks at my passport and calls me "Mister," as if I was my dad. She asks if there's been a death in the family or a sickness, perhaps they could expedite me.

I tell her no one died.

She asks if I could explain to her "the sense of urgency."

I say, "It doesn't matter where I start from. I'm backpacking and it's going to be an adventure."

Her eyes dart to the cash on the counter and the stack of bills peeking out of the envelope in my hand. She looks at the computer screen, types on a few keys, and smiles at me.

"Would you like an email confirmation?"

I say, "Paper's good."

She tells me the flight starts boarding at five-fifteen tomorrow morning and please check in two hours early, so I'll have enough time to go through security. She hands me a printout and says, "Have a pleasant adventure." I think she means it.

I smile as soon as my back's to the counter. Soon, I'll be gone. There're clocks everywhere in the airport. It's just past noon and I go to the concourse mall to waste some time. There're coffee shops and stores with junky plastic toys, a bookstore where I browse, but can't find anything I want to read.

At an internet cafe, the coffee is bad so I leave it while searching for Miloš again. Only a few pages are in English. I find the picture, the same that's in my newspaper cutting. It's clearer, so I stare at his face, but it still seems that the longer I stare, the less focused it gets. There's nothing new but that, so I leave it.

There's a food court and I'm hungry, so I order fast-food Chinese. Even though there're still hours to waste, the food court makes me want to hurry. It's all the people moving around that makes it that way, always moving in the corner of my eye, dragging cases and carrying bags.

The foreign exchange booth near the food court has a countertop gap in security glass to pass money through and back, a little metal box set in it to talk through. I ask for Euros, and he nods and counts out my bills onto the counter. I keep a few cash dollars because there's still time to kill before my flight takes off. He does the math and gives me fewer Euros than I gave him dollars, but apparently it's all worth the same.

I want to call Angela to thank her again for letting me crash at her place. For some reason, I feel like I should let her know I'm okay, and that I'm leaving the city. It's probably because she was nice to me when I really needed it, so I feel I owe her.

Hunting for a pay phone, the terminal seems to go on and on, just wandering into forever. After a few minutes, I find a phone to put some coins in. I search my pocket for the page Evelyn wrote her number on, bringing you home, but can't find it, so I hang up the receiver again. The phone doesn't give my coins back, so I hit it and walk away.

With hours to go, I make my way back through the concourse mall. At the travel store, I buy a toothbrush and a little tube of toothpaste and a power converter so I can charge my iPod in Europe. The lady gives me a clear plastic bag and tells me to put any liquids in it when I go through security. I buy a pack of gum and a chocolate bar too, and she smiles at me like a mom would when she hands me the change. I like the way she looks at me, but I don't want to think too long on it, so I move on.

With nothing better to do, I stand in line to be scanned and screened by security. I figure to go to the other side because there's nothing left to see on this one. Maybe I'll write in my journal. Maybe I won't. Maybe I'll just listen to Angela's iPod. Maybe I'll sleep some, but I doubt it.

Hours to go and I'm still at security because I'm selected for a random search and can't help thinking of Lydia, back at the ticket counter, that maybe she typed something in the computer and had them pick on me. So, now I'm in a room with windows looking out at the security lines and a tinted bubble camera in the corner looking in at me. I'm asked to unpack my stuff onto a table, so I do. A stern-faced guy puts on blue rubber gloves and picks through my clothes and rubs some of it with cloths to see if I have any bombs hidden in my packed underwear. In this situation, I'm worried that maybe, somehow, a bomb did wind up in there, even though I've never seen one in my life.

He says, "You can go."

Hours to go and I drop my last quarter into an old Pac-Man arcade game. There're some other games, but they're all old, from when arcade games were just new and only cost a quarter to play. The sound and graphics are bad, but it doesn't matter because it kills the minutes better than sitting and staring at the runway, or sitting and just thinking too much. Instead, I work my Pac-Man through a maze, dodging ghosts and finding power pellets so I can sometimes eat the ghosts instead of them always eating me. My eyes are dry and itchy, so I can't do as good as I should. After a few levels, the pink ghost gets me. My last Pac-Man turns inside out and pops like a bubble.

By the time I walk out of the arcade, the sun is gone. I sit facing a runway, loop my arm through a backpack strap and stare out at the city buildings, lit up and faraway small. I think about Angela and her boyfriend, the sounds of them having sex in the other room from where I laid on the floor. I think of Mr. Langman standing over me, holding a rock against the black. I think of Evelyn and what she told me about my parents and about the astronauts, then I think of the guy from the parking lot semi-truck, didn't know his name. I hate having only one-night people, the way it makes me a one-night person, and then gone.

I pull out the newspaper bookmark from my pack and re-read the article. I stare at the picture of Miloš surrounded by the text, a picture of an old, bearded guy sitting on a wooden chair under some kind of flowering tree. He doesn't look at the camera, he looks at something hidden past the border of the picture instead. He's not smiling, but he's also not sad. After a while, I can't see him anymore. I've searched the image too deep and there're just a bunch of black ink dots on grey paper.

Then I just stare out at the runway again.

5

The sun isn't up yet when they start us boarding. Most of the seats in the waiting lounge are full when the announcement comes overhead and I think of how short the night is when you see it through. I've seen a lot through, but it never stops me wondering what I miss whenever I'm asleep, that the idea of days means nothing. There's just the idea of how little time there actually is between sunset and sunrise, here sitting in a boarding lounge in a plastic chair and waiting for it to cycle.

I sit forward, put my elbows on my knees and knit my fingers to rest my chin on them. This girl next to me, she's about my age and only seems to notice me when I lean forward, like I just appeared there. I've noticed her though, since she sat down and looked the other way.

Now she looks at me and I can tell she's figuring on talking to me like I've been trying to figure out how to talk to her for a while. It's weird, being nervous to talk to someone, but a body is. We look at each other. She doesn't turn away, but she doesn't say anything either.

So, I do it. "What's your name?"

She says, "Mon. It's short for Monica, which I hate the sound of, so everyone calls me Mon."

I nod and say, "I don't think it's that bad."

She shrugs. She has brown hair, brown skin and light green eyes. She has a sharp chin and really white teeth compared to her lips. My eyes slide to the space on the bench next to her. There, two backpacks and a hoodie.

I ask her if she's travelling on her own and she tells me no, that it's her and her boyfriend going backpacking around Europe for a month or two, depending on how long their money lasts.

She says, "We have some friends we're meeting in Brussels. My boyfriend's older brother is over there already, backpacking, coming from Krakow to meet us in Amsterdam."

She tells me she always wanted to see Rome since she was a little girl and it sparkled in her imagination, put there by some fairy-tale book her dad read to her over and over again. She's always wanted to visit the Spanish Steps, since she first saw Audrey Hepburn on them in some old movie she watched with her mom. She tells me she thinks Audrey Hepburn was so pretty and really tiny. I don't know different, so I nod.

The attendant calls to seat the fancy rows. Mon and I check our tickets and we're both in the back part of the plane, but not in the same row. Mon introduces her boyfriend when he comes back. His name is Kai and he's bigger than me, but not in as good shape. He's handsome, but in a boring way.

He says, "Hey, bro, what's up?" Which I think sounds dumb, but we chat for a little bit and he seems okay. He smiles a lot and he obviously loves Mon because he's always looking at her, even when he's talking to me. He's always touching her leg or her shoulder, like he can't believe she's really there and has to keep checking. I understand why, she's pretty and when she laughs it sounds really good.

They say we should hang out in Amsterdam together, since I'm on my own and all. "Maybe we could travel together for a while," they say. "If we're heading the same way."

I can tell Mon means it, but I'm not sure Kai does. I tell them I'd like that a lot.

Mon asks me where I'm going and what I'm going to do.

I say, "I'm heading to Paris and then maybe Italy." I tell her I like art and want to see some. I say, like her with Rome, I saw a book of the paintings in Paris and I'm going to see if the reality of the place can match my imagination. She believes me and I feel bad about that, but it was my mouth's first instinct, didn't even think not to lie.

Kai says, "The line's short now. We should go."

Passport and boarding pass, down a tunnel that smells like nighttime and jet fuel the whole way to the plane at the end. Kai and Mon sit together three rows behind me, talking quietly, and it makes me so lonely that I've never had someone like that, and how bad I've wanted someone I could be with. I stow my backpack under the seat in front of me and put my foot on it, so I know it's always there.

The cabin lights dim and the plane is left lit by scattered reading lights and the blue glow of the safety video playing the same on every seat-back teevee. The flight attendants stand in the aisle, clipping a buckle and then unclipping it again, to make sure we all know how a seatbelt works. They're telling us what to do when the plane crashes and how to jump out, unless it's even worse outside.

Sleep is coming on me when the plane jolts and starts backward across the tarmac. We aren't going fast because there's a guy walking beside the plane, carrying a glowing orange stick. All I see is his outline, the flash-cross of his reflective vest catching light and the orange glow stick held above his head. The safety video ends and the captain tells the crew something about checking the doors are all closed. Our plane starts driving around the runways, looking for the one we'll leave from.

The little girl next to me tells me about her dad and about how they are going to see him. She's seven or eight or something around there. She says, "My dad works in Holland and we might move there next year."

I nod and tell her that's great and say, "I'm sure your dad's really excited to see you."

The girl's mom sits in the aisle seat. She watches me out of the corner of her eye, but keeps her head facing her magazine. I can tell she's not reading, that she's listening. Then she decides that I'm okay and she goes back to reading.

I think about how exciting it must be for the little girl and I open myself to a bit of that excitement, too. It tempers the loneliness, but it's a weird mix of feelings, pulling in opposite directions.

The little girl asks if I'm going to visit my dad, too.

I tell her that I'm not, that I'm going to Europe to go to school to study magic and potions. Only one of these things is true, but it's okay.

She looks at me sly, like she's almost sure I'm lying, almost. She asks, "Do you know any magic yet?"

I say, "I do."

I tell her, when I was little, like her age, my dad told me that on my birthday, and only that once in a year, I could do a magic spell. He taught me the words that I had to say, that it had to be said just right, at eleven-eighteen at night, because that's when I was born. I have to be barefoot when I say the words, he told me, like when I was born.

She says, "Has it ever worked?" And I say, "Not in the thirteen years I've tried."

"What does the spell do?" she asks.

"I don't know for sure." I fake puzzlement to buy time to think up something. Then, "My dad just said it made everything good for the whole next year."

"Do you still believe in it?" the kid asks.

And I say, "I can't not. What if it's true and what if it works? It's easy to do, so it would be silly to waste the hope of it. Shouldn't ever waste hope."

The girl asks to know the words and I tell her.

The girl's mom smiles at her magazine. She's been listening.

The sun's just coming up as the plane tremors and bumps faster down the runway. The little girl cranes to watch the ground drop out and I lean back against my seat so she can get a better look out. The plane banks sharply, offering us a view of the sky, and the girl loses interest. She turns on the seat-back teevee and watches cartoons.

My eyes want to close, but I don't let them yet and I glance back between the chairs, where I can see the top of Mon's head and Kai's beside it. They're tilted together, touching. I can't tell if they're sharing earphones or talking, but they don't see me watching. The man in the seat right behind me gives an annoyed look, so I turn straight again.

I stuff my pillow against the cabin wall and it slides down the plastic a few times until I find the right way to wedge it; then it stays. I put in the earphones and turn on Angela's iPod. Some electronic fog comes on, which seems so perfect for the moment, a buzzing hum and shifting tones and slow beats. Not much sense to it, like a snow globe of music that swirls around, all liquid sounds. I listen, the air in the background, cold and fast and screaming by the plane, only a few inches from my cheek.

I don't know when I fall asleep, but sometimes, I don't know when I'm really awake either. My head drifts through the fuselage wall and I feel the wind on me. My seat bumps across the sky, not connected to anything, just suspended by the speed we move. Sometimes I wake up, but just enough to check we haven't crashed, to check the backpack still rests under my sneakers. It's not really waking up, and then I'm asleep again.

6

The little girl is sleeping when I'm woken up. It's the stewardess and she's smiling and reaching over to my seat, her fingers gently on my shoulder. She says something and I look at her. She makes the motion for me to take off my headphones, which is when I realize they're still in, but there's no music playing anymore.

She tells me that we're getting ready to land and asks if I'm buckled in. I lift my blanket to show her I am and she nods and carries on down the aisle, smile, nod, smile.

It's dark out the window and I can't tell if it's cloudy or if we're still over the ocean somewhere. I wish I could see something, the lights of a city below, the moon on the edge of night, anything, just to get a sense of which way is up and how far away things are. I think through the romance that we're flying upside down, but it doesn't last long. Gravity tells me what's down and the teevee map in the seat-back shows we're close to Holland. It shows that the local time is almost ten at night and the temperature at the airport is thirteen degrees Celsius and we're not long from being in it.

Thoughts rush me. I don't have a place to stay. I don't know anything about Amsterdam. I don't speak the language. In the span of time I slept, I crossed an ocean away from anywhere and anyone I know. The thought of that makes me lonely and a bit chicken.

I glance back and between the seats to see a sliver of Mon, the steady blue glow from the teevee on her face. She must sense me because the one eye that I can see, it looks up. I don't flinch away and neither does she. I want to ask her if I can stay with them for tonight because I have nowhere and they're the closest things I have to someone familiar.

Can I stay with you and Kai, just until I feel safe again?

We look at each other for a few more moments, and of course mind-reading isn't a thing, so she doesn't know how bad I want to be with them.

The cabin lights come on and the pilot tells us about how we're close to landing and what time we'll land at and what to do if we have any connecting flights. The plane bellies through the clouds, into the streamers of rain hanging underneath. It spatters and streaks, stuttering horizontal trails across the window. There're wet, sideways lines in the air between my window and the flashing white beacon at the wing tip. The ground's close, the runway lights already quite far apart. The black gap of the tarmac between them catches the occasional strip of light and reflects it strong enough to see in the hazy drizzle, and seconds later, everything in the cabin jolts as we touch ground again.

The little girl wakes with a start. She had slept through the entire descent with her cheek pressed against her chair back. She cries for a little bit from the scare, but not loud or for long, more just a whimper. The sound is muffled by the machine around us screaming down. The girl's mother makes soothing noises and tells her things that I can barely hear, just in bits once the machine stops whining and pieces of her mother's voice come clear over the rhythmic bass thumping of the wheels over gaps in the tarmac.

I want to hear what she's saying, want to know what words stop the girl's fears. I want to hear the words that make her scared just disappear and be forgotten. But maybe it's not the words themselves, maybe it's just her mother's voice in her ears. I imagine she's saying obvious things like, "It's okay," and "We're here," and "Just a bump. Nothing to worry about," which is fine because that's probably all the little girl worries about anyway. And that's all I can think that she might be saying, which makes me realize I've forgotten the sound of that voice at my ears, telling me those things. What did she even sound like?

The plane drives and turns and bumps over more gaps. I pull the backpack from under the seat in front and hug it close, curving forward to look out the window. The wheels stop moving, and for the first time in hours, my body is still. The only motion left travels inside me. It's in my ears, like wind past the fuselage, and I close my eyes for a moment.

I smile at the little girl next to me, say, "Bye," to her when she says it to me, and then she's gone. Her mother holds her hand and leads her up the aisle. The girl has a pink backpack with a rabbit face and rabbit ears, and I still clutch mine to my chest.

The plane empties of people. The air smells different than last time I smelled it. I don't rush. I stand and hunch under the luggage compartment, just to stretch some blood back into my legs. Mon and Kai wait in the same way, her tucked under the compartment and him standing straight up in the aisle beside her. They look at me and say something, but say it too quiet to hear. I point at my ear and shake my head a little and Mon nods like she understands and holds up her finger to tell me to wait for them.

Kai grabs the overhead bags and hands one to Mon, and as they pass, he says, "Don't go without talking to us. Meet us on the other side of customs, 'kay?"

I nod and try to fall in line behind them, but the next couple doesn't let me in, and like it makes any kind of difference, they scowl at me as they go by. I get in behind them and exit the plane behind them too. Kai and Mon head to the baggage claim and I go to customs.

I fill out a form at a table. I carry less money than they ask about and there isn't much else in my pack they'd be interested in. Nothing to declare. I go through a gate, expecting it to be hard, and am surprised when it's easy. I just walk through into a new country.

I find a water fountain and swish out my mouth. There's an information booth near it with racks of brochures. The lady there says something in Dutch and I ask where I can get a flight to Belgrade. The lady tells me Jat Airlines, in English. Then she tells my blank stare where their counter is, weaving a finger in the air with all the different turns to get there.

I figure Mon and Kai will wait a while for their backpacks, so I go. Departures is a big warehouse echoing with grey lights and hard walls. It's busy and I have to walk quite a way to find the right desk, but they're closed and a desktop sign says they'll be back in the morning. I take a brochure from the counter and then start back.

I read the brochure while riding the escalator back down to arrivals. The next plane for Belgrade doesn't leave until noon tomorrow. Someone brushes past me, too close, walking down the escalator steps, and crumples the brochure. He says something to me over his shoulder and I'm mad at him, but maybe he said he was sorry, so that thought soothes it a bit.

I lose my way back to the gate once and then once more, every hall looks like the next one. When I finally find the right place again, I wonder if Kai and Mon have already been through and left without me. I don't expect they'd wait long if I wasn't there, even though they'd said it. I watch the customs exit for them, my backpack slung over my shoulder and the airline brochure in my back pocket. When Kai and Mon come through, they both have big packs on, straps over both shoulders because they're heavy, heavier than mine, with stuff. They both smile at me, but I think Kai's is a bit forced where Mon's seems real.

They talk like I'm part of their trip, like I've always been part of their plan and I'm happy for that. The guy who brushed past me on the escalator made me feel foreign, lonely in a place where I don't know anything and can't even speak the language. Could make a person sad and then angry by turns, like it does me. That's what Kai and Mon cure.

Mon asks if I have a place to stay at and I say, "I don't, but I'll probably only stay in the city until tomorrow."

Kai seems to warm up to the fact of me then and offers me a loose smile, says, "The place we booked probably has room. It's a hostel in the Jewish Quarter. Pretty cheap, good spot, right on the edge of the old town."

I tell them that's great, but can only think that Kai shouldn't really be cold to me because he's handsomer than me, and I'm not the threat to him and Mon that he seems to think I am. Of course, I would be with them if they wanted, but that's just jealousy in my head, not theirs.

They talk like tourists as we follow the overhead signs, pointing us to the train station. They talk about meeting up with Kai's brother. Kai talks about the cafe he was at last time he was here, and it's decided that's where we'll go once we drop our bags off. There's talk of different names of pot and how we'll all smoke it. I think that sounds okay because being a part of something will help kick this feeling that I've already happened, like they already remember a future when I'm gone. It's a horrible feeling that I can't dwell on for long or else I'll disappear to myself too. So, I try to be excited. I smile. I nod my head a lot and try to be funny, which I think I am because Kai and Mon laugh at some of the things I say. We go under a glass roof and then down an escalator. We buy a ticket from a machine, talk some more on the tunnel platform, and then a gust and a train comes, heading to Centraal Station, so we get on.

I watch the tunnel wall through the window, tight underground spaces lit by little yellow lights and glowing red signs above doors in the walls. Then the train breaks surface and I'm looking at my reflection. It's dark out there and there're tired faces all around, the hushed chatter of nighttime passengers, English, Dutch, French, something else. I catch none of the meaning as the motion of the carriage sends me into a lull. And I drift.

Outside, the lights could be any city. They don't remind me of the dark, little town I left behind though, somehow they're different. The words that come from Kai and Mon make sense, but only when

I concentrate on listening in. I fade in and out, lulled by the speed, the thrum of the engine, the sway of the tracks.

My head nods as I bounce off the bottom of sleep and back into consciousness and then away again. I'm aware I'm ridiculous, having slept so long on the plane already and still not being able to keep my eyes open. Ridiculous because I can't stay awake except for when I'm still and can't sleep except for when I'm in motion. The difference between the two, for me, is so subtle that it's sometimes hard tell one from the next and, a lot of times, I never really fully inhabit either.

Kai and Mon talk. Some of the things they say to each other makes me wonder if I'm not really here. They're talking about the hostel, but I miss the point because I drift. I think I hear them talk about the sex they had, or are going to have, and again I feel like I shouldn't be here and shouldn't be listening. I can't help but picture Kai standing naked in front of her sitting on the edge of a bed. I picture myself there, too. We touch him first, then each other.

I glance through an eyelash haze when their voices stop. The train jolts and slows, and they're kissing. I open my eyes and they don't stop, so I look out the window. The night's set in tangerine and the city's constant now, not just pockets of unfortunate houses and low-rise apartment blocks along the tracks. The train slows more and I watch Kai and Mon's reflection and think of the taste of them in my mouth, like they're tasting each other right now, like I'm part of both of them. The city slides behind their translucent reflections, as if they're projected on it, bigger than it, rippling across the stacks of the lit and dark windows. I lean my forehead to the glass, to see if I can touch my reflection to theirs, but I can't get close enough and the window is cold and hard against my forehead.

My eyes are drawn to focus outside again as we pull into Centraal Station. It's a huge hangar of light and concrete and a lattice metal roof. The train stops with a jolt. Kai and Mon break apart, smiling at each other and in no rush to move on, even though people start leaving the car. They laugh, mostly to each other and mostly not out of embarrassment that I saw them. We get up, sling our backpacks, and move.

7

The sounds Kai and his brother make start while we're still separated by a length of platform, bracketed by tracks, in the industrial hiss and clang of the train we came in on. It's a desperate machine-gun chatter, their language, travelling faster the closer our feet get, lost in the cathedral space above the slender fingers of concrete platforms.

They talk like they haven't seen each other in years, though it's been only months. They have their own language at times and speak it as we stand under the spidery architecture, framed by deep green and glass, a brick wall, a pub, a newsstand, an information booth. They hug. They slap each other's shoulders and they laugh. I can't help but like them both, and there's a pinch of envy, too, for being left out of their life so far, for not being part of their shared space right now.

Kai's brother is Darren and he's a year and a half older, but looks more than that. He looks worn, in a good way, like he's been out here a while, exposed to the strange weather of foreign places, far from home. There're crow's feet wrinkles at the corners of his eyes and his teeth are whiter because his skin is tea, the colour of sunshine and travel. He's lanky and wiry and not as big as Kai.

He hugs Mon for a long time, says, "It's good to see you," over her shoulder. And she says it back to him. It shows in her that she means it, that she really likes him.

Darren shakes my hand, muscles make lines up his forearm. He says hi with the vulnerable openness of someone who makes new friends fast wherever he goes because we'll be friends tonight, and then tomorrow we'll be gone from each other again, like we need to smile more and move at twice normal speed.

He asks where I'm from and the blank look tells me he's never heard of it.

I say, "It's small," like the way people usually say, it's okay.

I ask where he's been, and he tells me he's just come up from Ibiza and he looks surprised when I don't know where that is.

He smiles and says, "You've got to go. The music's crazy and the party never stops. And the girls, the girls are the most beautiful I've ever seen."

I say, "I'll go."

And I'm not sure he believes me, but he laughs and puts his arm around my shoulder and we walk. He says, "We'll get along, you and me. We can be friends." And I believe him.

Darren walks with me. Mon and Kai follow, and Darren asks if I'm meeting anyone here and I tell him I already have. He's easy to laugh, which is one reason I think we'll be friends for tonight. He asks where I'm going and I tell him Paris, and he says something French at me. He tells me that it's the name of a place that's been a bistro for the last two hundred years, or something like that, and that the pastries are really something else. His words. He takes his arm from around my shoulder and promises we'll talk more and then he turns his attention to Mon.

We walk, backpack nomads across the platform. The station's not very busy, I think it's because it's pretty late, must be past eleven o'clock, but I'm not even sure what day it is here. It may be tomorrow from where we left, or maybe it's yesterday. I'm not sure which way time moves around the world, but I'm certain, given a minute to think, that I could figure it out. It doesn't much matter because the next day'll come and with luck I'll be on the noon flight to Belgrade. Until then, it's a matter of waiting out the minutes and it sounds like that should happen pretty easy tonight.

I listen to Darren talking and Mon putting in a word or two where she can. Kai has moved to walk beside me and his company is friendly enough, but chillier than his brother's, talking is harder so we fall into a march-step and doing that together feels good, like we're paying attention to each other even though he may not notice.

We walk, following Darren to a stairwell in the middle of the platform, which takes us down to a narrow tunnel that echoes with people noises and thrums through from the train engines above.

It widens and there are a few narrow shops along the walls, but most of them are caged and closed. Someone plays a guitar and sings and the acoustics of it are disorienting. In one ear's the musician, in the other his echo. We move though a grand and dimly lit lobby, and then we're in the black, fresh air of night.

Darren talks about how we should drop our bags at the hostel and then go get a joint and some drinks. The brothers take the lead past a two-storey bike rack parkade. They both know when to stop at corners and which way to look as we cross the bike lanes and bus lanes and tram lanes and traffic lanes. Mon's beside me and we're following, looking at the lights and not knowing where the canal reflections end and where the skinny three-storey, four-storey, five-storey buildings begin. The city's double is upside down, and I can't figure out which parts are underwater and which parts are above. It must have just rained, still does, but not much. Wet cobblestones reflect the lights, just like the canals do. There's noise and engines and we glance at each other and smile. I can't help but feel an elated anxiety that I see matched in her face.

The air is damp and musty and old. I tell Mon that it looks like a movie, and she says she likes how all the little houses touch shoulders and lean forward or backward, some a little, some a lot.

I say, "This is the first time I've been overseas." And Mon says, "Same for me."

She says, "I went to the US once, but that doesn't really count." And I agree that it doesn't.

We walk along some busy streets, buses hung from electrical lines and cars in roads sunken down from the sidewalk. Headlights flash honey in the puddles and taillights flash red in the same way. There're some street vendors selling stuff, like salted fish and little balls of dough, and it looks like you can buy beer from them, too. We stop at one intersecting street and wait for some bicycles to rattle past, seeming oblivious to both us and the bus that narrowly misses them as they clatter along. Mon and I chuckle at the stereotype of the bicycles. Darren glances over his shoulder from his talk with Kai, but only occasionally.

I think about how fine everything is. My past isn't anywhere near me and I can tell them what parts of me I want to. I don't need to tell them about my hometown, my dad, the fifty that paid for my sex. I can tell them I'm going to Paris and I want to be a writer and I'm meeting a friend, only one of which is true, but it's okay. I don't need to tell them I'm running, even though nobody is looking for me, not anymore. Everything I've done is so far away. Mr. Langman is far from here. I steal a glance at Darren and Kai ahead, Mon at my side, and I can be whatever they need tonight.

It's an easy fiction I share with my new friends, and for the moment it doesn't make me feel hollow and fake, though I know by the morning it likely will. I can only be someone else for a short time before it takes payment, when the lies start chipping away. It'll all come back, but by then, I'll be gone. Right now, they like what they know of me and I'm part of their group. For the first time in longer than I remember, I don't feel alone.

We walk a quieter street that has little bridges humping over glassy canals. They remind me of the sea monsters drawn on old maps, like cobble-scaled serpents, like "here be dragons," and we just walk casually across their backs. Each is marked by a sign with an unpronounceable this and that printed on it. There're little flat houseboats moored to the stonework canal sides, up and down the light-rippled ink. The air is fish-tank and there're lights in most of the boat windows, tiny yellow rectangles or circles, with trembling sisters drowned nearby. I can't help but picture hunched dinners around cramped tables, gentle water tapping against the hull. I can't help but picture the liquid movements of dreams made in those little beds rocking on the canal.

A guy stands next to one of the boats. The glow of his cigarette flares. I can't see any details about him, just a silhouette, and Mr. Langman bullies into my brain for a second, even though he's impossible here.

There's no traffic on these streets.

There's very little light to cause these shadows.

There's a bicycle frame chained to the bridge railing.

The tires are gone. A shout echoes from somewhere, but I don't flinch because it doesn't seem out of place. I wonder what was shouted, excitement or anger, but I don't know the language.

And then the canal is gone and we walk up a narrow side street. It's so tight we go single file when someone comes our way. I try to peek in the windows we pass, but most have curtains drawn. A shadow moves inside as we walk by. There're people behind these walls, behind the windows, but I don't know what they're doing, even though they are so close.

Darren says, "This is it." And he pushes a door open.

There's a small sign with the address and hostel name bolted to the brick. We walk into a cramped, dimly lit reception area. Music plays. The desk is as wide as the woman behind it, and she's tiny. There's a staircase that seems to have been built by someone who'd only ever seen ladders.

The woman smiles and says, "Hello."

The space is tight with us. I move and try not to knock any brochures from the wire rack tacked to the wall. We tell her we're checking in and I tell her that I don't have anything booked, but she says, proper, "This is not a problem. The main dorm only has a few guests tonight."

Darren smiles and says, "We're roomies."

Kai and Mon have a private room, which is fine because the image of them kissing on the train is stuck deep and it's better they sleep somewhere else, that way I don't have to think about them or their mouths. I don't have to think of the warmth from Kai's skin or the place where Mon's legs meet. My thoughts are on sex tonight. I can't stop them.

The woman behind the counter takes our passports. She signs us in and gives us keys and points to the ladder-stairs. I ask if there's somewhere to lock up my bag and she tells me, "Complementary lockers are in the dorm bathroom."

Darren and I are in the main hall on the second floor. Kai and Mon's room is on the next floor up, top floor. Darren says, "Let's meet in a half hour and go."

Kai and Mon keep on climbing. The stairs creak and thump. The walls are thin and I can hear them talking even after the door to the main dorm closes behind Darren and me.

The room takes up the entire floor, minus space for the stairwell and another door that leads to the bathroom. The dorm isn't big, narrow and long instead, and it's full of bunks along the walls and a few chairs around a coffee table in the middle. Darren and I chat a bit with the only other person in the room. Darren knows her name and where she's from and a little about her. She's a decade older than us, easy, and lies on a bottom bunk across the room, her eyes half-lidded and her words sag, lazy with sleep or something else. She laughs at things that aren't really funny. She's got bad teeth.

Darren lounges on his bunk, crooked leg over bent knee, and picks between his toes through his socks while he talks. I toss my backpack on the bunk in the corner, rummage in it for a minute, then ask Darren if he has soap and shampoo I can use, and he says he does.

The bathroom has some sinks along one wall, a few shower stalls sectioned off by curtains hung on rusty dee-shaped rods. There're also a couple of toilets on one end, each in its own little room with a door. They don't look that clean, but I don't expect them to, so that's okay. Beside the toilets are a few lockers.

Darren's still talking to the girl and someone thumps across the ceiling above. I look over my shoulder and can't see Darren or the girl, so I walk to the counter and turn on a sink. I let the water run while I unzip my pack and rummage out three hundred Euros for the night. I have no idea how much the clubs cost or beer costs or weed costs, so I grab another hundred on top of that and stuff it all in my jeans pocket. I take the newspaper article from the paperback and slip it into my pocket, too. I look around once more to make sure no one saw the money, and then zip up the backpack again.

There're a few empty lockers, each with a little key that locks a padlock. It's not all that good, but it's the best it'll get right now.

I'm not over-keen on leaving my pack behind, but I can't take it, and there's no way I'm missing the night to babysit a bag when a lock can do the job. I figure nobody knows how much money's there, or that it's even there.

The locker key goes in the same pocket as the four hundred Euros. I go into one of the toilet stalls and close the door. Once I'm done, I strip and peek through a crack in the door to see that no one's in the room. I cross to put my clothes on the counter near the sink and then I have a shower.

I spend some time because the water is turned up really hot and it's good on my skin. It's the first proper shower since leaving the motel across from Big Tits. I use some of Darren's shampoo to lube a tug, because I have been so horny since watching Kai and Mon kiss and figure I can think clearer after rubbing one out. I listen to the sound of Darren and the girl talking while I do it. Their words are a muddle, but their voices go back and forth in the other room. I think of Kai and Mon kissing and I get close really fast, prop one arm against the slimy shower tile and come at the wall.

Refreshed loneliness settles heavy and quick. Voices in the other room I can't understand, and I let go of myself and wonder what I'm really doing here. I prop both arms against the wall and hang my head under the water to kill the other noise for a few minutes before I turn the faucet off. The bathroom is steamy and my fogged reflection in the mirror over the sink is small and far away. I don't have a towel, so I dry myself with my boxers and then get dressed, leaving them hanging on the shower rod to dry out.

Kai and Mon are sitting in the dorm. Mon's hair is wet and Kai looks like he showered too, and I can't help but think that they did it together while I was alone. The other girl is still in her bunk, smiling her bad teeth at everyone, half-lidded eyes, listening to Kai and Darren jab playfully at each other. I have my hands in my jeans pockets, fingers of one hand touching the money and locker key to remind me where I am, the others touching the newspaper article to remind me where I'm going.

"Ready?" Darren asks and I tell him I am.

I say, "Bye," to the girl on the bunk and she smiles and says something back. I don't understand her, so I just nod and follow everyone down the stairs.

The lady at the counter tells us she's locking the door at midnight. "If you come back later," she says, "the keypad code for the lock tonight is an easy one to remember." And then she shows us how to use it. She reminds us what the numbers are and goes back inside, leaving us between the tight alley walls. There's no clock anywhere, but it's late already so the lady will probably be locking up pretty quick. Still, we're all charged with being in a new city and don't feel anything but giddy. It's almost as if it's a waste to not be awake for everything all the time here.

Darren takes the lead because he seems to know where he's going and I'm all turned around in an old city that's a warren of canals and alley streets, all built like a tangle of string.

8

Kai and Mon talk a quiet buzz behind us. I hear them, but only in voices, not words. There're more neon signs stuck to the sides of old buildings. There're more neon puddles splashing neon stains on our shoes. There're more shadows moving in the alleys we pass and there're more shadowed faces in the streets we walk down. There're more languages being spoken, a lot of English and I recognize a few others, a lot I don't know.

"Check this out," Darren says and walks to the next building, a storefront of three tall and narrow windows in a row. Each looks into a small red room, lit bright by inward facing bars of light around the windows. Each room has a stool.

The first window has a tall, skinny blonde woman sitting on the stool. She's wearing some strings and may as well be naked. Her breasts are small and her nipples point up, which I like. She's beautiful and she smiles with a gap between her front teeth. She's around my age and she moves her legs and I get a glimpse of her.

Then she tilts her head, like she's all shy and embarrassed about it, like she hadn't meant for us to see.

Kai and Mon catch up and Kai says, "She's hot." And Darren says, "Her tits are too small." Mon tells us that it makes her sad that the girl is here like this.

Darren and I move to the next window, which has a bigger woman in straps and lingerie behind it. She's a brunette on top but her pubic hair is ginger. She stands and does a little twirl when she sees us watching. Her butt jiggles a bit when she moves. Her thighs are chubby and dimpled. She's older than me, probably in her thirties, but she's beautiful too, even though she's totally different than the first girl. She squats down, rubs her hand against the window and of course I'm hard, ever since seeing the first girl. I instinctively take a step back, forgetting the glass is between us and not realizing how close I was standing to it.

Darren laughs and tells me not to be scared.

I tell him I'm not.

Kai joins in teasing, says, "She would eat you alive."

"I'm not scared," I say again.

I blush and don't want them to think I'm new or anything, but I still don't take a step closer. I ask Darren how much they cost and he tells me it depends what I want them to do.

Then he asks if I like the older one and I tell him honest that I do.

Kai asks how much anal would cost, but Darren doesn't get to answer because Mon punches Kai's shoulder hard, says to him, "Fuck you," and walks away, not waiting for us. I can't tell if she's really pissed or joking, but if it's real, I think it was just a question and she shouldn't get too raw. These women are here, someone will pay them, facts can't be changed. It's like Cheryl, like how the trucker paid me, nothing us four can do to change how it is and we don't even know enough to really judge what it is.

Kai runs ahead to talk to Mon. I watch him jog and hunch down to walk beside her. It has started to drizzle, which hazes them gauzy, black inside with a cherry-red neon outline. They walk apart for a second. Then they walk together, Kai with his arm over Mon's shoulder. I guess he shouldn't have said what he said, not when she's here, and not when he's her boyfriend. I think if I said anything to rile her, but I don't think so. It's a prideful lapse if I stepped over. I just wanted to be a part of them, to fit in. I was just interested. I've never seen anything like this and don't know how any of it works.

In the next window, there's a short woman, shorter than me anyhow. She has dark brown skin. She stands with her back to the street, to me and Darren. I feel I can stare at her proper this way because she's not watching me back. She has long, straight black hair twisted into a braid that follows the dip of her spine. There're small goosebumps all over her body and I wonder if it's cold in her little room. I run small circles with the pad of my thumb against the tip of my fingers and don't realize it for a minute, but I'm dreaming that it's the sensation of running my fingertips over her goosebumps, reading her skin's braille. Her bottom is heavy and round and beautiful. Her legs are smooth muscle curves and her feet are wonderful. The arch of her foot is a perfect bow, the ball of her foot is tinted grey with dust.

I let out a breath I didn't realize I've been holding.

Darren has been watching me and asks me quietly what I think.

I tell him, "She's got beautiful feet."

And he says one word without inflection. "Interesting."

Kai and Mon are quite far up the street from us, so Darren and I run to catch them. The street cobbles are uneven and I trip but somehow stay upright. It takes my feet a few more steps to figure out how to run on these wobbly streets.

I don't know if my erection will fade tonight, doesn't feel like it ever will. I hope that Kai and Mon can't see it pushing at my jeans in the shadows and the drizzle rain. Then I wonder, what does it matter because Darren and Kai are probably the same. So, I guess, then, it's Mon who frightens me. It's her judgement I don't want.

9

Darren says, "It's just around the next corner."

This city is so tight, it's like I'm rubbing shoulders against bricks and bodies wherever we go, like being squeezed in a crowded room. It's hard to get a breath. There're people milling in the lane outside of a door, smoking and drinking and talking and laughing. The place is marked with a square sign bolted to the wall, not much bigger than a sheet of paper. No way we would have found it without Darren knowing it was there.

Darren says something to the big guy with the big arms at the door. The guy nods, takes some money and we go in past him, though he doesn't move much to make room. It's black and hot inside and people bump into me, rubbing up on one side and in the front and in the back. It's near pitch, so I put my hand on Darren's shoulder not to lose him in the mess of noise and bodies. Darren puts his hand on mine and holds it there. There's a tug of a finger hooked through my belt loop. When we pass through a black curtain and into the club, I look back and it's Mon and her other hand stretching back to hold Kai's, making a chain of us, anchored on Darren's shoulder.

And there's noise.

And there're lights flashing on and off and on.

There's a beat pushing a crowd around the room, from the bar to the dance floor, the dance floor to the tables around it. Some people are just dancing on the spot, wherever they are. I don't know if this place has walls, can't see them, just people. There're shirtless guys in jeans, with skin fit tight over muscles, and women in little tops and short skirts that make them seem more bare than not. There're a few older people, them mostly sitting at the bar with drinks close by for company, watching everything sidelong.

Darren leads us there and we order some drinks. I try to give him money, but he holds a hand against it. He pulls me close with a tight grip pinching where my neck meets my shoulder, close enough that his lips brush on my earlobe and he says over the noise that the next round can be mine. I nod, that's fine and that's good and that's what'll happen.

There're drinks in our hands and then there aren't.

Then there're more and then they're gone, too.

He juts his chin at a couple of girls on the floor and smiles to me. We go over and dance with them. Kai and Mon stay behind. I can't help but watch them in glances. They shout a few things at each other and then they kiss. I can't help it, I want to be them. In this room full of people, to only want to look at each other and no one else is something I've never shared with anyone.

I have to force my attention back to the girl dancing with me but she's seen me looking away and has turned to dance with Darren, too. I feel like crying because I don't have a Kai and a Mon. The strength of that sadness shocks me because it's unexpected, didn't even know it was in me. I just have a lonely me and a pocket full of Euros and I catch a guy dancing and looking.

This guy I'm dancing with . . .

It's like I notice him for the first time, and he's beautiful. The way he moves is amazing and the way he smiles at me is amazing. I can't help but dance close. Sometimes I see Darren flash in the mob, but mostly I'm watching this guy. The way he moves makes me want to hold him closer, so I do, my hand under his shirt, spread across the trench of his spine with my little finger dipped below his belt line. He doesn't fight it, taut skin, rolling muscle underneath, slick with sweat he bends, but he's still in power and he's still in control. I know it because he's comfortable being up against me. He tells me this just from the way his body moves over mine and I'm so charged by it I can't help but smile. Our clothes press between us, a second skin between ours and the sensation primes me. From the way he acts, it primes him hard, too.

A tear breaches my eyelid because I'm rushed by so much, so suddenly, that I can't think of the future or the past and it's such a release. In the lights and the noise, we stand still and he kisses the tear from my cheek, like it's a normal thing to do. All I think of is the pressure of him against me. I close my eyes to us falling through the beat. Then he's gone.

It's light and noise and movement and Darren's at my side and Kai and Mon aren't far away either, just past the dance floor. The guy is gone from me, but it doesn't matter because, for the first time in such a long time, I feel like I belong somewhere. I realize it's not just this place, it's these people who have let me in. It's Kai and Mon and Darren and what easy company they are. It's this place that doesn't care what I've done or who I am because all that was before this minute and it doesn't matter anymore. I can't remember the last time I felt I belonged anywhere so easily. Darren holding out another drink at me. Mon moving close and bouncing and holding me, telling something through a smile. Kai keeping me in sight, as if I'm a second away from crossing some line. Then him passing me a cigarette that's not a cigarette but a joint. The warmth of this night, this dark inside space, the people around me and the hands on my body, all make the scared in me disappear. Maybe not disappear, maybe just fade to the back, but it's still a relief to have it pushed back there for a bit instead of sitting up front all the time. The recent loneliness of my days of travel, my week in the motel hiding from Mr. Langman, watching for spacemen from Evelyn's front porch, sleeping on Angela's floor alone while she had sex in the next room, all that hollow is gone. I forgot that things could be beautiful, even if just for a night, even if just for an hour, or even just for a simple minute.

It's light and noise and I can't see, only feel. That feeling is a hand in my hand and bodies parting in my wake as I'm led to the edge of the strobe-light pulse. It's an arm around my shoulder and a voice in my ear, Darren, asking if I want another drink. My head nodding, my eyes closed, the brush of his lips on the rim of my ear so I can hear him over the pulse, hear him say, "Follow me." And I do.

He sits us at a booth on the edge of the room, him beside me, his arm across the back of the bench, over my shoulder because he leans in to talk. Heat comes off him. Drinks are watery rings left on the table, the glass in my hand and then gone. Darren tells me I'm going to have a great time in Paris, there's so much to see on every street, and like all the parts of this continent he's been to, there's so much time pressed into such a small place that you can't get away from it. Not like back home, where there's barely nothing seen of the past and such a dizzying stretch of time ahead that you can barely know anything but today.

He says, "It makes you think differently here because of it, when you can see it. The past isn't humble and hidden here. It's become part of this future."

I nod.

"It's not empty here," he says.

I ask him about him, Kai and Mon. I ask it again, but louder when he shakes his head that he can't hear me.

He tells me Kai's the best brother anyone could have. That Kai was always bigger than him, and when they were kids, Kai fought a kid two grades older to protect him and got a black eye and a loose tooth for thanks of it. He tells me how Kai didn't say a word about it, not a word, even when their mom grounded him to teach him that fighting didn't solve anything, even though this showed them the opposite, that sometimes it did. Darren says, "Sometimes you just have to fight, and that's the way it is. It's a universal language too."

Before I can say more, Kai and Mon find us. Then they're sitting across the booth, drinks on the table between us, and then gone. Drops in circles, left on the table from the glasses.

We're teeth-laughing and eyes closed, heads tilted back.

We're voices louder than music and then quiet again, looking out at the dance floor.

Darren holds a little tighter to my shoulder than before and he tells Kai what we were talking about and Kai says, "That fight was nothing more than a few punches back and forth, and a week grounded in my room."

"It was more than that," I say and Darren nods.

I say, "I've had my fights, both won and lost, but they were always mine and not someone else's. I think that's something less than what you did."

Kai tells me that my losing a fight says something about me. He tells me he hasn't had a lot of fights, but he hasn't lost any, and Darren laughs at his brother's brag.

We're shouting over the noise, the colours of it spin everywhere around us.

"That's a trick, never losing," I say.

"You never lose a fight," Kai says, "if whatever you're fighting for is always right."

He says, "It's not whether you think you're right or not, it's whether you are right or not. If those two things don't line up, then you won't be standing at the end of it all."

He says, "That's why it sucks, losing, why you'd better be sure you're going to win before things even get started."

Before I can think too long on Kai's slight, or of those fights I'd been wrong in, Darren has more drinks between us, in our hands, and then they're gone.

It's light and noise and we're all drunk and we're all high. Looking at the eyes around the table, we could all use another drink. We've smoked cigarettes and dope and we could all use a little more of everything.

"What's your real story?" Kai says. "Not the one you said before, and what's in the backpack?"

I blink at him because I can't figure for a minute what he's talking about. Then, once I do, I need time to figure out what to say.

Kai leans in, says to my face with a smile on his, "I've been meaning to ask all night. You're on your own. You got one little backpack. Doesn't seem much in it, but you tell us you're touring around Europe. You say you want to see art in Paris. I'm curious about that because you don't strike me as a guy to care about that. You don't even seem to know where you are right now."

Kai leans back, like he's done asking questions, but looks at me like he's still waiting for an answer. Then the music fills the space without Kai's voice and I expect Mon or Darren to tell him to leave me alone, but it doesn't happen. I can't tell if they're all interested in an answer or fading out on the night.

"I travel light," I say, but it's obvious that won't satisfy Kai. I know now he's been puzzling on me ever since we got off the plane. He's not been keen on me hanging out with them, just tolerating it. He wants to know, and I guess it's fair he does, fair he's getting in my face about it. I'd be wondering about me too, all being the same except our places switched.

Kai shakes his head and tells me to tell the truth. He leans forward again and gestures to Darren and Mon when he says, "We're all friends here, right?"

When he says it, I'm not quite as sure about the answer as I was earlier.

It's the light and noise and loneliness and dope and drinks and the late hour that make me resolve. The truth this time, though still maybe not all of it, maybe only what I'm okay to tell them because there's a lot I wouldn't tell anyone, or at least wouldn't tell to fresh friends right at the start.

I tell them I lied when I met them, that I didn't know them, and hope they will forgive me that lie.

"There were part truths in it," I say.

"From a sideways view," I say. "My mom and dad are no longer around. Dad disappeared from me a long time ago. Don't blame him, he had to work to keep a kid fed and all he knew was being a rigger. I'm sure it wasn't his plan neither, what happened, but he did what he could. Mom disappeared into her own brain when I was twelve, even though her body's still there. I'm eighteen, now."

I tell them how I got from there to here, living for some months with an uncle who was drunk and living for some months with a foster family who wanted me for showing to their friends, that they were doing something good. Mostly, I lived in a government house and it was easy to leave all that because they didn't really want me there in the first place. I tell them I always managed to make money, enough for a meal though often not enough for a bed under a roof, and though I managed to eat, sometimes the money wasn't easy-making.

“It’s only five years between there and here,” I say. “It’s not that long if you think of it, but minutes can change things more than months do. Some seconds last longer than hours.”

“Everything I own is in that bag,” I say. “Some clothes and money and a notebook that I write in.” I tell them I’m going to meet my granddad. That he’s the only family left, but he doesn’t know I’m coming yet because I can’t find much trace of him. That’s why I have to go looking. And maybe he might tell me to take a hike and maybe I might get stuck there, but he may also help me. I tell them he’s a writer, that I want to be one too, and hope he can teach me. I have to try because it’s what I want.

I stop and think in the lights and the noise. Sometimes the words don’t come like they should. I say, “What used to be and what is now are never the same thing. That can be a good thing or a bad one. Things are always getting better and always getting worse at the same time. So, when it’s bad, all I have to do is wait for the pivot. When it’s good, I have to try and ignore that, eventually, the pivot will come.”

Kai looks like he’s chewing on it for a moment, then he asks how they know this story’s really the truth, because I lied the last time.

Lies run out, like everything else, like money or time or people. I tell him, “There it is.”

Whether he believes it for truth or not, I say, “Of course there’re other things, other stories, but you can’t know a person in a night. Maybe not even in forever, and this has to be enough.” And after a moment, I can see that it is.

Kai asks, “Where’d you get the money to come here?”

“You’re boring me, brother,” Darren says to Kai and then looks away, at the crowd, as if he wants to regain the party. There have been enough questions.

Mon scowls at Kai and he ignores her and looks like he still wants an answer, which I give him.

“I worked for that money. I’ve found it isn’t always there when you want it, but it’s always there if you need it. It just happens that way,” I say and see he’s not satisfied with that, but I don’t care.

Isn't none of his business. I won't tell him any more and I won't tell him any different. I don't want to lose them, my new friends, but will if I have to.

Kai gets it. He sees the line and he smiles at me, then kisses Mon on the cheek, acting like me and him were never even pecking at each other in the first place. He nods like he's satisfied, like we're good again, but we aren't.

It's light and noise and Kai and Mon hold hands on the table and drinks in their other hands. Nobody says much for a while. It's not that we don't have anything to say, but maybe we're just too tired. I can't but focus on how my jaw is clenched tight on one side and how Darren has me penned into the booth. His knee is against mine, his hip to mine, his shoulder to mine. I feel trapped and he doesn't know it. I've been trying to figure out what time it is because I'm unhinged from its geography. Should I be tired or hungry or just waking up? I figure it's probably around three in the morning, which is tomorrow here already, but still yesterday from where we came from, and I realize, at that moment, I inhabit too many times, so I let it go and don't think of anything else for a while.

Kai and Mon, their eyes are different than they were before, which is probably all about the drinks and smokes we've had. Kai stares at the dance floor, held by the lights and moving bodies. Mon looks exhausted. Her eyes are dark rings staring into the table, into a middle space, only snapping back into this place occasionally.

I'm a bit too lost in my own mind and can't have the drink sitting in front of me because I'm sure I'll throw up if I do. Even without it, I'll probably puke, so I reckon it would be good to be somewhere outside to do it. Darren notices all of this, too. He's still looking pretty normal even though he's probably drank and smoked more than any of us.

He says, "We should turn it off for tonight. You guys look done. Maybe swing by the IJ and look at the water on the way back," he says. "It's not far. Fresh air will be good. There's none fresher because it blows in from the arctic where there's no cars or people to use it up."

It seems like forever to cross the bar, just like we came in, my hand on Darren's shoulder, Mon's finger through my belt loop and her hand leading Kai's through the press of people. But we make it and then we're outside.

10

The light and noise are behind us, behind brick walls and trapped in the building back down the alley. Now, around the corner, my feet tell me I'm more messed up than I thought. Maybe it was the noise and light and movement in the club that made me think I was still functional. With everything else moving, I couldn't tell I wasn't standing still, but the drugs are in there, cotton in my lungs and cotton in my head, and I stumble.

It's raining and the candy neon cobblestones heave to trip me up. Each step is wet, raggedy rectangle outlines, cinnamon-heart red and lemon-drop yellow. The walls on either side of the street are slick with the colours too, like someone's clambered onto the roofs and dumped buckets of electricity down the brick face.

Our noises echo up and down the street. We've found new energy in our movement and I laugh and Mon laughs, and Kai and Darren talk. The noises are all double in the street. I can't tell who, but either Darren or Kai runs ahead, the applause of his footsteps bouncing everywhere around, and then he waits for us to catch up.

Laughter and we're alone, could be the only people in an abandoned Amsterdam, and that would be okay. Our shirts are quick soaked through. I shiver, but don't feel cold. A wave rides up my body and I find a dark corner to throw up on. There's a wracking strain, muscles squeeze ribs, and I chuck a ropy spew onto the ground. Someone's hand is warm on my back and it's Darren. Kai and Mon wait a few feet away. I'm embarrassed to be the only one to lose it, like I'm weak or something. I wish they would have kept moving and left me in private, pretending it never happened when I caught up. When I'm done we keep going.

And there's nothing left of the tight lanes and claustrophobia of the old town. We're in the open space in front of Centraal Station. I look at it for the first time, from the outside, a pretty, old building made ugly by the modernity built in front of it, the power lines and bus lines and back-lit advertisements for watches and perfumes. The bricks are scales spot-lit from above. The windows are full of knobby metal ribs.

It's quiet here, calm compared to the dizzy maze we'd just spun through. There're still a few cars and a guy on a bike rides by, but every once in a while, it's just right empty, vacant, except us in the middle of it. I find myself anticipating those moments because they trigger a simple peace in me. It's easy to picture this city empty tonight, empty beds with rumpled sheets and forgotten teevees entertaining empty rooms, their lights on and off and on.

Just as easily, we're standing on the seawall looking out over the black water. All there is, a cold wind from across the gap. I can't see the water but hear it moving close by in the dark. It's a threat, like a towering wave could be where we can't see, to take us and freeze us and drown the air from us, waiting just beyond the seawall lights. Then my eyes adjust and grey lights from across the water stitch the wave tops together with shaky electric lines. There's a distant strain of some machine humming, so faint that it's easily lost in a gust of wind.

The cold cuts through. It was easy to ignore earlier, protected by the buildings, but here the wind does it to us. Kai and Mon are curled over with their arms crossed in front, hugging fleeting warmth close. Darren climbs on the railing, leans out, and I picture him disappearing over the wall, the splash of him landing in the freezing water, so I hold him with a hand hooked over his belt. He's really not close to going over, I only think he is. In the rolling wind, he's laughing, telling me he won't fall, not even close.

He says, "I'm fine."

He calls me Mother.

Things get a bit worse when the wind and rain pick up. We're frozen, but none of us want to leave because the company feels good and we don't want it to end, like there's nobody else in the world so happily messed up as us and out so late at night that it's become morning again. We goof around on the edge of land. I wonder how many other idiots like us have climbed up on this seawall over the years, looking out into nothing from the very edge of something.

I let go of Darren's belt and he doesn't disappear over the edge, after all.

I give him a playful shove and he yelps, but stays put.

Kai comes out of the dark at me, laughing. I run and he chases me. I'm faster and after a sprint he sees it so he gives up and wanders back toward Darren and Mon, them distant and small because of the ground we've covered. Kai looks over his shoulder to see if I'm sneaking up on him. His shirt is wet, the fabric stuck to his skin, some ripples. The light draws a smooth and shadowed line down between his shoulders. He's smiling and Darren and Mon call out for us to come back. I'm winded from my sprint, so I lean my elbows on the seawall and look out at nothing, let my mind drift in nothing, catching my breath.

Things get a bit worse when a group of four guys our age walks by and one of them says something and the others laugh. I don't know where they came from, but they're here and when I look up at them, they stop and come back to me.

In accented English, they ask me what I'm looking at, and I tell them that I'm looking at nothing.

Had I thought about it, I would have said something different. What they seem to understand is that I'm calling them nothing, a bunch of nobodies, and they don't like that. Had I thought about it, I wouldn't have said anything because they were only looking for an excuse and anything would have been enough.

I look back to my friends and they're too far away to help when I get punched. It happens so quick that I didn't even know it was coming. The guy who punches me, he steps into it and knocks the wind from my gut and then another guy hammers me in the back, good and solid in the kidney. I let out a cry and fall down because it hurts too much to be standing up anymore.

I don't feel the rain anymore.

I hear my breath.

I'm crying even though I don't want to, but it hurts and it's hard because I don't think I did anything to deserve this. I don't know why it's me, here on the ground. I get two kicks in my side before there's a blur of motion. It's Kai taking down two guys with his arms stretched out to each side. He just runs through them at full speed from where he started down the seawall.

Darren is there and knocks another guy off his feet, and Mon shoves one, yelling at him something fierce. And there's nothing left to the fight because the guys run away. Kai and Darren chase after them for a bit, like to make sure they get the idea to keep moving. While their shouts and footsteps fade, Mon helps me to sit with my back leaning on the stone wall.

She asks if I'm okay and I nod, but she can tell it's a lie from how I grab my side.

I wish they had hit my face, wish there was blood on my teeth and a bruise near my eye, split lip Hollywood style, so she could see how it hurts. The body-pain isn't the worst of it though. It's worse being weak, getting beat in front of my friends, having to rely on them for help instead of me being able to help them. I don't want to be the guy who needs to be taken care of. Worse is the beautiful sympathy Mon wears on her face.

She puts her hand on mine, the one clutched to my side, and they rise and fall together, just breathing. That touch makes it a little easier. She leans close, other hand warm on the back of my neck, and with her face so close to mine, she asks what she can do. Her breath is the air between us.

Then I kiss her.

I forget about Kai and forget that Mon's still mostly a stranger, and I kiss her. It's because she's so close and her touch makes me feel better. It's because of the wet twists of her hair and the rain drops on her skin. It's because of the drinks and the drugs and this winding, alien city we're in together. It's because of the recent aggression and her present compassion. It's because of selfish want, riding me undeniable. It's because somewhere, in her voice and in her eyes, somewhere in how close she is, I think she wants me to.

Our lips are cold from the rain and her mouth is warm. I kiss her and she stops it, but not right away.

She says, "No," quietly and looks down at our hands, but doesn't take hers away.

A few moments later, Kai and Darren come back.

They didn't see it.

Things get a bit worse when I pull myself from the seawall and test out the parts of me that hurt. Everything causes more pain when I'm vertical, but I play it down when Mon says that we should go to the police or the hospital.

I say, "I'm okay."

I say, "I just want to go back to the hostel and go to bed."

Kai and Darren don't seem to care what happens now, so we go. I don't watch where we walk, just follow their feet down one street, and then down another; it doesn't matter. I hold tight to my side, otherwise it feels like a knife stabbing at me with each step, and that's one thing I concentrate on for a while because I don't want to think about kissing Mon. Kai and Darren walk ahead and laugh and re-enact their pursuit for us. By the end of their story, they're ready to tell it again with bigger feats, so they do. Slaying lions, they're heroes.

I don't pay much attention to anyone except Mon. She walks a little ahead and doesn't say much. I can't figure it out. I thought she wanted me to kiss her by the way she leaned close, by the way she touched me. Maybe I was right, maybe she did want me to, but now can't figure out what to do with it on account of her being with Kai. I think maybe she'll take that confusion out on me or maybe I was wrong in the first place and had no right. Any way I figure it, this won't end well. I'm already thinking how the sun can't come up quick enough and how I'll get to the airport and get gone before it gets even more complicated. So, I watch her to see how she'll deal.

Things get a bit worse when Kai accuses me. Somewhere, in the quiet whispers of our settled walk, Mon must've told him because he comes at me, a mess of violent motion that I don't understand at first because it happens so fast. He doesn't hit me. He threatens to, but when I flinch and stumble back against a wall, he stops short. I feel pathetic because I'm not even worth it in his eyes. It's then I wish he would because it'd be easier than having words about it and better to get it done with quick, just one more hit tonight. I want it, just so it can be over.

Kai's fist is pulled back behind his shoulder, but Mon says, "Kai, don't. It wasn't anything, just stupid."

And those last words hurt worse than anything. We aren't friends. I misjudged us from the beginning, and I'm nothing but lonesome without them and mad at myself for thinking we were anything more. From start to end, I'm the only mistake here.

Darren gets between Kai and me. He doesn't know what's going on. He doesn't say a word, only stands with an arm braced across Kai's chest, a hand on his shoulder, as if he could hold Kai back if Kai really wanted to get at me.

"What's your problem?" Kai shouts.

I can't think of anything to say, so I don't, which makes Kai madder, like I'm being an ass for not explaining myself. I can't tell him that some things are indefensible and he'll just have to think whatever he thinks about the whole thing.

"I don't want to see your face anymore," he says. "You're gone. Now."

He strains against Darren, who says, calm, "Take it easy, brother."

And there's nothing left to argue over. Mon doesn't meet my eyes when I look at her. She's got her hands stuck in her pockets and she's fixed on the ground at her feet. She's shivering. She flinches when Kai yells at me again.

"I'm right here."

I look back at him, his eyes bloodshot and shallow. They don't focus.

"Get out of my face," he says.

I can't make this right, only worse, so I turn and go back the way we came. It's quiet behind me and I glance back to see them walking away, shoulders hunched against the rain. I turn a corner and lean against the wall, prod at my tender side with feather fingers and figure probably nothing's broken. I have to go back the way they went because the hostel is that direction, but I don't want them to see me following.

So, I wait and wonder how a night could become so long. I wonder how I could have messed this up so quick and think about how it'd be best to just move on and try again. I don't think about how many more times I'll have to move on and try again. Surely a person will run down from it and have to settle somewhere, maybe just in hope of a place that's less hostile than every one he's left. I think, maybe it's me who makes places hostile, which is a hard thought because I can't move on from me. That's somewhere I'm stuck and I'd hate to think too much on it, so I don't.

I check around the corner and don't see anyone, so I walk slowly after the way they went. The hostel's not too hard to find again and I look up and there're no lights in the windows, only rain from the sky. The keypad clicks with the code and the lock clicks to let me in.

Things get a bit worse in the dark quiet of the lobby. The door blocks out the rain noise and there's a soft glow from a lamp on the reception desk. I climb the stairs as quiet as I can. The creaks stop me a bit, but soon I'm in the main dorm. The only light is the pale grey coming from outside. The girl that was in her bunk earlier isn't there anymore, and in the dark, I listen to Darren breathing steady from across the room.

I go to the bathroom and turn on the shower to let it run hot. While I wait, I peel my wet clothes off and hang them over the other shower rod. It feels like I might throw up again and my brain is still out of it, but not as bad as it was before. As the steam starts to come from the shower, I inspect myself in the mirror. I can't stop shivering even though I'm inside. I poke at the bruise surfacing on my side. Looking at it, that's the only proof of getting beat, and I expected more judging how sore I am.

I go stand in the shower, hang my head under the water, heating me all over, watch it scald my skin bright. I try not to think back on the night, but can't help it. There's nothing left behind me, and it's time to move on to what's in front. Why I waited to move on, I don't know. Maybe I'm chicken of what's in front because I don't know what's there. Maybe being chicken of it's just being stupid, because the good times here weren't that good, even though they are the best I can remember. It was nice having people again. It's what I wanted, but people are tidal in places like this and no one's meant to stay together or for too long.

Exhaustion comes pretty thick, but I won't sleep, there's too much spinning too fast. Then I remember my backpack, and can't remember how I got so stupid to leave it behind. I rip the shower curtain back, two hooks come off the rail and it hangs dog-eared behind me. I root through my jeans pockets, the wet newspaper article falls apart in my fingers, wet Euro notes, some coins fall a bouncing clatter across the floor, and the locker key falls out with them. I ignore the coins and snatch the key from the floor and bolt across the room to the lockers.

It's stupid, how I stand with the key in my hand for a locker that's been pried open. It's stupid how I stare at it, and then open it, and then reach my hand in to check, even though it's clearly empty.

I go throw up in the sink. There isn't much left in me, just heave out a few strings. The mirror is steamed up around the edges, and in reflection, my jeans and my shirt hang from the shower curtain rod, a wad of Euro notes in the pocket and some coins on the floor, and that's all I have. Even the boxer shorts I left drying on the rod earlier are gone.

I sober up quick.

What used to be and what is now are never the same thing.

I'm right screwed and don't even have underwear anymore.

Things get a bit worse when I think about how far there still is to go. It's not easy anymore, not like it was a few hours ago. I lean back against the wall and slide down to sit on the cold tile. I just stare at the steam rolling out from the shower and the dots of coins scattered across the floor. The wad of newspaper, it's all fallen apart and done with being read.

I'm crying, quiet and to myself. I don't know when it happened, but it's there, tears on my face and snot from my nose. That's all I can do because it's a hard truth to realize I've been so dumb. It hurts to cry on account of my bruises, but in a way, that feels good. It wakes up my brain, makes it clear what I'm in for. I've been in harder spots, sure, but I've cried then, too.

I settle a bit and make my way around the bathroom picking up coins from the tile. They matter now. I check my jeans, and all in, there's just over one hundred Euros and some change. Not enough for a plane, I'm sure. Maybe enough for a train, though I don't know. I put it all on the counter to dry before going into the shower again and standing there and thinking. I pick at the stitches on my arm for a few minutes, trying to focus. They're loose and most of them come out easy, leaving tiny holes in my skin.

Time passes and I can't tell if I'm still crying on account of the shower running over my head, but after a span, I can breathe to the bottom of my lungs again and I turn the water off. There's no towel so I use my hands to run the water off me the best I can before going to the dorm to lie down. Darren moves, but he doesn't say anything and I don't know if he's awake or asleep. I stare at his shape in the dark. He wouldn't have done this, none of them would. My eyes stay on the bunk where that woman was when we left. The sheets are messed there, but she's gone. Of course, she's gone. After a little while Darren's breathing goes deep and regular again, sleep breathing.

I don't sleep the rest of the night, but what's left is not long to wait out anyway. I have to get gone from here. When the sun starts up, before the hostel wakes, I quietly get dressed, sign out, and get my passport from the lady at the desk. She smiles because she doesn't know what happened. I smile back, but it's a lie. I don't tell her my backpack was stolen. The need to be gone is stronger than my want to talk to the police and wait around for them to do nothing to help. I've stayed too long.

I head to the train station in the ashes of morning light. It's not raining anymore, but it's cold and my clothes are still damp.

I'm too early for the ticket counter, but it's only a short wait. When it opens, I look at the board and the closest I can get to Belgrade with the money I have left is Rome. It'll leave me with just under twenty Euros.

I buy a ticket.

And then there's nothing left but for things to get a bit worse.

BOOK III

1

I don't want to fake a missing leg like the woman sitting on these steps, on the cold cream stone half a flight below this terrace. I can't do it as well as she can anyhow, droning on and rocking back and forth, looking like the most broke-down thing on Earth, like the next step for her is dead. She's dressed her body in rags and her face in wrinkles and sunspots. Her voice sounds like tears and she's begging for money I'm sure, even though I don't understand what she's saying.

She's got one leg sticking out from under her dress. It's wrapped in dirty and colourful fabrics and she wears a black Nike with a dirty white swoosh. Her other leg is missing. She's got a sideways bent spine, bent over so horrible it's painful even to look at, her unsteady hand held out like a shaking cup to show off her swollen knuckles and bone bent fingers.

She glances around, and when she thinks nobody's looking, she tucks her leg under her skirt and the other one comes out. She rolls her ankle in a circle, like to get the blood flowing again, then adjusts her skirt to hide her newly missing leg. She bends her spine the other way and starts again, hand out and droning in the saddest voice ever heard. There's a rag in front of her, stain-smeared too, with a couple coins on it, marking the passing of a few generous tourists. Most people ignore her and just walk by, and a few have sneered and called her a gypsy.

I imagine her when she's tired of sitting there and can't even guess what she does when she's not on the steps. I have no idea where gypsies go or what they do in their time off. I've seen them in a few tight alleys, sitting on bulging plastic bags like on chairs. There's been a few of them walking the streets, hunched over and begging too, but surely there's more to it than just begging or sitting.

A few weeks ago there were Kai and Mon and Darren. Before that, there was Mr. Langman and Molly and a fresh ladder of stitches up my arm, a goose egg on my head. And before that, I couldn't have even guessed on everything that's happened. If I could only remember the future like I can the past, I would have tried not to be here. If I could have made a difference to it turning out this way, I would have. But maybe the future is as set as the past is, and there's nothing can be done about either of them. I feel like I slept the whole way, came from that desert valley through Amsterdam and to Rome in a dream, like I fell asleep in the desert and woke up here.

I never thought of Rome, not in one way or the other. It was just never in my head until my cheek was vibrating against the train window, and waking up as we rolled to a stop in the station. My heart skipped faster in the seconds I searched for my backpack, and it didn't slow down when I remembered it being gone. The lady sitting across from me watched and then smiled when she caught my eye.

Out of the train and into the station, the weightlessness of my shoulders was all I could think about. The backpack had been an anchor and now there was nothing. I had to pee bad, so I found a washroom and did. I washed up in the stained sink, in front of the spotted mirror, and there was someone in one of the stalls who suddenly shouted and punched the metal door. I froze first, then snuck back to the hard spaces of the station full of yellow lights and sneaker squeaks on the tile.

I was starving and out front of the station there was a place to get a hot dog, just a cart on wheels with a guy standing at one end. When I ordered, he spoke English at me, which sounded good, like at least buying a hot dog could still be easy. I put some ketchup and mustard on it and ate it in a few bites because it was that good.

The sky was the grey of a sunrise or sunset, I couldn't know which. The street lights were on, the air drenched in the light of them. Watching for a while, people going by, cars going by, more people, it became clear that it was morning. People drinking coffee, like they'd just woke up. People with the newspaper they hadn't unfolded yet.

I couldn't stop checking for my backpack. Every once in a while, I'd grab for it on my shoulder or look around for it, firing a panic to flush my skin hot. It had been so important for so long, checking for it was going to be a part of me for a while, too.

There was a map of Rome on a stand near the train station entrance. I looked it over and then walked to the Spanish Steps. I had no reason to go there except remembering Mon talk about it, about seeing it in a black-and-white movie she watched with her mom when she was still a kid. It was only a half hour walk through the old streets and I felt a lot better for moving, because I slept a lot on the train.

The streets were crowded and the sidewalks were crowded, both smaller and tighter and noisier than anywhere I'd ever been. It felt like one street held more people in it than I'd ever met in my life. I came to the steps from the top, in front of a big white church that looks down them onto the crowds of people. That was the first time I heard the woman's sad voice.

2

A few weeks ago I was punched by strangers, and pushed away by friends for being an idiot. I shouldn't have kissed Mon. I know it. Before that, I was sitting on Evelyn's porch, eating frozen pizza, and watching the space station track an orbit just above the valley edge. And before that, I bought a thrift-store laptop and waited in the chat rooms for the Mr. Langmans to show up.

Now, I'm on the other side of the world watching a beggar with a fake bent spine and fake missing legs. Now, there's just the numbness in my arm where I cut it climbing out the motel window. I pump my fingers because if they stay still for too long, they tingle for a bit and then disappear entirely.

There doesn't seem to be a connection, from back then looking forward; only looking from here on back does it make sense. It makes me wonder what I'm not seeing now that'll come a week from now. That thing Mr. Langman told me when he was walking away in the desert, that thing he said, it's been bugging me, repeating in my head like echoes. I know why, too. His words were true. He put me in the bone dust and then told me something I should have known already.

"Probably time to find some friends who'll miss you, who'll come looking for you when you're lost out here," he said.

Or something like it.

I thought I was good on my own, maybe not good, but at least okay. Now, I know I wasn't and have never been. I think that's why I clung so hard to Angela and her boyfriend when we smoked up and they let me spend the night in their apartment in the city, why I latched onto Kai and Mon and Darren so quick. I don't want to think about the week in the motel by the gas station, but the image of the red marks on my hips from his grip flashes to mind anyhow, showing the past doesn't go away, just piles up and waits to visit whenever it wants.

I don't want to sell fake Prada bags to the tourists like the guys at the bottom of the steps do. I don't even know where they get them from, but they're always picking them up and putting them back on a sheet spread out on the ground. Motion pulls the eye toward it, I guess.

Those guys, I've watched them for a week. They're good. Their eyes always on, as they pick up their bags and put them back down again. They watch for anyone who glances at the bags, then they try to put one in their hands. Once it's there, I haven't seen it go back. Most of those guys are at the base of the stairs, on the cobbles of the plaza in front of sparkling stores, clothes in the windows that ask for more money than I've ever known. I looked through those windows, the first day here. Behind the glass, there're pants that could feed me for months and shirts that could put a safe roof over me for a good long while.

I watch the bag guys from the middle terrace. Some of them venture closer to try to entice a sale from the crowds clicking pictures of the fountain, a half-sunk stone boat in a pool of water that looks melted down a few feet into the cobbled roadway, like it's eroded out its own lake to sink in over the hundreds of years it's been there. There's hope that the boat won't sink though because one of the fountains squirts water out, bailing it and keeping it part afloat. Problem is, there's a troublesome spout shooting water into the boat as much as the hopeful one shoots water out, meaning they get nowhere in the end, and the boat stays half-sunk in the road. The sculpture's by someone famous. I read the plaque, don't remember the name.

A week ago I figured out how to get the money to keep moving toward Belgrade. It didn't take much to sort it, just watching people move up and down the stairs. The Spanish Steps are sweeping, and from the bottom, a broad staircase goes straight up to a terrace in the middle of the hill. From there the stairs split into two arms, hugging the outsides to where I first stood, at the plaza atop.

Looking out from up there with a hot dog burp, over the stretching huddle of squat old buildings, everything was already busy. There were too many people to count, all of them moving, too. The rooftop restaurants, set randomly at the corners of buildings amidst the prickle of teevee antennas, they were setting up tables for the day. There're thousands of wires and antennas on the roof tops, stretching to the hills back beyond. This strata of time's not seen from below, hidden even, to keep the modern world separate from the old one, but each church has electric lights and loudspeakers so the bells for mass can be lost in the echoes better.

Looking down, there were two guys dressed like costume gladiators on the terrace, one curving flight of steps down from me. Them talking. Them smoking cigarettes. Their costumes like how a kid thought ancient Romans would look like, and for a Euro, they'd hold their cigarettes behind their backs and pose with you for a picture. The one-legged woman was there, the first time I ever saw her and the first time I ever heard her sad voice. Back then, I still thought she only had one leg, and only later knew her for a fake.

Back then, I didn't know the regulars, like her and the costume gladiators. I didn't know about the guys with the knock-off purses, or the old men with their paintings at the top of the stairs. I hadn't met Sam and Maria, even though they were there, sitting on the railing, one flight down from the top and one up from the bottom. Sam's skinny legs were drawn up and Maria stretched hers out front. I hadn't met Gio either and didn't know yet which of them were bad for me, or which were good. I wasn't yet scared of the cops watching the tourists.

I didn't know much right then, right off the train and new to it all, but it only took me a few minutes to figure out how to get the money to keep moving. I was standing with the tourists at the top of the steps looking down at everyone else looking up. I had only been there a few minutes before this guy asked me to take a picture of him and his girlfriend. He handed me his camera and I told them to smile and they did. I took their picture and gave back the camera. He thanked me and I just nodded and watched them go down the stairs, holding hands.

3

Walking the city every day, I always wind up back at the steps. The stone stairs look polished smooth by people going up and down them for the last three hundred years. Pigeons weave through crowds of feet, gathering and scattering like schools of startled fish. The guy selling chestnuts on the coals makes the air around him heavy, earthy, like warm wet clay. I listen to Italian I don't understand and Chinese I don't understand. There's enough English in the air that I don't feel too alone. Guys in track suits lean against the walls, smoking and talking and watching the girls. I stay away because there's always trouble in groups of guys that only needs a wrong word or wrong look to set it off.

Looking out at the basin of buildings and people below, I watch clouds of cigarette smoke dissipate. Hidden in plain sight, tinted security camera bubbles are bolted to the buildings and terraces and looking down from light posts, also watching over everything.

There're always police around, a few different kinds. There're the ones with cloaks and feathers in their hats, who seem to be there just to get their pictures taken with tourists. There're ones that look like the cops I know about and there're ones that look like army. The differences don't much matter, they all carry guns, carry them in the open, like they want you to see, like you can't miss them.

I don't want to sell paintings like the old guys gone grey, sitting and smoking and talking up a good gossip, like they don't care if they sell anything, like their paintings are only a reason to hang out with friends for the day. They sure try to sell something when their buddies aren't around though.

That's where I met Gio. He sat under an umbrella and had stacks of paintings. I was staring out and he said, "I painted this."

I don't know about paintings, good or bad. I told him, "It's nice."

He said, "For you, a deal. Twenty-five Euros, but just for you." He shook his finger and winked, like telling me not to let anyone else know.

I figured him to be as old as the steps, with deep wrinkles and weepy eyes, with thin grey hair and a few teeth of his own, the rest fake. His voice was weak but his smile wasn't.

I smiled back, genuine, said, "I have no money."

He laughed at that and told me he didn't either, or so his wife kept reminding him.

He said, "Been married fifty-four years, so I tell her we're rich in history, in love. She tells me a Euro doesn't buy as much as it used to."

He laughed and I did too, not because I found what he said funny, but because I liked him.

"Who the fuck knows?" he said. "I've only ever known Lira."

He asked where I'm from and I told him.

"A long way," he said. "A long way to be without any money for a painting."

He raised an eyebrow, like telling me it's okay to confide in him. I didn't know what to say. I couldn't tell him how hard it is to be here and waiting on sunrise by the river. I couldn't tell him how cold it is down there or I'm chicken to be alone in the dark, hiding, always listening to the shadows. I didn't say anything, but I think he saw me true.

He told me his name and told me he's there all the time, that I should come by to talk again and we could get to know each other. A few other guys showed up and started putting out paintings. They said, "Ciao," to Gio and he knew them each by name.

He told me to bring him a cappuccino with sugar in it when I came back. He laughed and gave me twenty Euros. He told me it's for the coffee and that the cafe up that street will pour one to go that I can bring him. He pointed vaguely and said, "But no big rush, I've had two already today."

I nodded goodbye as more of his friends showed up and talked to him and set up their own paintings. They all looked the same, the old men and their paintings. They talked in Italian, waved their hands around at each other. Their backs were to the steps, like they didn't care for the view that everyone else came to see, like they were tired of it.

Every day the old men are up there, under the spire of the big white church. The bag guys below and the painters above, the costume gladiators wandering the steps between them.

4

Every day, I start at the steps, or wind up at them. I don't know why because my plan could play out anywhere in this city. Maybe it's because it's the first place I came to. I like the steps even though they aren't much to look at. I think it's the crowds of people always here, the different languages in the air and everyone waiting for their friends to come meet them, or the people from somewhere else, just happy to be here.

There're lots of people my age and I like to watch them, too. Most of the time they're with someone, and it always makes me lonely because everyone has someone they're happy with. It's still nice to watch them, even though they make me feel that way, the girls smiling and their guys preened and handsome.

After the first day, I don't go near Gio and it's because of the money he gave me. I want to give his money back at some point and buy him his cappuccino and thank him. All of that will have to wait a bit though, and Gio knows it. Like with the money he lent, he didn't have to say he's got time to wait, not with words anyhow. We see each other on the steps, greetings in a nod or a smile, and there're no bad feelings there. The money was to help me, not for a coffee. It was way too much and the way he said, "We'll have a coffee sometime," means we will, but not right now.

With Gio's money and the bit I still have from my train ticket, I last some nights on the river edge and days in the city. I get hungry, sure, but I've been that before. When I get too hungry there's a McDonald's near the steps, a few minutes' walk down to Piazza di Spagna. It's cheap and I like the burgers. The strawberry shakes are good, too. Most nights, I sit at a table there for as long as I can. I watch people. They kick me out when I drain a coffee and add an hour to it. That's usually where I clean up too, in their bathroom, as best I can. It's so busy that it's easy to disappear inside, so there's never trouble. The money lasts a few weeks, but barely. I know I smell bad by the end of it. There's nothing I can do about that.

5

At the steps, I meet Maria because she asks me, "What the fuck are you looking at?"

I'm shocked to hear English directed at me after being so long in my own head, didn't even know I could be seen anymore. Her accent tells me she's Italian, but her English is really good.

While I'm being shocked, she says, "Seriously, I've seen you here the past four days, and you got this stare that's starting to worry me."

"I'm sorry," I say. "I didn't know."

She looks at me, as if judging, and then she says, "You didn't know what?" But her tone's softer, her face is softer, and she's not mad like she seemed at first.

I say, "I don't know. I didn't realize I was staring. I'm sorry."

She nods, apology accepted. She hikes her butt onto the railing and pats the stone beside her, like calling a dog to sit. I go there and sit. She doesn't say anything while she fishes a cigarette out of a crumpled pack and then lights it with the last match from her pack. She glances at me and I'm staring again, so I look away, only to have her image stuck in my mind. She's pretty, brown hair and brown eyes and skin the colour of a suntan. She's not skinny, but she's not fat either. She's the perfect in between and the perfect height, just a little shorter than me.

She clears her throat to get me to look her way again. She's offering a cigarette, so I take it.

She smirks at me holding it and says, "You don't smoke."

I say, "I do."

And she says, "Then light it."

Her cigarette is in her mouth and she's looking at me like she's waiting for something. I shrug my shoulders and shake my head. She leans closer to me and I get it. I put mine in my mouth, lean in like to kiss her, but touch the end of my cigarette to hers and we both inhale. My cigarette is lit and I'm coughing hard because it's horrible.

Maria laughs and looks down the steps and says, "You're so new."

I can't say anything back because I'm still coughing, now wiping tears away, too. She's laughing at me, but I'm not hurt about it, it's nice she can. I'd laugh, too, if I wasn't choking.

I meet Sam because he asks, "Maria, who's your boyfriend?" He's coming across the terrace at us, dodges a guy, dodges a girl, and then he's close. He's all smiles and holding out his hand. "I'm Sam."

I shake his hand, still coughing. He's got thick black hair, cut close, which I like. I don't trust his smile yet, it doesn't seem true, just kind of goofy. Maria calls Sam an idiot and slaps his shoulder.

Sam takes my cigarette and says, "Give it. Don't want you to hurt yourself." He takes a big drag and blows it out, like to make a point that he can do it and I can't. I don't mind him taking the cigarette and appreciate the out.

Sam and Maria are friends. They make each other laugh while

they catch up. I watch people on the steps, hear them talk. The costume gladiators, they have their hands on a girl getting her picture taken. Best I can figure, Sam sometimes lives with his older brother, who, he says, "is an asshole, but it's better now I'm bigger and he thinks twice about hitting me when he's drunk." Maria squats with her girlfriend and a few other people in a room somewhere close by, and so it seems like all of us are in need of a solid place to crash.

They seem to remember that I'm here and ask where I'm from and I tell them. They think it's cool, so I shrug and say, "I guess."

"Where are you staying?" Maria asks.

I tell them I have a place by the river.

Sam isn't fooled and says, "Watch out for the gypsies. But then," he looks me up and down with an appraising kink in one eyebrow, "you got nothing to steal, so you're probably fine."

I don't know to laugh or not, so I say, "I'm good."

Maria asks, "Where are you going?"

And I say, "I'm trying to get to Belgrade."

They both nod.

I say, "All my money got stolen, so I need to make some."

Sam laughs and says, "All us three then, hey?"

He says, "No roof for our heads and no money for our wallets. A sad bunch."

And I can't but agree.

Sam says, "And how are you going to make that money?"

I say, "I got a few ideas."

"I'd love to hear them," Sam says, "because I've tried a lot of things, short of getting blown by old men in the park, or getting a real job, which is impossible without the papers." Sam takes a pull on the cigarette, contemplates me. "We can help you," he says and Maria agrees.

"I don't know," I say.

"So, what are you going to do?" Sam asks. "You going to sell knock-off purses or paint pretty pictures for the tourists to buy? Or are you going to just beg, like an old one-legged woman?"

I'm nodding to each of these things and watching the people crowd the steps. Maybe Maria and Sam can help. My plan could be easier with them than alone.

"Every day," I say, "I watch people here."

"I know," Maria says.

I ignore her and keep on. "I watch them and there's something most of them are doing." I stop. Sam and Maria wait, each with the stub of a cigarette smoldering between their lips. I feel smart for once and ask them, "Don't you see it?"

They look around.

"Tourists," Sam says.

Maria nods and says, "Mostly."

I say, "And they're all taking pictures."

They nod, but still don't get it.

"Watch," I say and push off the railing and walk out into the crowd.

On the middle terrace, I lean against the railing and look down at the statue of the half-sunk ship below. Not two minutes gone and someone steps close and asks me to take their picture. It's a guy and his girl and he hands me a big camera and points at which button to press. They stand against the railing and I count to three out loud and then take a picture. I hand the camera back. They huddle and look at it and smile and thank me without taking their eyes off the screen.

I go back to Sam and Maria and say, "That's it."

And they blink and Maria says, "You're going to take people's pictures for free."

Sam looks up at the church and says, "I've heard better plans."

"They gave me their camera," I say. "That one was worth a thousand bucks, easy."

Maria says, "And when the security cameras see you again and again?" She points and says, "And those police down there near the fountain? What about them?"

Sam shakes his head. "This is a stupid plan."

I ignore him and tell Maria, "The top terrace on the south side and the middle part, there on the left, I don't think the cameras see those spots. If they even work at all."

She nods, seeing that I have thought it out a bit. "And the police?"

I say, "I guess that's a matter of my legs against theirs."

I say, "They're always down there talking to each other, so I just won't go down there. I figure halfway up the steps is a decent enough head start."

Sam flicks his cigarette and says, "A stupid plan," again.

"Maybe," says Maria. She swings her legs like she's running in the air and watches them for a bit. "What do you need us for?" she asks.

"I got nowhere to sell cameras," I say, "and I got no backup in case something goes wrong."

6

I meet Sam and Maria at the McDonald's that night. It's busy like always and I wait in line. It's noisy and people shout and laugh loud, each trying to be heard over the others. I order a coffee. I want to order a burger and some fries too, but I don't have much money left. I guess another reason I don't buy a burger or fries is because, once my money's all gone, I actually have to do this plan, not just think about it. Sam doesn't order anything and Maria has a hot chocolate.

We wait for a few minutes and a table near the window clears out, so we take it. Maria's girlfriend is there too and I wish she wasn't, because I don't want too many people to know what we're doing. She doesn't say anything and Maria only talks Italian to her, so I figure she doesn't speak English. They talk together, share the hot chocolate, and they're pretty together, which makes me happy. Then I think it's fine she's here because they're like one person really.

Sam fidgets the whole time, bouncing knees and fingers knotting together and coming apart again. He says, "I talked to one of my brother's friends. He knows someone who will take the cameras." Sam says, "He'll take a cut, but I don't know anyone else who'll do it."

"That works," I say.

"How much do we get?" Sam asks.

"We split everything three ways," I say.

"Equal?" he asks.

"Equal," I say and he smiles.

Maria tells me that she'll be hanging out near me, and if something goes wrong, she can make a distraction. Sam asks her what she's going to do and wiggles his eyebrows at her and smirks. She smacks his shoulder and laughs and calls him an idiot. Then, she says something to her girlfriend, who flicks her fingers from the underside of her chin. Sam laughs about that too. And that's all the talk about stealing tonight.

We talk while the city goes by, blue in the window beside us. It's late when I get back to the river, and there's barely anyone on the walk there either. It's dark and the water slips quietly by. I don't want to do this but there's nothing left and I can't think of any other way. I don't like stealing from people who don't deserve it, but there's nothing else I can see to do. I know, because I don't sleep trying to think if there is.

7

Maria is at the steps the following morning and I ask her where her girlfriend is.

"She works in a shop," Maria says. "Selling clothes."

I nod.

"That's how we can even afford what we have," she says.

I ask her how long they've been together and she says, "Four years."

"Do you have a girlfriend?" she asks and I tell her no.

"A boyfriend?" she asks and I tell her no.

The begging woman switches her legs. She stops chanting while she does it and it's the absence of her I notice. I watch as she adjusts her skirt and then I scan the crowd for Sam. The costume gladiators aren't here either. Gio's at the top, in his regular place, his back turned to the steps.

I ask, "Do you have family here?"

"Sam's late," Maria says.

We watch people for a while, and then she points him out and gives a quick wave. Sam spots her and comes over. He's smiling and I don't think I've ever seen him not. He hugs Maria and does me one, too. There's a dark bruise on his neck and something behind his smile today, but Maria and I don't say anything.

"So," he says, and rubs his hands together.

Maria stays quiet. I say, "So," back to him.

"What do we do?" he asks.

There's not much left but to get started. Gut a knot of nerves, I walk to the side of the terrace where I think the security cameras can't see. My heart's thumping pretty good. I look around and spot Maria by the railing. Sam is where we left him and I wish he would stop staring at me.

The cops are down near the fountain, like always, and I'm thinking of their guns when someone asks me to take their picture. I say, "Sure," and look through the screen on the back of the camera at a middle-aged woman, her face starting to soften and her body starting to follow. She wears sneakers and has a bandana wrapped around her neck to keep off the sun. The city is the background and all I can think is that this is how old my mom is, this is my mom on a vacation she dreamed of and saved up for her whole life. I think of Evelyn and the warm light of her house.

My fingers shake.

I take the picture.

I give the camera back. She thanks me and is gone.

Sam comes through the crowd and asks if I was scared she could outrun me, and then he laughs.

"It was a cheap camera," I snap. "And stop staring. You want more people watching?"

Sam's smile slips a little.

Maria comes over and asks if everything is okay and Sam tells her it was a cheap camera.

Maria contemplates me for a moment, and then her and Sam disappear into the movement of the crowd again. I'm left there standing, watching their backs go from me until they are lost in it.

The old men talk above me, their paintings are backdrops and they could be sitting on a watercolour coffee-shop patio overlooking the acrylic city skyline for all they care. The bag guys rearrange their bags below. The police hold tight their weapons and talk sideways to each other, always glancing around, always watching the people looking at the half-sunk boat.

"Can you take our picture?" a man says and I tell him that I will.

They move to the edge of the terrace, a family of two little girls, their mom and dad. Arms over shoulders and smiles plastered on their faces. Him wearing a Mickey Mouse teeshirt and a fancy wristwatch that flashes expensive sunlight, her a striped blouse with a glitter purse slung over her shoulder and a few bands of gold around her neck. Their two girls are in summer skirts, even though it's not that warm, and they seem bored to be here by the way they fidget and the sour looks on their faces. All of them, there in the camera-lens crosshairs. My finger trembles on the button and I push it down firm to give it something to settle on. The camera clicks a picture, but they don't know, they don't hear the shutter sound. They don't know my fast heartbeat and my short breath and that I tell them to get a little closer together because I'm trying to delay the moment I run, to firm some courage and not turn chicken right now.

They shuffle closer together and I say, "Good."

Dad nods and smiles when I tell them I'm going to count to three. One, two, I run.

I'm across the terrace and four steps up when I hear him shout. After that there's no noise, just steps, two at a time, flying under me and surprised faces flashing past. Someone grabs for me, but I'm moving too fast, too much inertia to stop, and the hand slides from my shoulder.

I don't look back.

I don't know if Dad is chasing as I run past the old men, run past big white church. I just run as hard as I can and will for as long as I can. It doesn't seem fast enough, but my legs won't move more even if my brain wants them too. I bolt down a side street, the camera tucked football in my arm, a little baby held safe in the crook of my elbow. I don't stop when my breath comes hard and I don't stop when my legs burn. Being scared keeps me moving, like the dad is on me, like the police are close behind.

Burning out, I thread narrow streets and duck into an alley. I can't go any more, so I lean against a wall, heaving full belly breaths in and out. My eyes are stuck on the end of the alley, watching for anyone with the chase on me. I'm ready to run if someone comes around the corner, but I don't know how much farther I can go.

And a minute passes and I'm smiling, still sucking air, leaning forward to have my hands on my knees, cross-eyed watching the sweat drip from the tip of my nose. When my breath comes back and my heart slows down, I stand and lift the front of my teeshirt to wipe the sweat from my face. When my legs stop shaking and I can breathe normal again, I walk to the far end of the alley and join the people in the street. No one pays attention, just another guy.

And I go and look for Maria and Sam.

8

Every day since I got here, people take pictures of the steps, pictures of each other at the top with the city background, and pictures from the bottom with the steps reaching up behind them, the old church up there, sat high. There're pictures of the fountain and the buildings and the cobble streets. There're pictures of hugging couples, cameras held out at arm's length and pointing back at their faces. They always look at the picture, together, and nod their heads, or try it again. Just by standing there for an hour, I'm somewhere in the crowd of a thousand people's pictures.

I hang out on the middle terrace, south side, or the top terrace on the left.

They say, "Please take our picture with the guys dressed like Romans," and I do. They thank me when I hand their camera back.

They say, "Take another one. I think I blinked." I take another and give the camera back for a "Thanks, buddy."

They say, "Try and get all the steps in the background," and I do. I count, one, two, three, and click, I take it. Then something distracts them, someone calls out or a car horn blasts down in the plaza. That's what I wait for, them looking the other way for just a fraction of a second, and I'm gone. Sometimes I have to run, but I figured out that a lot of times I can just walk away and disappear into the crowd. They can't spot me when I do that because they didn't look at me close enough to know how I look in the first place.

Maria is there, always in the crowd somewhere and ready for things to go wrong. They haven't yet. She hasn't had to make a distraction for days now.

We find Sam after things calm down, usually a few hours later at the top of the steps because the cops are always at the bottom. I give him the camera and the next day he has turned it into some money that we split up at the McDonald's. I don't do too many cameras, one, sometimes two, a day. A few days I don't do it at all because I'm so chicken of the cops.

Sam is there quite a bit, but not always. I don't know where else he goes, but he always meets us at McDonald's after sunset to give us our share of money. It's never much, being sold to his brother's friend for cheap and then split three ways after that, but Sam usually buys a burger now, which he didn't before.

I keep going back to the same spot every night, down by the Tiber. It's late and I say bye to Sam and Maria in front of McDonald's. We hug and Sam tells us he'll see us tomorrow. Maria's girlfriend is there usually, too, Eva, and she teaches me a few Italian words every night. I tell her, "Good night." And she says, "A dopo," back to me. I say the words back and she either nods her approval or twirls a finger and has me say it again, and then corrects the way I say it. I hug her goodbye, too, then we walk in different directions.

I weave through the same skinny streets west every night. There're stores I pass, windows gated and doors barred, but there're still lights shining on the diamonds in the windows. There're stores with mannequins wearing fur coats in the windows, the fur so rich it looks wet. There're stores with pale-coloured bottles of perfume on shelves in the window, sparkling just like the diamonds do.

I reach the road that follows the river. It's busy with cars all the time, day and night. Where I come to it, there're two cop cars stuck in traffic with their blue lights spinning and angry sirens bouncing off the buildings around, back and forth across the river. I watch them for a minute and they don't move an inch. I cross through traffic, not caring about lights or crosswalks because nothing's moving anyhow. Someone honks, not at me but at their frustration. Then I'm on the other side, following sixty-some steps down to the cobble pathway that follows the river's edge. Most of the noise is gone by the time I get there.

Along the Tiber, it smells like piss under the bridges and the stone walls are wet even though it hasn't rained. It's colder here than up on street level. My breath is clouds and I tuck my hands in my armpits to warm my fingers. There're lights at distant intervals along the slick walls and under the bridge arches. The walking path undulates like shallow waves, like breathing. Sometimes there's wreckage down here, brought from the city above and tucked out of sight. A bent-up shopping cart lying on its side, a garbage bag leaking out a wet line, a pile of clothes, all come over the course of the day and are gone in the morning. There's darkness down here too, between the cones of pathway lights.

In the night, it's quiet even though the road's just sixty-some steps above and always busy with cars and cops with their blue lights whirling and angry sirens bouncing around. Down here, there're a few guys fishing, talking quietly, the smell of their cigarettes, waiting for something to catch even though I don't ever see anyone catch anything. I guess that's not the point at midnight down here. The point is smoking and talking and fishing and waiting it out for tomorrow.

I walk under a bridge, going toward my spot. I buried my passport there, buried it with my money in a plastic bag and covered it with dirt and rotting leaves so no one could find it unless they know exactly where to look.

Along the Tiber, it's like the sides of a canyon, steep and smoothly carved out of travertine blocks, straight up to the city level. There are little weeds hanging from some of the cracks and there's a guy in a shadow across the water. All I see of him is just little movements in the dark and I don't know if he's alone, but I'm glad he's on the other side. I don't look there more than I need to because I don't want him to see me, like not making eye contact keeps me invisible.

I go under another bridge and I'm at the spot I've been staying the nights. It's a place in the curve of the river, off the path where dirt and logs have piled up and made a narrow peninsula. A few skinny trees have grown in the right spots. Them and the short bushes make it so that no one can see me watching the light off the black water going by, not even the occasional jogger running the path twenty feet away or the drunks leaning into a phantom wind under the bridges.

It's cold tonight and I shiver for it, but there's nothing I can do to warm up really. I walk the pathway for a while, but that doesn't help much so I go back and just hold my arms around me and hug warmth tight, sit and wait and watch the water.

I think of Sam. Maybe he's got a place at his brother's tonight. I think of Maria and Eva holding each other, warm together in sleep. They live in a broke-down squat and share a shower with a floor of other people. They say nobody cleans it. Eva seems really sad sometimes. I think of all the people on the steps, the pictures of the guys with their girlfriends I've taken and then given the camera back. Or stolen it.

The water turns from black to grey, and sometime in the early morning, the guys fishing leave. I watch the valley walls change, colours drifting from grey to white. Some stones stay stained black with hundreds of years of water seeping between the joins, but all of it grows clearer as night lifts to morning. There're more people. There's more city noise from above and I stand and stretch. My butt's damp from sitting on the ground and I'm sore from clenching against the cold all night.

I go to the McDonald's and buy a coffee and a hash brown. It warms me up some. I have some money again but have to keep it building so I never buy more than's really needed. I'm fifty Euros from a ticket to Belgrade, which means only two or three more good cameras.

Back at the steps, I wait for Maria. The begging woman loses one leg to gain the other. I wait for Maria and she comes an hour later and we start. I take a few pictures. Maria's faded into the crowd and Sam's there or he's not, just always seems to be when he's needed.

"Can you take our picture?"

"Yes," I say.

And it's a guy and his girlfriend. Usually, I only take from people I know can't get me, but for some reason, I know I'm going to take this guy's camera. It's heavy and expensive in my hand and as I hold it in front of my face, that's not the reason I'm going to take it. It's their picture, he's handsome and she's beautiful. They're a few years older than me and they're happy and it's them seen together through the camera that makes me want it, want them, want to be them, that feeling, safe and perfect together.

My hands shake a little, not enough for them to see, but it's my body getting primed to run. I'll have to run faster than ever because this guy'll be fast, probably as fast as me, so my only advantage is the time it takes him to realize what's happening.

I tell them to smile and they do.

I say hold it and they do.

And I go.

The guy knows me right away and he's quick after me, so quick I feel like slow motion in front of him. I glimpse over my shoulder at the way he moves and I know I'm caught. It's just a matter of now or in a few steps from now. Either way, I'll only have time to regret this decision for a few seconds.

I don't look back again because I'm taking the stairs two at a time, past the costume gladiators before they can exhale their cigarette smoke, past the begging woman so fast she pulls both legs in.

The only thing in my ears is the sound of my breathing, hard and harsh, exertion and panic. I don't know where the guy is behind me because I'm focused on not stumbling over what's in front of me. He's coming though. His noises are close.

He pulls my feet out when we're halfway to the top. I twist and hit the ground hard, putting my body between the camera and the stairs because I'm still thinking to save it. Pain shoots through my hip and arm. His hand is a clamp around my ankle and I kick without even thinking. I look back and he's down flat on the stairs too. He lets go.

His girlfriend is coming up the steps behind him. I push myself up, but then she's on my back with her arm around my neck before I can take a step, her weight forcing me down again. The camera breaks under me this time. My chin bounces off the edge of a step and my teeth grind over each other. I spit out some blood and there's a chip of tooth in it. It's the same glossy white as the old stone.

I can't breathe with her on me and it's hard to push up with her on my back. I can't hear anything because of the confusion in my head. Then she's gone and Maria's there, shouting at her in Italian, waving her hands and getting in her face, forcing her away from me by getting real close to her.

I run and Maria blocks the guy. He accidentally knocks her down trying to follow me and then stops to help her up. At the top of the steps, I look down. The two cops are running up. Maria is gone and the guy and his girlfriend are looking. I glimpse Gio's face in the blur of his paintings and then I'm gone, too.

9

Along the Tiber, I hear Sam and Maria coming before I see them. It's still light out, but that's slowly going away. They talk to each other, their voices off the stone walls. They're looking for me and I wish I never told them where I was staying. I wait all quiet and still, scared rabbit, hoping they'll walk right by me sitting with my back against my skinny tree, hugging my knees, with my forehead tucked down on them. I'm a dark box, as small as can be. Nothing's broken, but everything's tired and sore. My mouth hurts and I spit the blood out when I've had enough of the taste. My tongue won't leave the jag of my broken tooth alone. It's the front one on the top, snapped at an angle, a triangle missing.

Sam and Maria are talking close now, like where my piece of dirt in the river joins the path. I don't want them to find me, but they do. They come through the bush, but I still don't look up. There's a hand on my shoulder and it's Sam beside me, sitting on his heels. He smiles when I glance at him, his eyebrows lifted up and his forehead wrinkles. Maria crouches in front and there's a sad look for me on her face.

"You have blood from your mouth," she says.

I spit aside, say, "Broken tooth, too."

She says, "Let me see." And I show her.

"Makes you look tough," Sam says.

Maria guides my chin up by hooking a finger under it.

"Your chin is cut up," she says, tilts her head for different angles and then pulls away.

Sam squeezes my shoulder and pushes up to his feet. "It's Friday," he says and I didn't even know that. "My brother will work all night. Let's go to his place. You can clean up. We just have to be gone around four o'clock. He'll be back sometime after that."

Sam tries to help me up, but I tell him I'm okay and get to my feet on my own. I'm stiff but try not to show it. It gets better in the steps it takes to reach the path. Movement loosens my muscles.

Maria tells us she'll go to the market. She says, "We'll need something to eat."

The three of us pool money and there's not much, but she says it's enough and goes up the steps to the city. Sam and I watch until she disappears over the top and then we keep walking along the river. The clouds have piled up over the afternoon. It starts raining. We hunch our shoulders, but there's not much more we can do against it.

"Maria told me what happened," Sam says after a while. His hair's plastered, wet against his forehead.

I don't say anything back, so we walk a bit farther. I don't want to talk about being outrun, about being beat again, about failing again. There was always a chance it would happen, that worse could happen, but I'm too tired and hungry and sick of always losing to keep talking about it. I don't want to even think about it. The cold gets deep once the rain's soaked though my clothes and I'm shivering for it.

"I think you should stop with the cameras," he says.

I say, "I can't. I need fifty more Euros for the ticket."

He tells me he'll give me that much from his share if I stop. I can't say anything for a minute because I can't figure why he would offer. He's got nothing more than me, except a dangerous place to occasionally sleep, depending on his brother. I tell him I can't take his money, and he can't hide his relief.

We walk up the steps to the road and we're going slow together because I can't go fast.

I say, "I'll be fine. I just need a shower and some clean clothes."

I say, "If it's raining tomorrow morning, we'll take the day off, but I hope it's not."

We cross the street against the light, and the buildings huddle tighter as we go. Then Sam is hammering on the buzzer of an old building covered with flaking plaster and a scrawl of graffiti. "It'll make my brother mad," he says, "but at least we'll know if he's home."

Nothing happens, so he unlocks the door and we go up a flight of stairs and to the end of a musty hall. Stained carpet and stained walls, and I think it's sad that I'm so happy to be in here with the chance of a shower soon. Sam runs a quick check of the apartment and it's small so he's back right away. Once he's sure his brother isn't around, he says, "Come in."

The apartment is one room, a kitchen and a living area, no walls, just furniture telling the purpose of space. The stove is tiny and old and the colour of an avocado. A window beside it looks over an alley of close brick. There's a couch on one wall and a single bed on the other. A gouged-up coffee table between them has an ashtray on it. Only a small washroom opposite the front door is enclosed, private.

Sam is chattering, but I'm not really listening. I'm thinking about how happy I am to have met him and Maria and Eva. I'm shivering hard and still standing in the doorframe.

"Come in," Sam says again. "Here's a towel."

When he turns away, I hold the soft fabric to my nose and close my eyes. It smells so clean.

Sam says, "Go shower. You stink. I'll find something clean for you to wear."

Sam's real small, so I hope his brother is closer to my size.

I lock myself in the bathroom and it's a tight space, barely enough room to take off my clothes without banging into the walls. I leave them in a pile on the floor and kick it under the sink. I don't think to look, but I catch a glimpse in the mirror, and it's the first time I've seen myself since getting to this city. I've lost weight and muscle. It's like there're twice as many bones under my skin. My eyes are sunk in and slung dark underneath. My face is dirty, and when I glance down, my hands are too, dark dirt pushed in the creases of my palms and in half-moons under my fingernails. The scar inside my arm, it's deep purple set against my skin, harsh contrast set in from the cold.

I point my chin up and there's an inch-long scab and a rust smear there from where I kissed the steps. I can't tell how big the cut is because it's too crusty. My upper lip's split a bit and I angry-monkey at my reflection. The chip from my tooth is not as big as my tongue thought it was.

The reflection looks old and sick and I can't stare at it longer, so I go stand in the shower. The water feels so good and I turn the heat up until I can barely stand it. The tiny bathroom steams up fast and I breathe it deep. The chill from waiting out every night on the river starts to leave. My skin flushes and I scrub with a washcloth hanging on the shower curtain rod and the soap sitting on the lip of the drain. I use the bar soap on my hair too, because there's no shampoo, and then just stand and let the hot water flow over some more.

When I step out of the shower, I hear talking from the apartment and I hope it's not Sam's brother. I'm not putting my dirty clothes on again, so I wrap the towel around my waist and go out.

It's Maria. Eva's there too, and they stop talking to look at me. I can tell by their faces that they see what I saw in the mirror. I want to hide, but there's nowhere. Eva's eyes trail from my face to my arm, down my body to the scars on my legs. I want to cover up my skin, to explain everything, but there's no point.

Sam comes from the stove and grabs a pile of clothes from the bed on his way. He hands them to me and says, "Here. I would have put them in, but the door was locked."

"Thanks," I tell him and I feel their eyes on me when I go back into the bathroom to get dressed.

The mirror is steamed up, so I don't have to look again, and the clothes fit pretty good. The jeans are a little short, but nothing too noticeable because the waist is loose and they hang low. I run my hands through my hair and then dig through the medicine cabinet. There's toothpaste that I put on my finger and rub around in my mouth. There's mouthwash too and the taste of it lets me know how far down I went without even realizing. Farther gone than Sam and Maria and Eva, I was the bottom of our group, and didn't even have the shame to try to change it, to even notice it, really.

I spit in the sink and something catches my eye. A clear plastic tab sticks out from under the toilet tank lid. I flick it and it ticks a lazy cricket. Then I lift the lid. It's the corner of a freezer bag, like for a good-sized roast. It's full of Euros, dry and floating in the water, must be thousands given the stacks of bills. It must be Sam's brother's money, from doing whatever he does when he's not bouncing at the club, maybe from some sideline when he is there. I don't know much about the guy, but Maria thinks he's no good, and Sam avoids him when he can and gets bruises when he can't.

Sam calls out, "Everything fits?"

And I say, "Yeah." And I slide the lid back at the same time to hide its noise. I wipe my hands on my jeans even though they're dry.

I stare at the lid and tap my thumb against my leg. I'm thinking about the money in the toilet tank, thinking to take it. But Sam would probably get blamed. At a glance, the mirror is starting to clear, and I go back to the room so I don't have to look at it again.

The food smells are rich, thick, and there's a sudden tightness in my stomach. I go and look over Sam's shoulder and he's got a pot for pasta boiling and steaming up the small window beside the stove. He's chopping garlic with a paring knife on the scratched-up countertop. It's raining hard, gravel-clatter against the fogged window.

Sam stirs the garlic into a pan with a pulped-up tomato and a coin-sized bauble of olive oil floating on top.

"Smells good," I tell him.

And he nods and says, "It'll taste as good as it smells."

He says, "This is my thing, cooking. I love it. So, all you have to do is eat."

The smell of it makes me realize how hungry I am, how I've only had a little fast food and coffee since getting to the city.

I look at Sam while he's busy. He's happy cooking, tied up doing it.

If he's going to get hurt by me taking the money, then I can't.

Maria and Eva are sitting on the couch and Eva calls my name. When I go to them, she points for me to sit on the bed. She says it in Italian, slowly to teach me and I tell myself to remember the words, but even as I think to, they're slipping away. I'm too tired.

There's a bottle of red wine on the coffee table and Eva pours a glass and pushes it toward me. I take a sip and don't like the taste, but it warms me up a bit as it goes down, so it's good. Maria and Eva share a cigarette. They each have their legs tucked up, leaning on opposite arms of the couch with their feet touching in the middle, them passing the cigarette to each other, alternating drags.

"You clean up," Maria says, nods her approval, but I can tell she's just being nice.

"Thanks," I say, and before she mistakes it for meaning about her compliment, I say what I mean, "Thanks for helping me get out of there today."

She shrugs and takes the cigarette Eva offers. She leans forward, taps ash to ashtray and says, "Just earning my place." She looks at me and can tell that won't be enough, so she says, "You're welcome." She leans back and takes a drag.

"You have to pick them better than that," she says, shakes her head and looks away. She's mad. "Don't be an idiot so much."

"I know," I say.

She says, "He was a lot bigger than you, muscles where you don't have any," waving her cigarette in my direction, like to point it out to me.

"I know," I say, picking at some leftover dirt under my thumbnail.

"You have to choose them better," she says again and looks over to watch Sam. Her cigarette is held up, above her shoulder.

I want to get mad at her nagging but can't because it comes from concern and it comes from caring. I just don't know what to do with those things. It's been a while.

"Drink," she says. "It's medicine and magic. It'll make you feel better and make Sam's cooking taste as good as he thinks it does."

Sam says something and she laughs, "Fuck you," back.

Eva offers me a cigarette and I shake my head and say, "No."

Eva says something and Maria laughs, tells me, "Eva says your Italian is coming along nicely."

I laugh too, and drink some more.

"Sam," Maria calls with her eyes still on me. "Do you have any music?"

And a few seconds later there's the crackle of a radio and a song comes through.

After a few songs Sam tells us the food's ready. There's no table to sit at and there're no worries about that. We go huddle around the stove, all of us together and no waiting in line. There are four plates and some mismatched forks and knives. We bump shoulders and jostle and talk and load up our plates using the wooden spoon until there's nothing left but olive oil water in the pot and a red smear of tomato in the pan beside it. The little window by the stove is dark and the glass is steamed over, so I can't see if it's still raining or not. I decide not to worry about it tonight and decide to forget how their faces looked when I stepped out of the bathroom.

I still think about the money in the freezer bag, try to figure out how to take it without getting Sam in trouble. I can't work a way to have both, but can't stop thinking on how to try. The wine has hit me already because I'm feeling all right. There's been nothing in my stomach for so long and one glass is enough to get good gone.

I sit next to Sam on the bed and Eva and Maria sit on the couch across from us, them hunched forward all knees and elbows as they eat from their plates on the coffee table. Sam fills up the glasses and then puts the empty bottle on the table.

Maria says, "That's all there is, so . . ."

Sam frowns. "You bought food instead of more wine?" he asks and laughs.

"We've seen you with two bottles," Maria says. "So, I thought it better to only get one." She translates for Eva as we talk and we laugh, even though I haven't seen Sam drunk.

"This is great," I say around a forkful, nodding at my plate.

Sam's got food in his mouth, so just smiles with bulging cheeks and sauce at the corner of his mouth. I start to feel better and I'm happy the food works to soak up my wine. When I'm done, I put my fork on the plate and lick my lips. I lean back on the bed and prop my head against the wall so I can watch the others. They switch easily from Italian to English and back again when they think there's something Eva or I should know. Maria tells of the time Sam got drunk and wound up grinding against a cop. She says he was lucky the cop was having a good night, and that Maria and Eva were there to peel him off the guy before it turned into a bad one.

Sam furrows his brow.

"What?" Maria asks his face.

"I don't remember that," Sam says.

"I'm not surprised," Maria says.

Sam smiles goofy and tilts his wine glass. "You still here?" he asks and I nod and say, "I am. Just listening." Both of these are true, but I lie by not telling that I'm still thinking about the plastic bag of money in the toilet tank. Nobody mentions what happened on the steps today and I'm happy for that.

I watch Maria when she doesn't know it. She laughs at something Sam says. She rubs Eva's knee and sits back. There's a little wine left in her glass, a frost of fingerprints on the glass. She has purple lips. I know I don't have to say anything more to thank her for getting that guy and his girlfriend off me, but I feel like I haven't said enough. I force it from my thoughts and after a little while it stays away.

In the pale light from the kitchen, to the rolling sounds of my friends talking, my eyelids get heavy. It's hard to follow what they're saying, so I draw my legs up on the bed and Sam shuffles over to make room. I don't shiver anymore and I feel safe. I realize how tight my muscles have been wound from spending all my nights by the river and all the days on the steps.

In the warm smells of tomato sauce, to the sound of rain tapping again on the little window by the stove, I fall asleep. I dream of nights in the trailer like this, a bubble of soft light and my parents talking quiet, words indistinct because I'm so tired, but their very presence is safety.

I dream of Evelyn and she's real, like she's right in front of me. She's floating in zero gravity, her hair out in waves around her head. She's spinning slowly clockwise and holding out a plate with a slice of frozen pizza for an astronaut. I'm glad for her, that she got the chance to go to the space station and not just dream it from her porch step, and that she has someone to hang out with out there, that she's not alone in space.

10

When I wake, the apartment is dark and a soft hiss still rains against the window. I lie for a while, blinking at the ceiling, listening to Sam sleep-breathe, listening to the building noises. I have to piss, but don't want to get up because I haven't slept in a proper bed in a while. Someone covered me up with a blanket and tucked a pillow under my head. It smells like old books, like unwashed life, and it's not a bad smell. It makes me feel warm and heavy. I curl into a ball on my side and breathe it in.

I see the shape of Sam in the bits of blue light coming from outside and from the crack under the apartment door. He's on the couch. The coffee table between us is covered with dirty plates and wine glasses and cutlery. I watch him and match the whisper sounds from him to the rise and fall of his side.

After a few minutes, I sneak to the bathroom to take a leak. With the hand that's not aiming, I'm flicking the corner of the plastic bag where it sticks out of the toilet tank. Each time I flick the corner, the plastic ticks off a list of what's inside. A way off the river, off the steps, out of this country. It's a way to give my legs a break, to stop running with cameras. A way to get to Belgrade, to find my granddad, to have a family again. It's food in my stomach and fewer ribs showing underneath my skin.

I'm done. I flush. I lift the tank lid and take the bag out. I drop it in the sink and slide the lid back in place. The ceramic grinds like sand. I pull the garbage bag from the can beside the toilet, dump the contents and put my dirty clothes from under the sink in it instead, and put the plastic bag of money in there, too. I stare at the bundle for minutes before stepping back into the room. Sam's still asleep.

There's a rattle from the door and I stand still to listen. At first, I think it might be noise carried in from a neighbour's place. When it happens again, I'm sure it's not. There's mumbling and dropped keys shatter on the floor, just outside. The door moves with a click in its frame.

Sam whispers, "What time is it?" He sits up and looks like he's been caught.

I say, "Someone's at the door."

"It's my brother," Sam says and bolts to the kitchen to flick on the light over the stove. In the light, his panic is clear.

"I thought you lived with him," I whisper.

"He kicked me out weeks ago," Sam says, his voice climbing tones. "He says I stole his stuff."

The plastic bag in my hand suddenly feels heavier and I want to ask Sam who he's been selling our cameras to.

"I never stole anything," Sam says, "but he's always drunk or high, so it doesn't matter what I say." He's vibrating, agitated eyes darting for an escape, but there's only the door. The apartment is too small, one room, a cage. The keys scrape in the lock and the mechanism tumbles.

"Okay," I say, but I can't think what to do.

Sam says, "I've been coming here when he's not around. I don't know where else to go." He says, "I can't believe I'm so stupid to fall asleep."

Then the door is open.

Sam's brother isn't more than a silhouette to start, a big frame blocking the light from the hallway and I wonder how two brothers could be so different. Where Sam's small, his brother is a monster. I'm closer to the door and he says something to me in Italian. The part that scares me is not that I don't know what he says, it's that there's no confusion in his voice, like I'm nothing or could quickly become nothing, a stranger in his living room that may as well not even exist.

Sam says something and his brother sees him in the kitchen. He shouts something and then is a wall of fury crossing the room. His arm sweeps me aside like I'm not even air. His breath is meat and booze. His touch is violence. I brace my hit off the coffee table, but still get my side jammed on the corner and it knocks some wind from me.

I'm up quick again, and have to be, to catch up to Sam's brother as he rails past.

Something in me is going to fight him. Kai's voice in my head says, "The only way to win a fight is to be right."

I'm right.

Sam fidgets, a cornered animal standing by the stove, as far away as he can get, looking for a path to flee as his brother gets closer. Then he's thrown into the wall, not far in the small space, but so hard that I feel it shake through the floor.

Sam's brother is raging at him, his back to me, and his voice rattling the air.

In a few steps, I'm right behind him. I take the pan from the stovetop; a few hours ago there were four of us around it dishing plates full of food and now I swing it as hard as I can. Sam's brother staggers sideways and drops to one knee. He's got a hand up on the side of his head, slurs something, then slumps to both knees.

I help Sam up and get him behind me just in time for his brother to launch himself at us. He's too fast for something so big. He swats the pan from my grip. It clatters off the wall and spins across the floor. His hand is tight around my throat, lifting me from the ground, pushing until my back crashes against the fridge. And he holds me there. Just the tips of my toes on the ground. I can't breathe. My hands fly up, clawing at his grip, but unable to ease the pressure. His face is right up in mine, ruddy and red. His eyes tell me he won't let up until I'm done. Blood comes from his ear. Stars start fuzzing out my vision.

Sam's on his brother's back, hanging by an arm locked around his neck. He can't do anything. He's too little. I'm fighting with all I can, but it's not much because we're pushed so close together. I punch a few times at his gut, from the side. It doesn't do anything. My hand scrambles around, pushing against him, then reaching out to the side. The paring knife is in my hand. It was on the counter, the handle still sticky from Sam chopping garlic. I'm so desperate to breathe. My body acts without me. I stick it in Sam's brother, in his side. I'm amazed by how easily it goes in, metal into meat, the short blade smooth to the hilt.

He shouts and his grip falters, but he doesn't let go.

I pull the knife out and push it in again. The handle is slick-warm now. This time's harder to put it in him because I'm aware of what I'm doing. I'm horrified to be capable of this. I want to plead with him to let me go, so I don't have to stick him again, but I can't even choke out a noise.

He hauls me off the fridge and slams me back into it. The room shakes to me. I hurt all over from the hit. My throat is crushed closed and all I want is to breathe again. All I can do is sputter and spit.

Sam's brother lets go when I put the knife in him the third time. He steps back and I gasp a breath as deep as I can and cough when it comes out again. He swipes a hand across his side and it comes away with blood. His drunk eyes look surprised to see it. I'm on my feet, rubbing my throat, staggering and dropping the knife as we back toward the door. He leans against the wall, staring, like memorizing me, like burning me into his brain so he can find me someday later. I don't care about that day right now.

Sam and I make it to the hallway and are almost at the stairs when I stop him with a hand hooked over his shoulder.

"I have to go back," I say and turn around. I hope Sam'll keep going, but he doesn't. He asks me if I'm crazy, but I hear him following close.

"Why?" he asks.

I don't tell him it's to get the plastic bag from where I dropped it. I don't tell him about the money. I just pat the air, to tell him to be quiet. We slow-step toward the apartment, being quiet, not to tell on our approach. The stains in the carpet, the crack and gouge in the plaster, the door still open from our flight, noise comes from inside the apartment, a crash and water running. There's mumbling and Sam's brother moves around in there like a threat. That threat's read by my body, in my trembling arms, in the quick train of my breath.

We reach the doorframe and Sam's hand is on my arm, pulling me back. I shrug him off. I need that bag of clothes. Even more, I need the money stashed inside it. There's another sound, something metal rattling around in the steel sink until it quiets. The knife.

The apartment is cast in deep shadows from the bulb above the stove. Sam's brother is at the kitchen sink, his shirt off and he's a block of muscle. He holds a wet dishcloth to his side, a few pink strands weeping from underneath. When I see him, I hear him breathe, heavy like a big animal. The sound was always in the air, just I didn't connect with it until I saw the cause. He hasn't seen me and the bag is on the floor, only a few steps into the room.

I flinch at Sam's hand clasping my arm again.

I bolt. Two steps into the apartment and snatch the bag from the floor. I spin and am gone as noise erupts from the kitchen. I have to shove Sam down the hall ahead of me. I have to not look back, even though the sounds of pursuit are close. If I look back, I'll stumble and then I won't be moving forward anymore. It's like we're trying to outrun a storm, like a stampede.

We launch down the flight of stairs, falling down them as much as taking them with any amount of control. Sam's at the bottom and I'm halfway down when Sam's brother swipes me in the back. I slam against the railing, miss a step, and my ankle rolls. There's a sick grinding in my knee as it splays out sideways.

Without thinking, I grab at the banister to slow my fall. The plastic bag flies from my hand to the landing below. Sam's brother kicks into me, knocking some noise out of me. Then he's going over top, tripped up and moving as fast as gravity can pull him. I watch when he lands on one shoulder, his neck bent sideways, and wonder how anyone could last through that. The silence is as fast as the thump of him landing, and everything is frozen.

I lie tucked up on the stairs, still clutching the banister, my eyes locked on the crumpled body a few steps down. It seems like forever passes and it still doesn't move and my mind spins up a panic that he's really dead. Then, past the stillness, things come back to life. I hear the sounds from the street. Sam pops his head around the corner from the sidewalk, his lips ringed to match the shocked look on his face.

A door opens upstairs, and someone calls out, "Okay?"

Sam's brother lets out a snort and then starts a heavy, rumble breathing. He's out cold, but alive.

I get myself upright. My knee throbs so bad I can barely stand on it. I draw a breath through my teeth against the pain. My leg holds a little weight, not completely useless if I really need it. I hobble down the remaining stairs and work my way around the bulk of Sam's brother on the landing.

"Okay?" The question comes from upstairs again and Sam calls something back. A door slams.

I move around easier by using Sam as a crutch.

"Help me move him," I say and Sam looks at me like I'm nuts, like I've asked him to give the devil a back rub.

Sam shakes his head and says, "Let's go."

"He's landed on my bag," I say.

And Sam says, "Then leave it."

"Come on," I say and start to pull at his brother. "He's out cold and I can't move him on my own."

Sam comes to help, and the two of us, we manage to shift his bulk enough to get the bag out from under. The lump of him mumbles something, like he's coming to. Sam's already ten feet away, out on the sidewalk and looking back at me and dancing anxiously to go. It's still raining hard and he's orange and shadows under the street lamp, flashing clear when passing headlights sweep him. There're snaking puddles across the cracks in the concrete and asphalt, reflecting every little bit of light they can. I leave when his brother's eyes start to flick around and then his eyelids open a crack.

"What do we do?" Sam asks when we get to a corner.

The tacky tires of cars splash by and we wait because my shocked thoughts make no sense.

"Find a place to get out of the rain," I say finally. I'm shivering, thinking of maybe going to the McDonald's we always go to, but Sam tells me there's a better place. We watch for a gap in traffic and then cross.

On the other side, there's a drinking fountain and I stop to scrub my hands in it. They're shaking and I want to think it's because of the cold, but know it's because of being chicken. I can't stop thinking about the feeling of putting a knife in Sam's brother and it terrifies me that I did it. I could have killed him. I never thought I could put a knife in anyone. It's not knowing myself that scares me. The water in the basin is pink and we go.

Sam and I are soaked and it's hard for me to move fast because my knee is messed up pretty bad. Sam helps for a bit, but then I can put a little more weight on it and don't have to lean on him anymore. In a few blocks, we descend a staircase and it takes me forever because each step shoots pain up my leg. Sam waits on the tiles at the bottom, fidgeting, looking up past me for his brother to block the lights.

I have to break a fifty Euro bill to get metro tickets and the lady behind the glass looks mad about it. I buy tickets for me and Sam. We go through the turnstiles and thankfully, there's an escalator to take us down to the subway platform. Sam keeps looking behind him, looking behind him, and I tell him to relax.

"Relax?" he says, shakes his head. "You don't know my brother then."

"He's going to be hurting for a while," I say.

"He won't be coming after us anytime soon," I say.

Sam says, "If you knew him, you'd be watching behind you, too."

I glance back as we round the corner onto the platform, when Sam can't see me do it.

It's a few minutes to the train and we stand in the dim tunnel, fluorescent lights casting our skin a slick pale green, both of us quiet and waiting. It's later than I thought, the clock says it's close to six in the morning. Sam's jittery and his nerves are about to send me crazy when a soft exhale slips through the tunnel, the train pushing a breeze out in front of it. A moment later headlights slide up the track from the dark. We board, and when the train starts moving, Sam finally relaxes.

"You're crazy," he says. "Going back for a bag of dirty clothes."

I say, "You're crazy for hosting a dinner party at your homicidal brother's place."

He looks confused.

"Homicidal," I say. "It means your brother wants to kill everyone."

"Ah," he says, nods, and looks at people up the carriage. "It's true."

The train breaks ground to cross a bridge over the Tiber and then we're going back underground again. The rattle and clang gets quiet, then loud again. An old man walks into our car from one farther back and starts playing an accordion. He sends his chubby grandson around the car to collect coins in a beaten paper cup.

"I like this song," Sam says and nods along.

I don't say anything because the music sounds a bit dorky to me. I drop some change in the kid's cup and he smiles. The accordion man and the kid move through the rattle and clang to the next car. The same song starts again, farther away and over the train noises.

I pull a quick breath and clench my teeth when I stand up for our stop. I don't know why it helps with the pain, but it does, like something else to focus on other than what's happening. I mostly pull myself up using the railing. My knee's swelling. It feels stiff and tight under my jeans. The train jostles to a stop and a fuzz of noise comes from the speakers, announcing the station's name. The doors slide open to an empty platform.

Sam watches me hobble off the train and shakes his head and says, "We should get you looked at."

I say, "I'll be fine, just need a place to rest it."

Getting up to street level is escalators mostly, thankfully. Black signs bolted to polished tile read Piazza della Repubblica and have arrows pointing the way up.

"You should ice it," Sam says as we ride the escalator.

I call him Mother, which he laughs at and shrugs, says, "Just trying to help."

I have no reference for where we are because we got here through tunnels, in directions I didn't know and at speeds I couldn't judge. We come up on the edge of a giant traffic circle. In the middle, there's a lit-up fountain throwing water high up into the rain. The sky hangs black and close overhead. A car drives by, headlights reflecting saw tooth lines across cobblestones.

"This way," Sam says. He's hunched shoulders in the downpour.

I follow him along a crumble-brick wall, not far, to a door. It's a church and there's someone sitting on the cold marble in the portico, out of the rain, hand held out for money when she sees us. I gave my coins to the accordion kid, so we walk past her. I help Sam close the door. It's sticky, probably from being hundreds of years old and with wood that's still able to swell from the moisture in the air. Through a little window in the door, the beggar watches us with sad eyes and I watch her back. Then, when it's closed, she looks out again to the empty street.

Sam whispers, "I like coming to this one when it's raining."

He says, "The roof's so high it's like being outside, and the priest doesn't hurry you out if you're hanging around for too long."

Sam's whispers echo and the room is silent when they're gone. We stand for a second. The sound of the rain and the noise from the traffic circle are nothing in here. The red brick outside is a lie to the white and rose marble inside. Everywhere, it's polished so fine that there isn't need for much light, just a few spotlights anchored up high, hidden and easily illuminating the place because it all reflects back so bright.

We walk from the entrance to the main hall and the ceiling soars even higher. It's absolute silence as we float to the middle of the room. My vertigo rises when I look straight up because I can't judge how high the ceiling is, the sensation's like falling up a cliff. I don't know much about God, but here, the hall is so big and the ceiling is so high, I wonder if this feeling of falling up is the feeling of Him. I don't much care for the old paintings up there, the people with suffering eyes aimed at angels who don't seem to notice; the shapes and colours are beautiful anyhow.

"So now what?" I whisper because speaking normally here feels wrong.

Sam says, "I don't know. We wait out the rain, maybe later go see if we can find Maria and Eva, maybe wait at McDonald's for them. Or the steps."

He says, "Whatever it is, we stay away from my brother."

"Okay," I say. "We're done with the cameras though."

Sam looks at me like I'm an idiot and I smile cross-eyed and put my tongue out a bit, which makes him laugh.

Standing beside me, Sam looks around the hall. He seems peaceful and I fake it to seem the same. My hands tremble again. I stare at them because I can't connect with why they're doing it right now. I try to stop them because it brings a hiss from the plastic bag.

My knee throbs and I still ache from being taken down on the steps. And here, this big room offers no distraction from the fact that I'm worse than I ever thought I could be, that I'm disappointed in who I was forced to be. That I deserved the marks I've got on me, the scar on my arm and my chipped tooth and the bruise from being knocked into the coffee table and the ones that'll soon rise up on my neck, in the outline of a clasping hand. I am owed the grinding pain in my knee.

Nobody did these things to me any more than I did them to myself. I know it's true, but still try to justify it, that there was no choice except to do the things I've done.

Where'd I be if I didn't keep moving? Hiding in a motel in a canyon or stuck down by the Tiber, starving and freezing and not even realizing it? Would I've lived the rest of my life in Dad's broke-down trailer, waiting for him to come back and knowing he never would? Would I chase him and go work the rigs, too? Sometimes hope is a lie, but I can't make any of these ideas stick because it's not what happened. In a government home, then on my own, then out here, farther away from anything familiar and still not even as far as I need to go, all of it done by me.

Sam's watching me and when I look at him, he says, "Come on, check this out." And he's off through a door at the side.

I follow into a small, dark room off the main hall. This one has a ceiling that's normal height and I can't see much but for contrast because there's one window and one door, open on the far side of the room, letting in the sound of rain. There're soft noises of Sam moving around and I see his silhouette in the shadows, like black on black, like a new moon silhouette against the night sky.

"Come on," he says and I stumble on the uneven floor, grit teeth against a new round sparking up my leg. His outline blots out the door and then we're out in a tiny courtyard. There's a pool of water, not deep, in the corner. There's an open door on the other side. Light spills from it, along with the words of someone talking quietly. A stone statue of a man, the height of two, stands solemn, too big for the little space. There're plants growing, vibrant and green and hanging from gaps in the bricks all the way up to the heavy sky above. We sit on a bench in the sheltered arch, out of the rain, and watch the sky get brighter and the rain get weaker. It feels good to get weight off my knee.

"This used to be public baths," Sam says. "From hundreds of years ago."

The intimacy of the space overwhelms, the depth of time, an empty hidden pocket in a too-crowded city, a little secret hole in the middle of life. Hundreds of years of whispered feet and echoed voices are still here, like a movement in the corner of my eye that's nothing when I turn to look.

"It's neat," I say. "Like behind a secret wall."

Sam doesn't say anything. We watch raindrops ripple the water's surface. We listen to the gentle sounds of it on the brick, and the voice coming through the amber-lit door on the opposite side of the pool. The rain turns to a mist, leaving nothing but damp on the ground and a steady drip from the plants growing up the cracked brick.

Sam looks at my knee, says, "Can you walk again?"

I say I can, so we go.

We're back into the church and Sam wants to go to confession and I look at him because I didn't know he believed in that stuff. He sees it in my face.

"Stay here long enough," he shrugs like it's an explanation, "and you will, too."

I tell him I'll meet him later. "There's something I have to do."

I tell him we'll meet back at the steps in a few hours. The sad beggar at the door is gone.

I find a city map behind scratched plastic near the metro stairs. I walk the streets back north and after a while, my knee feels a bit better. I stop when it says to, and favour the other leg like it wants me to, but it seems to like the movement. As the morning gets deeper, the sun comes out as erratically as the people do, like they don't trust the rain's gone. Cars weave by on tight streets threaded through old apartment blocks.

I come to the Tiber pretty close to the piece of land I've been sleeping at and look down on the pastel grey water from the sidewalk railing above. I think of Darren leaning out over the dark of the IJ near Centraal Station, which takes me to Kai and Mon and how her lips were cold from the North Sea air, how warm they were underneath, deeper in her skin, and how sure I was both of us were in the kiss, not just me. And now a car horn sounds and my knee throbs and I think of how different things can get so quickly. I want to stay with Mon, in my thoughts, cold there like I am now, but in my memory the cold isn't as lonely.

I find a flight of stairs down and go to the river edge. I haven't been down here during the day and it seems much smaller now the edges aren't hidden in the shadows. There're more people here, a woman walking two little dogs and some old people arm in arm. I walk by them all, to my spit of land, and look around for anyone watching. There's no one, so I step into the brush.

The water gurgles past and I dig a hole at the place I've been wasting the nights. The dirt is loose and easy. No one can see me here, unless they're craning over from the bridge above. I hear a few people pass by on the path and don't stop digging. My hands are black and my fingernails have dirt crescents when the hole is deep enough. I find the plastic bag with my passport and the money I already have. I take the bag of money I stole, take twenty Euros out and put the rest all together in the hole, then push the dirt back in, too chicken for getting caught or getting it lost to take it all with me. There's a debt I owe and will pay back. I have to or I'll hate myself that it's left undone. I push some leaves over and mess up the ground so there's nothing left to tell on what I've done.

My hands ache with cold when they go into the river. I rub them together and watch the cloud of black dirt drift away in the current. I toss the bag of my old clothes into the bush and wait until there's nobody passing by before leaving.

Climbing sixty-some slow stairs up to the road, I start toward the Spanish Steps.

11

I come to the steps from the top, with only the big white church above. The street I'm on cuts an angle leading to it, so it comes on me a bit unexpected. The open space seems massive in contrast to the warren I've been walking through. The sky has settled on being low and grey, and there aren't many people around. The guys dressed like gladiators aren't here. The tourists taking pictures aren't here. It's still real early.

Gio's setting up under a few giant umbrellas, their stalks set in metal stands on the ground. He doesn't see me, so I step into a coffee shop, the one he pointed out when he gave me the twenty Euros a while back. It's empty but for the guy behind the counter, the pastries, and bottles of mineral water. The guy behind the counter, he speaks English, and I order two cappuccinos. He smiles when I tell him it's for me and Gio, and tells me he'll bring them out.

The cobbles are wet and the steps have puddles that fake the sky, reflections like bits of it have fallen down for people to walk on. Gio sees me when I'm halfway there and he waves and unfolds his chair to sit on. When I'm closer he says, "Hello again, my young world traveller."

He says, "Is this the morning you buy me coffee?"

I wait until I'm a few steps closer before telling him it is. He pulls a collapsed three-legged stool from behind his paintings and unfolds it and pats it for me to sit on. It's covered with comets of dried paint and he says, "Then you get the artist's chair."

I tell him thanks and sit, delicate at first until I'm sure the wobbles don't tell on the stool's collapse.

"You've been busy. Always on the run." Gio taps a finger in the air, waiting for me to say something about the cameras, of course he's seen, but I don't say. So, he examines me, says, "Your travels have been trouble."

I think to get hurt by that, but he says it with an honest face and it's true, so I nod and tell him it's been hard lately.

"Well," he says. "I would love to travel the world again with good knees, money or no."

I tell him that it's not good now and he scrunches his face, then shrugs his shoulders and says, "And it'll get better soon, then it'll get worse again after. But when you sit in a chair and sell your paintings, an old man at the end of it, you'll remember it with a longing heart, whatever the past was."

I've never thought of myself at Gio's age and laugh, and he asks what's funny so I tell him.

He says, "You shouldn't worry about it too much. The older you get, the more time you have because you can always retreat to the past. And at my age, so much has passed. But you know this all already, I guess. Don't you?" He laughs and twirls his fingers in the space between us.

He says, "At your age I knew it all too and the more you think you know, the less you believe." He glances at the church and then settles back on me. "But you'll come to find, the more you truly know, the more you need belief, because it'd be absolute craziness for all of this to be without purpose."

I don't want to tell him what I think about the church, that I don't think of it much at all and am just fine without it, so instead I say, "I don't paint."

I tell his confused face again, "I don't paint, so I won't be your age sitting and selling paintings and longing back for the good old days, for today especially."

I don't tell him, but I won't miss the loneliness, the weeks of hunger broken up with crappy fast-food punctuation marks, always being cold and waiting for something else to go wrong, feeling so tense for so long, that I sometimes welcome when it finally does go wrong because it means I don't have to wait for it anymore. I won't look back on any of it with longing, but I don't tell him any of this.

We're through into the breaking sun, and the morning crowds start to gather on the steps. The air starts to warm to the light. The guys selling bags set up at the bottom of the steps by the fountain. The one-legged woman is there, seemingly from out of nowhere. The costume gladiators wander by, talking, smoking cigarettes, and the guy from the coffee shop is coming our way, a cup on saucer held in each hand. His eyes go back and forth between them, so not to spill any.

We watch him and Gio says, "Well, what do you do if not paint?"

I say, "I like to write, or at least I think I can."

"Those are two different things," Gio says. "Thinking you can and being able to."

Gio says, "Read me something you wrote."

I tell him I can't, remind him that my backpack with all my stuff got stolen a few countries away, and I don't even have a notebook to write in now.

The coffee guy gets to us and Gio says, "Salvatore, thank you for bringing our coffees all this way."

Salvatore hands Gio a coffee, hands me a coffee, tells us that it's not that far. He says in English, "I'd stay, talk, but no one's watching my shop." With a slight bow and a smile to us both, he makes his way back across the plaza.

"You have been to the Keats museum then?" Gio points with his cup to a brown building down near the fountain, siding onto the steps.

I shake my head and wrinkle my forehead at the building. Gio sips his coffee and I sip mine.

He asks, "The Colosseum, have you seen that?" And I shake my head.

He asks, "St. Peter's? The Public Forum? Vatican City?" And I shake my head the whole time until he falls silent, thinking about it, and then telling me that it's okay because I'm still new, that there's plenty of time.

He swats his hand my way, says, “The Pantheon isn’t going anywhere anytime soon.” And laughs. Then, “So, if you haven’t seen the sights, what have you seen?”

I sip my coffee to think on it for a moment, what have I seen? From the prairie I’ve seen outer space and had the rare feeling of bleeding out into bone dust. I’ve breathed air coming straight from the arctic and it smelled like a million-year-old ice. I’ve been lost in a city of neon with naked women for sale behind shop windows, and it made me lonelier than I ever thought was possible. I have been kicked to the ground only to suffer the sweetest kiss. I’ve never known how to regret a kiss, until I had to regret that one.

From the bank of the Tiber, I’ve seen the water go by in the dark, my eyes on it all night and surrounded by a city that’s so old it doesn’t even know I’m here. I’ve run through these tight streets and when people turn to look, they don’t see me. I’m gone. There’s just the echo of my shadows off the walls. All they hear are fading footsteps.

When I speak, it’s slow because I’m thinking. I say, “I’ve sat at McDonald’s trying to see how long a coffee can last and I’ve seen the look on the face of a guy who fears his own brother more than anything. I’ve seen a church so big that I felt like I was falling up into it, and the silence there was so still it was like being dead, and that scared me.”

I laugh and don’t know why, and I glance at Gio.

I say, “I’ve seen my lies run out, like everything else, like money and time and people run out, like everyone I’ve ever known and everything I have ever owned to right now, sitting in your chair. And I’m so tired now, I’m not even really here.”

Then I shut up because if I don’t, I think I’ll fill the whole day saying these things.

We’re through into silence and Gio looks out at the city. I sip coffee from a trembling cup and watch people coming up the steps, people going down the steps, them going by the church that looms big above us. And as we sit, I’m so sick of the sound of the one-legged woman that I want to scream at her to shut up.

I'm so tired of the way my body feels, always cold or sore or hobbling around on a blown-out knee, always in some kind of pain. I hate the costume gladiators and the smell of their cigarettes and can't stand the sound of everybody here, around me, talking a language I can't get and feeling stupid for it, stupid for how I got here. Mostly, I'm sick of how I can't seem to do any better than always the bottom of it all.

But there's nowhere else to go and there's no one else to be and there's nothing else I can figure to do, except what's already been done. I have Sam's brother's plastic bag of money and my passport buried next to the tree by river and it's time to leave, today, without another night under the bridge.

It's like Gio was waiting for me to get the thought out. He stares for a moment, then says, "In the end, we'll both become other people's memories, for however long they last, and then gone. We're important only to those who loved us."

Gio watches two little kids play a chasing game up and down the stairs, squealing. Their mother shouts something at them and they stop and run back to her.

"Only to those who loved us," he says to himself. He looks at me sideways, says, "You drank McDonald's coffee?"

And I nod.

"This is Italy," he says to the empty space beside him, like there's someone there. "And the boy drinks McDonald's coffee."

"It's not that bad."

He shakes his head, digs through his stuff, then holds out a sketchbook. "For you. It's empty."

I take it.

"Fill it up with your brilliant ideas, if you have any," he says and flips his hand at me like to shoo a bug. "Maybe this notebook will be taken from you like the other one was, or else it'll be forgotten by you on a bus seat, but no matter how it happens, full of words or empty, you'll leave it behind, too."

He says, "Write this down. Write these words for the first ones in there." He points for me to open the book. When I don't, he reaches over and opens it for me, then gives me a pencil. "At some point, everything and everyone, we are all of us left behind. Not a single one of us isn't, in one way or another."

I write it on the page and look at it. In the silence that follows, I can't look at Gio. I run my fingers up and down the pencil, over the braille of his teeth marks in the wood. I'm embarrassed by my complaints and feel stupid about them now. I don't know Gio and I don't know what Gio has done in his years, but he's probably right.

"The only thing we have to worry about until then, is who loves us." He considers me for a bit before he says, "Understand."

It's not a question, and he clinks his cup to saucer and sets them on the cobblestones beside his stool. He smacks his lips together and sighs. I look to his face with the noise, and he smiles and slaps my shoulder, says, "Good coffee."

I shrug and look in my cup. "McDonald's is better."

He swats me again and laughs. "Did you bring me change?"

I dig in my pocket for the coins. I give them to him, and when I stand to leave, he gives me another pat on the shoulder and wishes me luck, says, "Goodbye."

I go down the steps, past the begging woman, and I don't care about her noise anymore. I glance back and Gio has one of his paintings in a man's hands, a tourist by his clothes and the attention he pays. I run my thumb over the sketchbook.

At the middle terrace, where I first met Sam and Maria, I sit on the railing and pull my feet up. I rub the teeth marks on the pencil and then I write notes on how it is to be here, how it is to be left behind, how I got here and who I've met. I write for a long time, disconnected pieces passing over pages in grey lines, like it's been pent up in me since Amsterdam, or since the hole in the prairies, or since before all of that even. The sun's overhead before I notice it's moved and I put the pencil between my lips and rub at my knee to see if I can distract the ache, but it stays put.

One thing I know now is people are always there, those I've met and those I haven't yet. I know this because I hear someone call my name and it's Darren. His smiles, says my name again, like it's a question, and he walks across the terrace. How long has it been? Only a month maybe, but his face makes me a lot less lonely.

He's in front of me, telling me that he's glad to see me and I believe him.

His arms are around me tight, and there's nothing to do but put mine around him, too. His body feels good held close, because I can't remember the last time anyone touched me that wasn't meaning for it to hurt. He was never a part of what happened in Amsterdam, only to hold Kai back, and I tell him quietly, over his shoulder, that it's good to see him, too. We step back from each other, look at each other with smiles. Darren shows his teeth and I hide the chipped one of mine behind closed lips.

He says, "You didn't need to leave." And I tell him that I did.

He says, "Kai would have gotten over it by now."

And I say, "I doubt it."

His eyes travel me up and down and he asks if I'm doing okay.

I shake my head, say, "It was stupid. I'm so sorry for it."

I say, "What're you guys doing here?"

"Mon always wanted to see Rome, the steps," he says, and I remember her saying it. "So here we are." He holds out his hands to either side. I look around to see where Mon and Kai are, but I don't see them.

Darren tells me they're meeting here, that they had to go find an internet cafe, that Kai's expecting an email to say whether he's accepted to university or not.

I nod and picture Kai and Mon back across the ocean and living in a house together, having kids together. Am I still out here somewhere? I can't picture my future as easily as theirs. I can't help being jealous for the life they haven't had yet, but probably will.

Darren asks again, "You sure you're okay?"

I tell him I am, tell him that I came here after Amsterdam and have been seeing the sights. He doesn't believe me, but he doesn't say it. I can't ask him for help. He's been out here much longer than me and I'm ashamed of the time I'm having of it.

I say, "I'm just waiting here for a friend to show up." And he nods.

He asks what I've seen of the city and I tell him pretty much everything and I'm thinking of moving on today.

I say, "Belgrade's the next stop." And he tells me he hasn't been there and hasn't heard much about it.

He says, "We should get a beer, catch up before you go."

He says, "We can all go once Kai and Mon show up."

I nod and am about to say that I don't think it's a good idea when I catch sight of Sam by the fountain in the piazza. He's already seen me and is heading up the steps, two at a time.

I say, "My friend's here." And Darren looks when I point.

Sam's distracted when he gets to us and just nods at Darren when I introduce him. He excuses himself and says that he needs to tell me something.

Darren says, unsure, "Okay, it was good seeing you again." He tells me to find him after we're done talking and we can wait for Kai and Mon, then get that beer.

I tell him that sounds good. I'll do that. That I'm glad we saw each other. And only one of these things is true.

He tells Sam, "You should come, too." And Sam nods again, but it's obvious he wants Darren to go. Darren gets it and leaves with an uncertain goodbye, his eyes from me to Sam and back again.

When Darren's out of earshot, Sam tells me that he heard from the guy he was selling the cameras to that Sam's brother is tracking me. Sam asks if I took anything from the apartment and I tell him I did. I tell him about the money and Sam's look is not of disappointment, like I thought it would be, it's one of fear instead.

Sam says, "My brother won't be talking if he finds you. He'll be getting his money back. Who knows what else." He lets the threat hang there.

I run a finger across the notebook Gio gave me, and after a bit, tell Sam that I'm leaving once I get my passport and the money from where it's buried by the river.

He says, "That's a good idea."

He says, "Be careful going back there." He tells me that his friend told his brother what he knew about me, that I was hiding along the river at nights when I wasn't running away with people's cameras.

I watch people go by while Sam talks. I'm searching for his brother, because if he knows that I've been by the river every night, he probably knows where we've been taking cameras from. I tell Sam that he should leave Rome with me, but he says he can't, he doesn't have any money.

I say, "I'll give you everything that's left after I buy a ticket. It'll be a lot. Enough to come with me."

Sam shakes his head and tells me he doesn't have a passport and he doesn't want any of the money, that he has to watch out for his brother now, too, because in his mind we're one and the same. The money in his hands will only make that worse.

I tell him I'm sorry for taking it, sorry for getting him in trouble.

Sam glances around, says, "Trouble was already there. A bit more doesn't matter much."

"You should really go and not come back. Seriously," he says, "best thing you can do."

I feel bad for the place I've put him in, worse that I can't change it back.

I ask, "What about you?"

I say, "You have to come with me."

Sam says, "I'll be fine." And I can't help feel he's blaming me, which I know I've earned.

I shouldn't be surprised it got this messed up. Of course Sam's brother would find the empty toilet tank and of course Sam would catch trouble from it. From here looking back it's easy, but early this morning, with Sam's brother raging around the tiny apartment trying to kill us and all, it made sense. I needed it and it was there to take.

Now it's just a matter of getting gone and while I'm thinking all of this, Sam and I have been nervously scanning the crowd for a cause to run. I can't run though, not on my knee. That leaves my options hiding or fighting, and just in that order, because there's no chance for me if it comes to fighting.

"Let's go," I say.

Sam says, "Yes. But in separate ways."

When I hear it, I get it. Sam's more sore at me than comes across and I won't see him again. A beat of silence between us acts as goodbye, and then he walks away.

To his back I say, "Tell Maria and Eva bye for me." I don't know if he hears. It feels wrong to leave without seeing them, but all I can do is hope Sam heard me and isn't so mad to pass along my words. I watch him go until there's just the crowd left.

Darren's still there, down below by the fountain of the half-sunk boat. He's talking and I see it's Mon and Kai there with him. Kai laughs and Mon does too, and my gut twists, the flight of stairs is nothing compared to the distance between us. I can feel that night, their friendship in the club, the way we played through the twisting streets and on the seawall. I can almost feel Mon's lips again.

They don't see me, so I go up, slowly back past the begging woman.

Gio's talking to another painter and he doesn't watch me go.

12

I have to go back to the river, to the tree where my passport and the money are buried. Everything narrows down to these two things, the only things I have left and the only things that can get me out of here. My panic overpowers, focuses, each corner I turn and each street I hobble down. There're no other voices left in the air now. There're no old buildings hemming in the streets and no traffic sounds bouncing around off them. I can't see anything but faces, watching them for the one that's trouble, the one that's a fight.

And going this way, cautious, on the uneven roads and sidewalks with my blown-out knee aching tender, it takes me a half hour to reach the road bordering the river. Traffic is a snarl, unable to move but straining. Bumpers close and exhaust-rumbling engines lined up make it easy to weave through to the stairs to the river path. It takes a bit to get down, but that gives me time to watch for Sam's brother along the water's edge. I take my time because it's easier going down than it will be going up, especially if there's a chase on. Once I'm down, the stone walls and high stairs are a trap. A man walking, he scowls uncertainly at the mess of me as we pass.

I lean against the wall and watch. The stone is cold in shadow and lingering damp, still from the morning river dew. I wait for my knee to catch up and look downriver while I do, past this bridge to the next one, to where I'm going. There's no one, in the sun or in the shadows, under the bridges or between them.

And there's my little piece of land off the path, and there's the skinny tree with my stuff planted in its tangle of roots. I can't tell if anyone's there, can't see into the brush. The one thing that worked for me staying hid is the one thing working against me now. It's an easy guess that's where I've been camping out. It's the easiest place around to do it, so it's both hidden and obvious.

I look back up the path, the grey water lazy beside it. The scowling man is a ways gone and a jogger on the other bank isn't a worry for me. I think there's someone standing in the shadow at the base of the next flight of stairs, a good distance away. I squint, trying to make it clearer, and then think nobody's there but in my mind. The walls are claustrophobia and my breath is short even though I've rested a few minutes.

I can't wait any more. I push off the wall and walk toward the tree, there's no choice in it, so there's no point in waiting any longer.

The shadow of the first bridge passes over me and I can think of nothing but getting gone. A car horn blasts from above. The stone passes under my feet as I come into the sun on the other side and wish for nothing but the feel of dirt in my hands as I dig up the money, nothing but the struggle back up the steps and the sway of the train to the airport. I won't relax until then.

I approach slowly, watching the bushes for movement and listening for any sounds that shouldn't be there. I don't even breathe, stepping from the path, because I'm set on searching out anyone who may be here. A branch rustles and I freeze. My heart pounding is the only thing in my ears, and I wait, breathe deep and slow, and it gets a bit easier when I figure the noise was from a rat or a bird or something. I push through the brush and hate it touching me because of the noise it makes and the way it grabs at my arms and shoulders.

I reach the skinny tree I've sat against for weeks. The ground where the money is buried looks the same as I left it, and I rush at it, easing onto my good knee and wincing at the shot from my bad one. Digging fast and focused, the earth smells like rot, musty vegetation, stale water.

Once I get the bag, I'll buy a change of clothes and rent a hostel room for a shower. I can't go to the airport like a mess. I won't stay for the night or to watch teevee or anything, only long enough to clean up, change from my old clothes into some new ones, and then gone.

It's these daydreams that do me in. I hear him too late, Sam's brother coming through the brush, all noise and movement like a charging bull. I look up, but too late, the plastic bag slippery between my filthy fingers.

An immeasurably short moment ago, the plastic bag was the only thing between getting stuck here and getting gone. Now, it's Sam's brother on me. I don't know if he was waiting or followed me or just figured rightly that this would be the place I'd be, but it doesn't matter because he hits me with a brick fist just the same. My head sparks instantly. My sight becomes stars. My ears become a ringing noise that's louder than everything else.

I fall to my side.

There's only dirt left in my hands. The plastic bag is gone.

One thing I know now is, any pain a body has can always get worse. I'm lying on my side in the rotting grass and leaves and Sam's brother is raging about something. I can't figure what he says and it's worse because of it. I can't talk to him or try to figure this out with words, there's just my body versus his. I don't know where the plastic bag went and I think for a moment that maybe it's gone into the river.

Sam's brother kicks me, his boot in my side. I shout out with it because he grazes my knee on his way to my stomach, and that hurts more than anything. Then the air in me is gone and I curl up into a ball, trying to pull some back in. He's on top of me, laying his body on mine and crushing me into the dirt. He's got his hand on my mouth, so I can't call for help, if there's even anyone close enough to hear.

I struggle against him, try to bite him, but he holds my jaws closed. I manage to wriggle onto my stomach, trying to get his weight off my injured knee. It's not something I think about, just running from the pain, trying to hide from my own body. He's on me, chest against my back, both hands clamped on my mouth and tangy like metal to my lips. Then he's pushing the back of my head, forcing my face into the wet ground, dirt in my nose and eyes.

I try to push up, to punch out, but can't do anything. He's like a house sat on me and the whole time he's talking, his mouth to my ear, his breath hot, whispering words I don't get.

He lets go the back of my head. I turn to the side and gasp. I can't breathe right for the mud in my nose and I can't see clearly because my eyes water from the dirt in my eyelashes. A glance of grey sky out the corner of my vision, the river there, peaceful to my struggles and the sounds of my panic: the grunt of me fighting, an unintentional whine, brief and fleeting from my throat, the spit and rumble of his voice. It's a confusing mix of our noises.

He pushes his chest more on my back and bumps his butt up into the air, the full weight of him off me there for a moment. He fidgets between his waist and mine, a fleshy fist working in the pressure between our bodies. I hear the ring of metal on metal and it's his belt coming loose, the tine on the horseshoe clanging a bell as it swings free. There's the machine-gun clack as he yanks the belt through the loops of his jeans, a fluid motion. His hips drop and he's full-on me again, our shirts still lifted a bit because of our struggle, his bare stomach pressed into the arch of my lower back. Panic makes me battle harder, because of what I think he's going to do.

I wish I could get his words clear, the spoken intention of him about the money, the money that could be in the water until I glimpse a corner of plastic in the brown deadfall a few feet away. It's a bit of hope, but quickly crushed under the weight of the man on me, something horrible before he took his belt off, terrifying now it's gone, and I try to yell as his hand works its way between his stomach and my back again. Nothing comes out of me but a choked noise, a pathetic vote of protest when it's hopeless, and the pressure on my back and knees as he inchworms his butt into the air again to make room and he grabs a handful of the waist of my jeans.

My whole consciousness is drawn to his fingers sliding between my skin and jeans, them tightening against the fabric, bunching at the belt line with his knuckles digging against the flesh of my lower back. I'm crying, manic because I don't want him in me. His knees slide to either side of my waist in a straddle and he growls wet words. His hand slips from my lips and curves around my throat, choking the noise out. I buck, uncontrolled and hopelessly desperate to throw him off.

He pulls on my throat and I arch backwards, his hips pinning mine to the dirt. Then his hand yanks the fabric at my waist. He picks me up, slams me back against my tree. I sit there stunned by the strength of him, the way he lifted me for the moment before gravity took me down again.

I glance at the plastic bag, mostly buried in debris, so close I could point it out, maybe end this, but I don't say anything. Part of me thinks there's still a way out with that bag in my hands and my body relatively intact. Part of me thinks even if I pointed it out to him, there'd be no mercy anyway. He wouldn't just smile and say thanks and leave without having me pay for stealing it in the first place, and for sticking a knife in him.

Sam's brother lunges and plants his knee in my groin, his chest against my face. I squeal an animal noise and think I'm going to pass out. Instead, I puke against that unique pain a guy's balls can bring. It's not much puke, just what little's left in me.

He looks down at me in disgust, at the mess I left on his shirt, on mine, in the dirt beside us. He says something and brings the belt up in front of my eyes, like for me to see it. The leather slides smooth under my Adam's apple before I'm yanked back, neck and the tree bound. My hands shoot up to pull the belt away as soon as I realize what's happening, but they're too late. The tine and the horseshoe ring again and the belt is cinched and latched.

I draw a raggedy breath. Not much goes in, just a bit, enough.

I try to wedge my fingers under the leather, to pull it away.

Sam's brother steps back, his knee gone from my balls, and completely detaching from me for the first time in the long seconds since we met again, from the forever it's been since he's taken control of my body.

There's nothing more terrifying than the feeling of suffocating. I claw at the strap but my fingers are useless against it. I let out a short gasp. A gob of spit lands on my shirt. My throat squeaks to inhale. I don't mean for it and almost laugh at the sound because it doesn't belong here. I scramble for the buckle around back the tree, frantic fingers like if I can get it, I can undo it.

The buckle's on the back side of the tree and at the edge of my reach. One of my fingernails pulls back as I struggle at it, but I barely notice. Just before I can pull the leather tongue free, Sam's brother kicks quick at me again. I convulse and my head feels full, my forehead taut with pressure and veins swollen. I try to make myself as small as possible, hands clutched protectively, a knot of human belted to a tree. My eyes are clenched too, like if I can't see any of it, then it's not here. But it is. His breath in my ear again, crouched close to me.

I think to hit him, but I won't be able to hurt him, just make him mad, so I freeze, forcing the little bit of air I can, in and out. I open my eyes and his are right there, close enough to see tiny red veins jagging through the white parts, the brown feathers stacked around blackhole irises.

He doesn't say anything. It's like he's frozen there, like he wants to be close to smell my fear and hurt. It's in his eyes, that I'm an experiment, not a person anymore, and neither is he really.

I'm not going to give him the pleasure of squirming anymore, so my struggles stop dead. I glare at him, and him back at me. I stay curled up, not moving except for a trembling I can't make stop. My eyes are streaming, but I won't back my glare down. I think I may lose at this too, but then he stands up and takes a step back from me, contemplating.

If he kicks me, I'll get through it.

If he punches, I'll deal.

It's when he pulls a knife that I know it'll get worse.

Of course, I recognize it's the paring knife I put in him when we were fighting in the apartment.

Of course, all the words he'd been spilling out as he roughed me up, they make sense now.

He thought getting his money back would be great, sure, but it's become more about getting even. And I can see it in him, it's also about something else. The interest I saw in his face earlier, that wasn't in anyone else I've ever met. Mr. Langman, he was close when he had me in the desert. But he had been thinking on what to do when he held the rock over my head, like weighing out options, better against worse. I flex my hand, the numbness tingling a memory of that night. Where Mr. Langman wasn't sure about what he was going to do, Sam's brother knows. Certainty's on his face.

He slaps the flat of the knife against his palm, tapping the blade as if it was nothing but a pen or a comb. He steps closer, the flat smack of the steel on his skin is a meek noise over the wheezing through a choked windpipe, but I hear it still, a little.

One knee in the dirt, he crouches beside. I want him to smile, to show he's evil, but he doesn't. I want him to blink, to show some indecision in his want to do this, but his face doesn't waver.

It takes just a flash to bolster my resolve, because it's all that's left. If it'd help, I would beg and cry, but it won't matter. So, I won't give him anything of my fear, even though it rages inside. I won't give him any of my panic, though it twists up my guts harder than anything I've known. I'll keep this all, the last thing that's mine, and he can't have it. This is me earning that bag of money hidden in the dead leaves. After this, it'd be won, not stolen. In a way, he's earned this, too. We both deserve this. This is the last thing to do.

His fingers lace through my hair, like a caress, like a lover's touch. His hand traces down my neck, over the plumped flesh bracketing the belt. His face is close to mine, our breath together like the moment before a kiss, like foreheads together in consolation. His hand moves to my shoulder and then is a palm sliding down to my chest, forcing past where my knees are tucked up tight, pausing flat and gentle against my breastbone, like he's feeling my heart hammer behind it.

The whole time he's whispering things at me, but more like to himself. His lips are moving and his voice is low. He takes the knife and taps me on the shoulder with it, flat blade, like he tapped it against his palm. My breath squeaks in and out. My eyes on him, I work to keep the tremors from my body, though I'm sure he feels them crawling under my skin. His hand continues down to pause at my belly button. He stops there and waits, taps me on the shoulder again, and I hiccup with fear.

He withdraws his hand from my belly and nods. There's nothing on his face, satisfaction or pleasure or anything, and then his eyes break from mine. I watch them trace the same path his hand took down my body, head to neck to shoulder, chest down to stomach, and then he looks content. It's like I can think what he's thinking, where to put the knife in me.

He pokes at me a few times with his fingers, a few times around the side at my ribs and I glance to see his other hand mirroring the spot on his own body, the spot where I stuck him in the dark morning kitchen.

I say, "Okay," a croak as much as a voice.

He looks up at the word, surprised, like he forgot I was even there.

I try to draw a breath, as deep as I can, when the knife starts to part my skin. I choke on it and shake a bit, as much as I can, with the weight of him leaning slowly into me and being strapped to the tree, my face red and there're veins sticking up from my neck and from my forehead, I feel the pressure, and try to focus on only that until the knife is all the way in me. My hands are clamped around his wrists, trying to push him back, but I can't. The spot burns hot at first, but then it's too much and turns into the dull pressure of Sam's brother leaning into me, holding it in me, whispering something close by and hateful in my ear, sure, because he deserves this, like I do.

He's here because of me, not me because of him.

I'm here because I'm a thief and a liar and a bad person. And here we are, found each other.

We're more the same than different, right now.

My head swims sideways and I black out for a second until the knife pulls out again. It's brief, but the jump in the world tells me I'd gone away. I don't feel warmth spread from my side. I don't feel much of anything that I thought I would, just a numb hollow where he's split me. For an idiot's moment, I wonder if I even have blood. I would look, but can't move to see.

I snake my hand across my stomach and push it against the skin. It's wet and I hold it there, flat to keep my blood in, as much as it can. My eyes are still locked on his, his wandering my body again. The fingers of one hand prod me and the other hand mirrors the same spot on himself. I know he's going to do it again when his fingers settle lightly on me.

With a hand cupped softly on the back of my head, this time will be worse because I know how it'll be, something I never need to feel again, and anticipation is so much worse than surprise. I spend all of my willpower on staying still and staying here, conscious, even though my mind threatens to go away from me.

We're both drawn by a fury of quick noise and a blurred violence of movement. Maria and Eva rage through the bushes. Sam's brother is gone. My eyes race around to find him, the threat in the jumble. He's gone and Maria is behind me.

She says, "Stay still."

She says something to Eva, Eva by the river, watching the water.

There's a momentary constriction around my neck. A prickle crawls across my scalp at the sound of the belt's tine ringing on the horseshoe, then I can pull free breath. I grab at my throat and choke and cough and cough and rub the skin there. I gulp, greedy for air, slide to the side to lie in the rotting leaves, coughing and coughing more.

Sam's brother splashes in the water. Eva kicks at him, so he can't get a hand on the shore. The current pulls him downstream. Eva shouts and kicks at him again. It's a horrible sound and a horrible movement, but she keeps him from getting back here, keeps him pulled downstream by the current.

Maria helps me sit up. I cry out at the movement then bite my cheek against it. Eva watches the river and I watch the world swim, as I go upright. Maria steadies me against the tree and shakes her head as she looks me up and down.

She says, "Sam told us."

I look around for him, but Maria tells me he's not coming. She lifts my shirt and looks at my skin and says a swear. I don't look. I want to lie down again but she won't let me, makes me stay against the tree and fusses with my body. Eva holds a wad of fabric out to Maria. Maria's hands are on me again and I jerk away quick because they flash as Sam's brother's hands and instinct thinks another knife is coming.

Maria smacks the side of my head, stares at me to make sure it's sunk in, then says to sit still. She presses the fabric, and says, "Quit being stupid. Put your hand here. Push hard."

I nod and point a lazy finger at the dirt. Eva looks over her shoulder at the river. Maria takes my hand and tries to push it to the ball of fabric she's pressed against my side. I fight her on it and point at the dirt again.

I say, "Eva."

Eva looks and sees the plastic bag there before Maria grabs my hand and puts it to use.

Breathing is so easy now it's funny. How was it such a fight before Eva and Maria turned up? They fuss, chattering in the back of my ears as they touch me. Their hands hurt, but I don't move because sometimes hurting can help. I watch through an eyelash haze, sunspots dance through their shadows, them framed by the grey stone walls, grey water, grey light down here.

Eva keeps glancing over her shoulder, sometimes when she hears sounds and sometimes when she doesn't. It's just Maria who doesn't take her eyes from her work and she's got a scowl knit tight between her eyebrows. She's got thin pursed lips and there's a small smear of blood on her cheek. My blood, I think. I make to wipe it off with a thumb, but there's blood there too, so I use the back of my hand instead.

"Sit still," she says. "Stop screwing around."

She tells Eva something and then says, "We're going."

She looks me in the eyes for the first time and I get calm from her, even though there's still worry in her face.

She says, "Put your weight on us as much as you need, but you should be pretty good. You're cut clean and these bandages should hold up until we get help."

With help, I stand, hooked forward at first, because that's the only way it doesn't hurt as much. Then, slowly I straighten up, still stooped forward a bit though. It's hard to know how to move. My old body is gone now for this one. Even the pain seems muted though. It's dull and wet, just the echo of the knife that went in me.

Eva and Maria lead me from the bushes and onto the pathway. It seems like this world shouldn't exist anymore, that just a few minutes ago, it all disappeared, collapsed down to the size of me and Sam's brother. But it's still here and we move slow through it. I try not to show pain, but it's hard to hide it.

Eva says something. She has an arm around my waist, a hand on my hip. My arm's over her shoulder for balance. She points and I follow her finger to Sam's brother. He's out of the water and standing in the shadow of the bridge behind us. We wait for a few moments to see what he's going to do, but he doesn't move to come at us and doesn't seem like he's going to. A jogger runs past him, heading our way, and it's weird that people are jogging here, past Sam's brother. It's weird that Eva and I, hooked around each other, probably just seem awkwardly intimate at a glance and nothing more sinister than that we're out for a walk together.

We walk the other way.

The jogger huffs past, heading upriver.

The three of us, at one time or another, we all look back to see what Sam's brother does, but he only watches, and by the time we get to the stairs, he's gone. It makes me even more nervous because now it's like he could be anywhere.

I've stared after him for too long because Maria says, "Up." And I swivel to face at the stairs.

With a hand sometimes on the railing, sometimes on Eva's shoulder, sometimes over Maria's elbow, we make it up the sixty-some steps to street level. It takes a while, and at the top, everything's spinning with people and traffic. Cars seem to go every way on the street, engine noise and gas fumes and sunlight flinging off glass and red metal, blue metal, white metal. There are eyes, some glances at me, all go by in a blur of legs and arms and faces and movement. A pigeon zigzagging away. Leather shoes on stone. Sun, sky, concrete.

The first look that sticks is from a wrinkled lady. She starts talking frantically, her voice fast and rough, and she's touching my arm and gesturing at me. She's concern and a paper soft palm pressed against my cheek and then gone. Eva is calming her down with words and hands patting the air between them. Eva moves her along. I look down to what she's pointing at and it's me, the rusty blood on my shirt.

I say, "I can't walk around like this. I can't go to the police. Can't go to a hospital. They'll call the police."

Maria says, "Be quiet." She looks at me, judges my desperation, then says, "We're going to the Welcome Centre. It's an outreach place. There's a doctor."

She says, "You're talking to the police, if they come. You're getting help."

"Can you walk? It's not far," she says. "It's in Trastevere." She points one bridge down and to the other side of the river.

I say, "I don't have insurance. I don't know what to say." I don't know what to do, but now it's passed, the idea of what happened settles in. Panic comes with it. I feel cold, my skin a clammy wash. I sag and Maria hoists me.

"Can you walk there?" Maria asks again and I grunt that I can, so we go.

Maria tells me it's for the homeless and it won't cost anything for the attention.

She says, "I don't know about them talking to the police though. They probably have to. You're a foreigner, so the police will probably be interested."

The sun's out, through the clouds, loud flares that make everything a little washed out and blurry. I walk mostly on my own, slow and bent and caring where I put my feet a little more than I used to, so I don't jolt about much. Maria leads a few blocks and across a road.

Then I remember the plastic bag. I remember the money in it, my passport in it. I remember pointing, showing it to Eva, and my mind goes frantic for it. Eva is gone. I can't see her anywhere on the street.

"The bag," I say. "Where's the bag?"

Maria says, "Eva has it."

I say, "Where's Eva?" And Maria doesn't look from the road ahead.

I say, again, "Where's Eva?" And Maria is intent on ignoring me, or intent on getting me to the Welcome Centre, I don't know which.

The future of this new world settles in on me and it's so broken and frantic, and I don't even know how to get past this. Then, looking back, I never much knew how to get past anything except to keep going, to never stop going.

13

Trastevere is a twisting maze and I'm lost by a few turns in. Eva's up ahead, standing in front of a building that looks like all the others, three storeys and old. There's a woman with her, older than us, probably forty or something. She comes to me. She's a hand on my shoulder and she's in my face, speaking her language and gesturing at the door behind her. Maria translates that this woman's the doctor. Eva's talking to me at the same time and so is the doctor.

I look in Eva's eyes and say, "That bag. It doesn't exist, okay?"

Of course, she doesn't understand.

I tell Maria and she looks at Eva, then back at me.

I tell her again and Maria says, strained-like, "I heard you."

I take the doctor's offered hand and draw a breath to make the two steps up into the building a little easier. Maria's talking to her the whole time and she's shaking her head and saying, "No," a lot. The spaces inside the building are small and tired walls and dim light. We're too many for it, but we all pass through just the same. Eva drops off somewhere and then I'm in a little room and the doctor's focused on my body. She talks to it, to herself, not me. She's wearing blue rubber gloves. Maria's there too, standing out of the way in the corner.

Maria says, "I'll stay. Translate. In case you and her need to talk."

I nod, clench my hands into fists because they're shaking really pretty bad. They have been for a long time. The doctor sits me on a table, helps me take my shirt off, uses some cloths to clean me up. She's feeling my pulse. She's poking my stomach. Her blue gloves have blood on them now.

She speaks through Maria, "How big was the knife?"

I show her a few inches using a gap between my thumb and finger.

Through Maria she says, "Ah, just a little one," which makes me laugh, which makes it hurt. It also makes me less worried.

She's casual about it, like it's only a little stab, like stop being such a baby about it.

Through Maria, the doctor says, "Don't do that, laughing." And I figure I don't need a doctor to tell me that.

She says, "You're lucky." She points and I look and she says, "Just muscle tissue." She says it like it's no big deal.

Through Maria she says, "We don't suture these. We bandage. Change the bandages whenever they soak through and keep it clean every time. If you start feel worse, you need to come back."

The doctor dresses the wounds, wraps me tight in gauze and bandages, shows me how to do it. She looks at me and raises her eyebrows whenever she wants to point out an important part. She goes to a cabinet and takes a teeshirt from a colourful folded stack and hands it to me. I test my arms as I pull it over my head, gently to not tug at the bandages. It's a tourist shirt. It's pale pink. It has a silhouette of St. Peter's Basilica printed in black on the front.

In the end, she crackles a stack of plastic wrapped gauze pads onto the counter beside Maria. She puts two rolls of fabric tape on top of that, some butterfly clips, a granola bar. Then she loads it all into a plastic bag. The doctor turns to me with a smile and kind eyes.

Her eyebrows go up and she asks, "Okay?" And I nod.

She's still watching me, so I nod again and say, "I'm good. Okay. Fine now. Thank you."

The doctor says something to Maria. Maria shakes her head and says something back. They exchange a few more words and then the doctor leaves. Maria tells me that the doctor wants me to stay around for the day so she can watch me. She then tells me they have to report such wounds to the police. These words spike me to move. I lean forward to stand, but then have to sit back again.

"No," I say. "No police." And Maria tells me the doctor's gone to report it anyway.

I say, "I'm leaving."

I say, "We've got to find Eva. I need my passport and some Euros from that bag. The rest of the money is Sam's, for the trouble. I don't want it."

She says, "You're being an idiot." And I don't say anything back because I'll probably just agree. I'm already grabbing the plastic bag of gauze and tape and peering out the door, steadying my woozy balance with a hand against the frame.

I don't see the doctor anywhere, so I tell Maria, "Let's go."

Eva's outside, leaning against the building across the narrow street, heel to wall, and a thread of smoke trailing from a cigarette. She smiles and butts the cigarette against the wall when Maria and I hustle her along.

The streets are close and twisting and I don't think the police would come too fast. I'm sure there're better things they're doing, but we weave a path along roads and alleys for several minutes anyway. That whole time, I have to listen to Maria telling me in fits of English between fired-up Italian that I'm being stupid. But she quiets with distance because she sees I'm not going back and all she has are words to convince me and they aren't working.

We find an alley and stop for a moment to watch the neighbourhood. Maria and Eva talk and smoke cigarettes. Their exhalations are shawls from blue to grey then gone as they float past the shadows of the alley into the sunlit street a few feet away. I eat the granola bar the doctor put in the plastic bag and feel a bit better.

Eva gestures at me and then Maria jerks her head to the side and says, "Eva thinks you're an idiot, too."

I nod because it's easier that way, because there's no use to explain why I have to keep moving.

Maria says, "Eva likes you for some reason. She's worried you won't make your next birthday because you're being such an idiot."

Maria says, "I think Eva is right."

I say, "Well, it's unanimous then." I say it harsher than I mean to.

Maria takes a drag and exhales fast and says, "I like you, too, and don't want this for you. You need help."

And I look away, part ticked off at them for calling me an idiot and part overwhelmed by their friendship. I don't know what to say to them and can't put the words together to explain why I'm going, so we're quiet together. I think on it for a bit then tell them that

I'll make it another few days, then I'll make it another year, and all the ones after, just fine.

Maria cocks her head to one side, her cigarette held over her shoulder and her back against crumbling stucco. The city fills the gap in our conversation with the noise of distant cars, clapping pigeon wing echoes, and a quiet voice singing from the apartment above our heads, a teevee show laugh track behind it.

In the end, no police come running down the road. No cruisers speed up to catch us, no blaring sirens and flashing blue lights. No doctor from the clinic comes to lecture us and it seems nobody cares that we left, not enough to come searching anyhow.

Maria and Eva finish up their cigarettes and throw the butts into the street. We leave the shadowed alley. The urgency that chased us from the clinic is gone.

I ask Eva for a few hundred Euros and she fiddles with the plastic bag she has tucked under her belt. It should be enough for a cab and a flight to Belgrade. Maria is still mad, but there's nothing I can think of to change that, so it'll just have to be let alone that way. I tell Maria again, the rest of the money is for Sam. She nods and I trust she'll give it to him. Eva hands me some money and my passport and I put them in the plastic bag that holds my bandages, holds everything now.

The streets get wider as we walk. They get busier. We're all uneasy, a keener eye kept for Sam's brother as there're more and more people around. Maria is waving for a taxi and one comes jolting across the traffic. A horn blares when the cab stops. The driver yells something and flicks a wrist, a fan of fingers, through the open window. The other's engine roars by and fades to reveal the cabbie's muttering underneath.

I step down from the curb and open the back. Maria and Eva watch. I stand with my arm on the open door for support, the other one on the roof. I don't know what to say and my gut wobbles with the feeling that I'm going to cry. The feeling of loss is so big and final that I don't know what to do with it. Maria and Eva and Sam have been friends like I've never had, and I get the feeling I'm not going to see them again. And that thought is weird, never seeing someone again.

The taxi driver says something and Maria says, "He's asking what we're waiting for."

Then he says, a big voice in heavily accented English, "Kiss them goodbye and get in the car." And I cough out a laugh at that, which makes me wince. My eyes go watery, but I force my tears to hang onto my eyelids and not go spilling down. Maria and Eva see it and smile.

Cabbie says, "Meter's on."

Maria says, "Yeah, yeah, fine."

She pulls a crumpled package of cigarettes from her pocket and lights one, draws deep. She holds the pack out to me and asks, "Want one?"

I smile and take one, not trusting myself to talk. She puts her cigarette in her mouth and leans forward with it out to me. I put my cigarette in my mouth and touch the tip to hers, draw in, and cough. My arm jerks to hug my bandages. Eva and Maria laugh at me and I don't get sore about it because it's funny to me, too.

"Here," I say and hand the cigarette to Eva. "I thought I could do it. I can't." I look from one to the other. And those are the last words.

I get in the cab and say, "Airport."

The driver nods and rolls a delicate hand at the windscreen, mocking the most accommodating chauffeur. "Excellent choice, sir."

He pulls away from the curb and we're gone into traffic. I don't look back to see if Maria and Eva watch the cab leave.

Through the traffic in jolts, my feet won't touch these streets again, just hover here, above them. I wipe my cheek and it's wet. I don't want the driver to see, so I lean against the window and watch the unfocused world pass by. On the freeway to the airport, I'm gone from Rome. I'm gone from Maria and Eva, and I'm gone from Sam. I'm asleep to the vibrations of movement against my cheek and I'm awake again when it stops.

In the end, there's paying the driver and there's the long halls of the departure terminal. There's a six-hour wait for the flight.

There's enough room for me on it and enough money in my pocket to get a ticket for it. There're seventy-five Euros left, too, which is good. I don't have bags to check, and it's some effort to take off my shoes to go through security. The guy at the machine watches me, scans my plastic bag of gauze and tape with bored eyes.

I buy a soda and a cookie at a place on the other side, then sit between grey tile and fluorescent lights, staring at a tabletop. It's hard to get up again, so when I do, I just keep moving. It hurts, but it's easier than sitting and letting my knee stiffen up. I go from one end of the terminal to the other a few times, killing time, letting my tears dry up a bit, and because my legs have been moving for so long, they don't seem to know what else to do.

I lock myself in the handicap bathroom and it takes a bit to figure out how to take off my teeshirt because of the new cut and bruises. I peel the gauze. The cut is swollen and red and still leaking, drops slipping slowly over my skin. I clean it up with the wipes the doctor gave me, and put new bandages on like the doctor showed me. They don't look as tidy as hers did, but that's how they'll have to be. I put my shirt back on and run a hand over my throat. There're bruises there. I hope they won't get too dark.

I'm back on the concourse and find my gate and can finally sit without feeling the need for movement. I stare out at nothing on the runway. The walkway is extended, waiting for a plane. And for the first time I feel it, I exist outside this place. The friends I've made here carry me the same way. I can still feel them, Eva and Maria lying beside each other and Sam, cold and leaving the Spanish Steps to wherever he goes when the late-afternoon light fades, maybe the church again. The streets in Rome are all in fading light and they're quiet. Electric lights out there, my friends out there, and I have never felt such a happy loss before, because leaving them matters.

Everything's a high-speed rush when the plane arrives. People crowd from out of nowhere and announcements rattle through overhead speakers. People get off the plane and I watch their faces as they go. It takes some effort to get up and shuffle onboard with everyone else. Announcements come in some language and then in English, flight attendants standing in the aisle pointing at exits and showing everyone how the life jackets work for when we crash in the water. Then we jostle over the gaps in the tarmac to the sound of jet engines. The plane goes smooth and quiet when the ground falls out, every shadow shrinking fast below, the silhouette of the city on the horizon in the low sunlight, and then I'm asleep.

BOOK IV

1

Foot to tarmac and down from the little staircase stuck to the side of the plane. The air feels the same and smells the same as it did when I got on the plane about an hour ago. Hand to door and walk towards customs in a daze, sneaker squeaks on tile like a bird trapped in here. There're black arrows on yellow signs to follow. I'm barely awake from sleeping on the flight, barely able to move the first few steps because pain won't let me alone any more than exhaustion will. It gets easier though, with each step my body comes awake to forward motion again, remembers the speed to which it's grown accustomed.

Past the baggage carousel, no, nothing to claim, no, nothing to declare. Here for pleasure, here to see the sights, staying at a hostel, no, I don't remember the name of it, somewhere in the city.

The cut has leaked through the gauze and my teeshirt, making a coin-sized rust stain on my side. I hide it with a bent elbow. I hardly get a glance from the customs guys, hardly a word of broken English, if any at all. They take in just enough to see I'm nothing, couldn't be a threat to anything, and then there's another new stamp in my passport. The letters are a different alphabet, blocky shapes both familiar and foreign, spelling out something. I walk past and into the terminal.

I find a seat and wait for everything in me to start working again. I blink and watch the people meeting passengers from my flight. They're open arms stretched out and then they're hugging, kissing cheeks. They're clasping hands and smiles and hearty pats on the back, and then gone. I think of the picture in the newspaper article I no longer have and I can't remember his face, just seems like dots, and I wonder how I'm going to recognize him.

The roof is low in here. The tile is grey and the lights are fluorescent. The windows that frame the road outside are streaked from dust and rain, even though it's just evening sun and blue sky out there now. The concrete is wet. Potholes and puddles made the same by the evening light. I don't try to make sense of it, just blink and stand and then find the washroom.

I take my teeshirt off and clean myself up. The cut's deep purple edges, red and angry, bruised around the slice. My body still leaks, but I think it's less than it was a few hours ago when I last looked. I don't know. I come awake with the pain of rewrapping myself, like how the doctor showed me to. Nobody comes in while I'm skin and ribs exposed to the mirror. I use some paper towel and soap to clean the spots from my shirt as best I can. I hold it under the hand dryer and lean my forehead against the wall and close my eyes while the machine makes noise. The stain is still there, just a bit fainter, a bit smeared around, and still damp.

Out into the terminal, out past the people still waiting at the gate to greet whoever, fewer now than minutes ago. Outside, the last of the sunshine smells like gas fumes, jet fuel, until a gentle breeze brings the sweetness of a distant rainstorm.

There're people here, some smoking cigarettes and talking, seeming like they've nowhere to go. It's noise here, the conversations drowning in a plane taking off, the hollow scream of jet engines pushing a plane upward to thunder then silence.

I look around and don't even know where to start.

Across the road is a half-empty parking lot and beyond that are early-season fields with nothing green covering them yet, just black-brown dirt and straw stubble. There's no city between here and the horizon, just open land painted in shadows of low, late light. I wonder for a moment if I'm in the right place, the right dot on a map, the wrong words in another alphabet in my passport.

An old guy by the curb has a cigarette pinched between his knuckles. He's talking to a friend, both of them leaning against a rusty black car, a little thing with the word "taxi" written on the side. The dot over the "i" is missing, peeled off, if it was ever even there. It might be he put the letters on himself. He sees me confused and says something that I don't get.

I ask, "English?"

And he reels me in with a slow hand rolling at the end of his wrist, cigarette smoke clouding the air around his head. He says, "Yes, of course. Of course, yes."

He holds the passenger door open, still nodding and a friendly face, his hand on my shoulder guiding me in. He closes the door and talks with his friend for another minute, and then they both erupt in laugher and say their goodbyes. Nothing's rushed.

I lean my head back to the headrest, exhaustion like I've never known. The driver wanders around the front of the car, stops to work something off the hood with his thumbnail, then stores the cigarette in the corner of his mouth before dropping in behind the wheel. He looks at me and smiles from behind a tail of smoke drifting out his window. His eyes water a little and he says, "Yes?"

I tell him I don't have anywhere to stay, but I want to go into Belgrade. I ask if he knows any hotels there, any that don't cost a lot. He nods at everything, smiles, but I'm not sure how much he gets.

He says, "Yes, of course."

The engine turns over and over, and catches after a few seconds. There's grinding as he puts it into gear. The taxi pulls from the curb with two jackrabbit hops and then settles to steady acceleration. The terminal sinks in the dusty side-view until it's a dot and then gone.

Out onto the open spaces of a freeway, two lanes each way with a greenspace between, and us heading some direction I don't know. The radio squelches. Tinny music comes through a few speakers and it's hard to tell what's going on there, a swirling confusion of horns and voices. The driver hums along, an arm hanging out the window, cigarette now a smoldering stub at the corner of his mouth. Flecks of ash swirl through the cab. He works the gears up, engine shuddering until he settles on one. I don't know how fast we're going because the speedometer doesn't work. Doesn't seem to matter though, he hasn't consulted the dashboard once, flicks the cigarette butt out the window.

He says, "American?"

I say, "Canadian."

And he shrugs, tells me, "It's okay. Nobody's perfect."

Then he laughs and then coughs that to a stop.

He pats my knee twice and points through the windscreen at some buildings rising on either side of us, says, "You love Belgrade. Beautiful city, beautiful women, good food. Welcome."

I nod and thank him and watch traffic stack up in front of us. Fields bracketing the highway have sprouted apartment blocks. Sometimes there's a word I understand on a sign. Coca-Cola is spelled the same as I know it. Other times, I don't even understand the letters they're written in. The radio squelches under every overpass. Each overpass feeds more cars into the growing mess with long, cracked onramps.

A quick glance over and the driver asks, "Here for holiday?"

I say, "Kind of."

I say, "I've come to find someone." And there's a blank look as a response.

He nods and I'm not sure he understands.

I say, "He's a writer. He's family. I don't know him though. But I want to talk to him."

"Phone is easier," he says and laughs again, coughs, and kisses another cigarette directly from the crumpled pack pulled from the dash, offers me one, too.

I hold up a hand.

I say, "It's not a talk we could have on the phone."

And the driver nods like he gets it.

He lights the cigarette, holds it in his steering wheel hand, and gears down again as traffic gets thicker. Slower we crawl. The two lanes have spread out to three or four even though the road's no wider, the lines seem more like suggestions than anything else. The cars around us are so close I could reach out the window and touch the one beside us.

The driver says, "Everybody meet everybody at Hotel Moskva."

He clears his throat, says, "Moscow Hotel. Writers are there. Always since long time. Many can buy coffee, but most can't buy cake." He laughs again, rubs his thumb and fingertips together: money.

Foot on the break and we jolt and he mutters at the taillights in front. I wake up, didn't even realize I'd dropped off. Don't know for how long. We go a bit and we stop again. The freeway has narrowed down to a bridge across a wide, milky river. We creep across. There're buildings on either side, warehouses on the water, other bridges when I look up and down the river. Over the water and behind us, the sunset's a fingerprint, pulled swift from a red paint pot and smeared sideways in tangerine sky.

"This is Sava," the driver says. He points across the oncoming lanes of traffic and off the side of the bridge and says, "Over there is Danube."

He jabs a thumb over his shoulder, back where we came from. He says, "That side is New Belgrade." He points out the windscreen and says, "This one is old city. A famous poet jumped off this bridge."

I nod like it all means something.

Stop and go, a gasoline breeze through the window and I glance down at my shirt to see if any new spots have leaked through, and there're none. I rustle my bag and there's enough for one more change of bandages, then I'll have to find a pharmacy.

Across the bridge and on the other side, the streets twist and wind tighter. Cars are parked along the sides now. The street lights come on in the bluing, all of them, all at once.

We don't go much farther when he stops in the road, pulls the car out of gear, and says, "Belgrade City Hotel."

The building is four storeys tall and cream-coloured stucco. The lobby windows glow. Spotlights shine up the walls. There's a train yard down the hill, a train stop right across the street. A tram rattles by, old and dented, and I wait for the sound to go.

The driver pulls the emergency break and the engine chugs like it's about to stall out. He says, "Three thousand Dinar."

I say, "I only have some Euros."

He nods and says, "Of course. No problem. Thirty Euros."

I count out the money, then I'm out on the curb. The driver leans across and says to me, "Remember. Hotel Moskva. Very close."

And he points a direction that goes through some buildings before he drives away.

Standing on the curb, the buzz of traffic is all around. Someone shouts from somewhere down in the train yard. Another tram rattles past, its headlights on, lights inside show people, some sitting, some standing, hanging by their arms from the railing overhead. It's old looking, like from when trams were first put onto the streets, like from an old movie about Europe, old with washed-out colours.

With the sun gone down, a chill sets in the air, and I turn from the street and head to the hotel door.

Out off the street and into the hotel lobby, it's a small space, but a proper hotel, nicer than anything I've ever stayed in. There's white stone on the wall, shiny tile on the floor, and a lady with a smile on behind the counter. She's talking to me when the door closes out the traffic noise, welcoming me to the hotel I'm sure, but I don't get it.

I ask, "English?"

And she switches, tells me good evening and asks if I have a reservation. Her eyes look me over quickly. I don't think she meant for me to notice, maybe didn't even mean to look, but she did. I know what she sees and can't do much about the judgement of it except be a bit embarrassed, a little ashamed.

I say, "No."

And she says, "Not a problem, sir."

I ask how much, and she says a number that makes me think I heard wrong because it seems too little for how nice the place looks. I have money left for three nights, so I book two and pay her and hope it's all I need. I save the rest for more bandages and some food. She copies my passport information down, tells me there's a free breakfast for guests every morning in the cafe next door, then points me up the stairs to the second floor. End of the hall, door's on the left.

The room is just a little bigger than the bed. There's a teevee on the wall and a door to the bathroom next to it. There's not much else except a wooden chair wedged in the corner. It's street-side and there's the muffled noise of people and machines through the window glass. I open it and a cool breeze comes in, carrying conversations and engines noises.

I turn on the teevee, flip the channels, but can't find any in English, so I leave it on to some music and go to the bathroom to change my bandages. When I pull off my shirt, I have to lean on the counter for a bit to stop my head from weaving in and out of dizzying static. I breathe deep to push back at fever and nausea.

My gauze is still wet from leaking and I unwrap it and look at the cut mark. It'll always be there now, even when it heals up, and it was just today that my body changed forever. I lean on the counter and hang my head over the sink in case I throw up. After a while, I flex my hand to bring feeling back, take a deep breath, and put on new bandages. The last ones in the bag. Then I lie down for a minute to try and get more normal before going out to find a pharmacy.

The teevee noise is annoying so I click it off.

I close my eyes to the sound of a tram clattering by.

A cool breeze from the window creeps across my skin, lifts the sweat from me for a moment and it feels so nice. I open my eyes. The ceiling is lit up from the bathroom glow. I roll my head to one side and see the wad of old bandages in there, blooms on white gauze piled beside the sink. I roll my head to the other side, toward the window. The curtains slide over a hump in the breeze. Dim light creeps in, washed out, like from a full prairie moon.

Outside and close below, conversations walk by. I don't understand them. Someone shouts. Someone shouts back. A woman laughing. A car horn bleats, echoing off the buildings, climbing through the window and bouncing around inside my room. Another tram chunks by. Its bell jangles. Its clacking wheels on the track turns into a knock at my door, slow and rhythmic, like the now-faded noise.

There's knocking at my door.

I hold my breath to listen because there shouldn't be. Maybe it was at the door across the hall. There it is again, my door, a stranger's door in a stranger's city. I swing my feet to the floor.

I waver and sit, waiting for the steady to come back. I think on who could be in the hallway. The lady from the front desk with something she forgot to tell me? Or someone coming back to a roommate who kept the door key? Wrong room, sorry, we're in the next one over.

The knocking stops and then starts again.

I sway and blink until I can stand. I think to put my shirt back on but can't care to. It's only two steps to the door, not far, and I put a hand on the frame of it to steady my exhausted feet. The knocking stops. I wait. I listen.

I don't hear anything else, then say, "Hello," to the silence.

There's a muffled response that I don't get. I open the door a crack to peer through. It's forced from my hand, swings back and bangs against the wall. I'm knocked backwards in a rush of adrenaline as I fall onto the bed. I'm full awake now, charged and looking at the door, looking up at Mr. Langman coming from the hall shadows and into my light.

Faster than I can move, he's on top of me, my hair in his fist, my head yanked back and to one side. Faster that I can think, he sticks a knife in my throat, deep and to the hilt. I can't yell out because the blade is in my airway. He exhales a long, warm breath in my face, like he's been holding onto it for a while, like he's been waiting to get rid of it.

Mr. Langman lets my hair go and stands up, leaving the knife stuck in.

He looks down, says, "Molly, you're a mess." And then his back is to me, walking out the door, around the corner and out of sight. His noises grow smaller and his voice fades away down the dark hallway. "Probably time to find a new line of work," he says, "and some friends who'll miss you, who'll come looking for you when you're lost out here."

A trolley clicks by outside the window. Its bell rings as I lie there, sweat-drenched under a day-lit ceiling, sunlight streaming through the window. The bathroom light is still on.

I blink, roll onto my side, and take a deep breath. I bring my hand to my neck. It's sore, sure, from being belted to a tree, but there's no hole from the knife, no blood coming out. I rub it a bit, and for some reason, the pain's good, like it soothes to the fact that I'm alive. I lie on the sheets for a long time before I can move. My head throbs and I shut my eyes to that. The sweat dries from my skin and my heart trembles to calm as I reason through it, reason through Mr. Langman at my door.

I glance over and the door is closed and it's still bolted.

I sit up. My bandages have soaked through in the centre. I swing my feet to the floor. Elbows on knees, I rest my aching head in my hands, and rub my forehead. It takes a while to get to my feet, feeling sluggish, feeling ill.

2

I splash water into the bathroom sink and my reflection looks broke down, tired and grey. I drink water from a cupped hand then pull on my shirt with the St. Peter's silhouette on it. It's stale and smells a bit like armpits, but it's all I have. Maria's face flashes in my mind as it comes down over my head.

There're twenty-seven Euros left in my pocket before there's none again. I look around the room. No time to be slow now because there're only two days rented here to finish what I came to do, and it feels possible again, now being in the city.

I rest a hand against the door and put the other on the handle, but don't turn it. I listen, try to hear through the wood and into the hall. Listen for a voice, for breathing, for a heartbeat that's too quiet to hear, anything to tell on a person lurking on the other side.

I take a breath, open the door, and it's empty behind, like the stairwell is empty when I go down, like the lobby is empty except for a guy behind the counter.

He nods and says something.

I ask him how to get to the Moscow Hotel and he tells me directions in English. I say them back to him to make sure I get it right and I do, then I'm out onto the street, in amongst the people and the noise. The sun blinds me for a moment. The temperature is the remnants of a cool night with the promise of a warm day. A chill is still in it, but fading like a quick memory. The cafe next door has people in it. There's the talk and clatter noises of dishes from inside. There's a long table with food at the back. A waiter in a white shirt and black pants welcomes me at the door.

He tells me to sit anywhere and gestures to the room behind him, like to say, eat your fill, join these people for breakfast, these smiling vacationers, families and couples, friends, these businessmen reviewing their presentations. There're boiled eggs and cured meats and bread. There's some fruit and pastries. I load my plate full and find a window seat. I go back for coffee and orange juice. It's good to eat after so long, and I feel myself coming back a bit from last night, from when I could barely move, barely think. I take my time and eat. Cars go past on the street. People go by on the sidewalk. My stomach isn't a hole after a while. I hadn't even noticed it was so empty until it's full again.

A rolling nausea rises in me and I wait to ride it through. A cold sweat sprouts onto me, trickles between my shoulder blades, finds the trough of my spine and traces a tickling track down my back to the waistband of my underwear. My forehead is slick. My cheeks feel a clammy flush. I figure I've eaten too much, too fast, after too long without a decent meal. I leave bread and berries on my plate and go outside, still not sure whether I'll barf, so I stop at an alley and wait it out again.

I turn down this street and down that one until I hit the one the guy at reception told me about. There's nowhere that doesn't have people. There's no street not packed with cars and movement and noise. There's a scrawl of graffiti on every building corner, dusty plaster, crumbling plaster, dirty stone faces, all marked with the swirl of spray paint. The air sounds like the mufflers it comes from.

A few blocks more and I'm standing at the point of a triangular plaza in front of Hotel Moskva. It's surrounded by roads and stern-looking buildings block three sides. Set like a thorn in the stone slabs of the sidewalk, there's a fountain that isn't running any water. The plaza is a crowd. The fountain with people sitting on its rim like pigeons, the plaza with people wandering about, all of them waiting for someone, talking to someone, watching someone.

Hotel Moskva looks like a hundred years ago that hasn't caught up with today. It's a narrow building and five storeys high. A sloping green roof with two spires on the front of it and green panels painted under some of the windows. When it was still new, it was probably alone here out on a hill. Today, it looks over rooftops and across the river to the buildings of New Belgrade.

It all makes me feel new, not even knowing, never being able to know all that has happened here in a hundred years. I look at it for a while. In the plaza, there's a woman squeezing an accordion and pulling it apart again, what comes out is something like music. A man throws popcorn to pigeons. There's a magazine stand, postcards, tour books for the city in different languages. Talk and engines in my ears. Breath and exhaust fumes in the air.

I stop near the lobby door to read a plaque saying some famous writers stayed here. It tells the history, how World War Two treated the place, how Albert Einstein stayed here, how Richard Nixon stayed here, how Robert De Niro stayed here, and when I'm done with the words, I wait for a grey couple in grey hats and jackets to come out before stepping in.

I can't help but feel the lobby looks down on me. It's two storeys high and runs the length of the building. Ringed by a balcony above, white walls and fancy inlay, dusty-purple stone bistro tables and fat stuffed chairs, couches around. Above, heavy chandeliers drip crystals and rain light. There's the hollow racket of a cavernous room full of people talking, and the tables are topped with cakes and coffees, everyone leaning forward and sitting back again, listening and talking and listening.

I stand for a bit and look around, look at the people, looking to recognize Miloš's face, how I think he will look now, only knowing him from that pixelated newspaper photo that was long ago ruined, but so long studied it's permanent in my recollection. I don't know what I was expecting. Part of me wanted him to be sitting here, an easy coincidence, illogical and obvious, like at the end of a movie.

But of course, he's not in the room. Doubt settles in, like I was always thinking that I could just find him, and this would be so easy.

There's an empty chair at one end of the room, a chair with a small round table looking through to the plaza outside. I sit, run the back of my hand across my forehead and it comes away wet. I feel sick and think it's from the realization that this whole thing has been just a little boy's fantasy. I guess I knew all along it was stupid, but didn't want to believe it because there was no other plan but this, and I couldn't bear to think of it not working because then there'd be nothing. Coming here to find Miloš wasn't a plan, but it was better than having nothing at all to put hope in.

A guy my age and dressed in black pants and a white shirt and a purple tie, he asks me something. I look at him, shaken by his presence and so exhausted of hearing every language but my own.

I ask, "English?" And he says, "Yes."

He says, "Your order?" And gestures to the small fold of paper in front of me, the menu.

I don't look at it, say, "Coffee." And he goes away.

I watch but can't follow him in the crowd. Everyone messes together in my eyes and it's hard to focus because everything's moving. Their commotion makes me lonely. There's nowhere I don't feel like a stranger. Another wave of nausea rises, one that brings a bubble of hot puke to the back of my mouth that I have to swallow back down.

A thought settles in me, how wrong it was to come here, how it had to come to this point. Looking back, from this overstuffed chair in this old building, in this noise and light, I should have seen failure from the start, but just didn't want to. It was all a mistake from the beginning. Leaving the prairies was a mistake, but I can't see any way I could have stayed there, not even sitting with Evelyn on her porch every night, if she even asked me to stay. I'd always be worried about Mr. Langman and I'd always be watching for his white truck coming at me. That place I grew up, it became too small and too empty. I should have been out of that town in the valley long ago, but it still feels like a mistake when viewed from this chair, because at least I knew what to expect there. There was some safety from the close-in canyon walls. If it wasn't safety, than at least it was familiarity.

The waiter comes back and puts a coffee and a bill on my table. He doesn't say anything, maybe he doesn't know any more words that I'll understand, and he's gone before I can say thanks. Breakfast and coffee have done little to soothe my headache and I close my eyes to it for a moment. I open them and look out at the street, pigeons and people and the accordion lady. It's a mess of light and cars, movement and shadows and graffiti, the mess that I'm in.

And, looking around this room at these people talking, there's nothing but the regret of my ridiculous hope, which finally failed when I walked in here and sat down. It was ridiculous hope that drove my legs all this way from the motel in the valley. It was food when there was none, courage where it was needed. It was ridiculous hope that caused blindness to everything where there should have been clear sight, and then it abandoned me at the lobby door. It left me right over there, just on the other side of this room. From sitting in this chair, I can see exactly the spot it ran out.

Now there's nothing left but a coffee in front of me and a little money in my pocket. It's enough for the day, which is all there is now and that brings some calm to me, that resignation I should have had long ago, before I got this far. I try to picture myself here in a year, in this chair drinking coffee and looking out at the plaza all day, still waiting and waiting and waiting.

My coffee on the table, when I reach for it, my hand shakes. I work on steadying the little white cup as I bring it to my lips. It's muddy and strong. There's grit in it, suspended in the liquid over my tongue and then down my throat. The cup clatters back into its saucer, but the noise is lost in the room. Nobody looks over.

I'm not even here.

The light coming through the window is too bright. Every sound is a smack in the ear and I work on bracing myself against it. My heart beats fast and my headache pounds fierce to the same rhythm.

I can't stay here.

I'm going to throw up.

I place my hand down for support and the table tips to the side. I hang in the air for a moment, separated from it, watching it tilt and fall. The coffee cup slides off the edge and shatters on the floor, the noise louder than anything, black coffee splashing across white tiles, chunks of porcelain lodged in it, oil slick icebergs. Then, I tip over to follow it to the floor, hitting the tile hard. I look sideways, underneath tables, people's feet held on a sideways horizon by sideways gravity, socks disappearing up pant legs.

A few chairs squeal across the tile. My head vibrates with the noise. A bunch of feet rush my way, the sound close and echoes. A hand on my shoulder. A voice in my ear. I don't understand and weakly shake my head before heaving a load of vomit across the floor. The hand pats my shoulder. The voice says something. I glance at the lips.

The cool tile under my burning cheek is a relief. Pulled by the embrace of gravity is a relief. No more effort is needed, so I close my eyes.

3

"Good, you're awake."

She says, "My name is Sonja."

Her voice has an accent, but she speaks confidently. She stands beside me in pale blue pants, pale blue shirt, brown hair tied back and deep brown eyes, maybe in the middle of her twenties somewhere, but probably closer to the start of them. I panic for my backpack and work to sit up, but she puts a hand on my chest to give me a gentle resistance to relax into. Doesn't take much, just a little pressure and I steady.

"It's okay," she says. She looks in my eyes, from one to the other, like to check I'm in there somewhere.

I remember my backpack is long gone, long ago now, and stop moving and look at her hand. Her skin is warm on mine and that means I'm not burning up anymore. My blanket has slid down to my waist exposing the clean bandages on me. A flush comes to my face and she removes her hand and scrapes a chair up beside the bed. She sits with an exhausted sigh and explains that they brought me to this hospital, from the hotel cafe, after I fell over.

I'm struggling to connect that place to this one.

She asks if I understand, if I can hear her.

I say, "Yes," But it barely comes out as a noise because my throat is so dry.

Sonja hands me a cup of water with a straw in it. I drink and she tells me that I had a pretty bad infection, but it's getting better because they're running antibiotics through me. She points out the tube stuck in my arm, the needle into my skin, the whole rig attached to a bag on a rack. Sonja tells me that it's tomorrow from when I fell over, and she's about to tell me more when I interrupt her and say, "I have no money for this."

I clear my throat and my voice comes back better when I say, "I have no money and no insurance. I can't pay for anything."

She cocks her head to the side, says, "I know. I searched you before I let them do any treatments, to see if you had anything good to steal." She shrugs and looks out the window. "When I didn't find anything, I figured we better save your life anyway because you might have rich parents who would reward me. Are your parents rich?" My face is confusion and she sighs. "And now I think I've lost on that gamble, too. Anyway, it all worked out. If I'd let you die, there would be a lot more paperwork to do, and it's almost the weekend. Would've probably had to stay late writing out the forms and explaining how it was the right choice to let you die because you had no money."

It takes me a moment to figure out she's joking because she doesn't even smile to let me know it.

She stands to leave and says, "You're lucky you didn't collapse on a Monday. I'm usually in a bad mood on Mondays, and I've got a whole week to waste on paperwork."

I say, "I'm glad I didn't ruin your weekend."

She shrugs and says, "It's okay, either way, I don't have any big plans." She finally smirks, and is gone.

Alone now, there's a teevee that speaks a different language than me, so I turn it off as quick as I turn it on. There's a window with the view of the building across the road. It takes some time to figure out how to sit up, swing my legs off the bed, and wait with stilt arms propping either side of me. The blanket slips again, clean bandages covering the angry red skin around my wound. It doesn't hurt bad, but my arms feel like a hundred pounds, my body a thousand. I have hospital pajama pants on, and my face heats up again with the thought that maybe it was Sonja who put them on me, that she saw me without them.

I get onto my feet and it's okay to stand.

I grab the pole I'm attached to and wheel it over to the window. There's not much to see through it, so I cross to the other side of the room because there's a closet there. Inside, there's my teeshirt and my pants. I check the pockets. My Euros are there but my passport isn't.

Sonja comes back in, heading for my bed until she notices me standing at the closet. She stops and gives me a frown. She says, "Get back in bed. You shouldn't be up."

I'm holding my jeans in one hand and have the pole gripped in the other.

I say, "Where's my passport?"

Sonja says, "You had a stab wound and you're a foreigner. We have to report that to the police. They have it."

She says, "They were here this morning. You weren't awake, so they left. They said they would come back." She points. "Bed. Now."

I ask her, "What do they want?" And she tells me that they probably want to know why I got a knife stuck in me and who's the one who stuck it there.

I sit on the side of the bed and she flaps a hand for me to lay down, but I don't. I'm still not sure to run or not, not that I could run, but I could maybe sneak out or just leave and they'd do nothing to stop me. It's a hospital, not a prison. Sonja sees the look on my face and shakes her head. A few steps and she's beside me, gently pushing me to lie down.

She says, "Did you stab anyone?"

I say, "No."

She says, "There's nothing to worry about then. Police never arrest someone for not stabbing another person, only when they do."

She says, "They probably just want to know what happened, if they can do anything."

"Can you be here when they come?" I ask.

I can tell she's about to say no, but then she sees I'm chicken and softens up and says, "If they say it's okay."

Sonja settles me and then leaves again.

An hour passes and she comes back with a doctor who looks me over. He doesn't speak English, so Sonja translates a few questions about how I feel, about my family history, which I can't tell her much on. She points at the tube and tells me there's a course of pills I have to take when it's done dripping. I nod and tell her I'll take them.

A few hours pass and the light coming through the window grows ripe and then starts to fade out again. That's when a policeman comes in. His face is a wall and his eyes are flat. There's nothing I can read on him, like if he's mad or curious or anything. He says something, and I don't know what, or even if it's said to me.

My heart hammers at the sight of him even though I knew he was coming. I should have snuck out because I don't know what could happen here. A bit of relief comes when Sonja walks through the door behind him. The policeman crosses the room to sit on the chair beside my bed. It creaks under him and he leans forward, elbows to knees to look at me closer. Then he holds out my passport, and when I take it from him, he leans back.

Sonja sits on the edge of my bed. I move my legs to give some room, and when she smiles at me, I'm so happy she's here.

The policeman introduces himself with a name I can't pronounce and his English is next to nothing, so we mostly talk through Sonja. I answer his questions. I tell him I was mugged along the river in Rome, that most of my stuff was taken, that I had a ticket to Belgrade that I didn't want to miss using, so I came anyway. I tell him I came here to see where Miloš Milić wrote about and to see if I could meet him. I tell him I'm booked into a hotel, that's where I'm staying, and that my dad will send more money to get me to a good spot again.

He asks me the same questions a few different ways over the course of fifteen minutes, what happened, where I'm staying, what I'm doing here. I guess it's to see if he can fish out a lie from somewhere in my story, but this is an easy one to keep because it's mostly true. He tells me they couldn't reach the emergency contact in my passport. "Your dad," Sonja translates, "who will send you money."

I say, "He's hard to reach because he's away for work a lot, but I'll get him. He's home every few days, so I can get him then."

In the end, I figure the policeman's blank face is boredom and not much else. Through Sonja, he tells me he may have some more questions, that if I move from the hotel, I should check in with the local police to let them know. And through Sonja, I tell him I will.

He stands and the chair slides across the linoleum from behind his knees. He writes a case number on his business card and gives it to me. He contemplates me for a moment longer, eyes downcast to mine before they travel the length of my body under the blanket. He thanks Sonja, nods at me, and he's gone.

Sonja watches after him long after he's gone, stares at the empty doorframe, silent the whole time. People noise, conversation noise, quiet constant noises coming through the door and then Sonja sighs.

She looks at her watch and says, "I'm going to check your bandages."

She puts on rubber gloves and I let her pull the blanket down, the fabric of it soft and wash-worn. There's a quick pain when she pulls the bandage off and I look down at the cut, a deep purple mess around the clotted gap in my skin. She examines it, prods at the edges a bit. I watch her do it and it hurts a dull throb even though she uses tender fingers. She swabs the cut with a little towel that stings and leaves behind a sharp antiseptic smell. Without words and without looking at me, she repackages the cut with clean gauze.

She tells me it all looks a lot better than when I came in.

I say, "What's wrong?"

And she ignores me.

Sonja cleans up the wrappings and a few loose bits of tape from the bandages and crumples them up. Her face is tight while she does it. She's mad and she's not the kind to hide it well.

I ask, "Did I do something wrong?" And she doesn't say anything for a moment, her lips a straight line.

Then she says, "It's none of my business."

I say back right away, "What's not?"

She shrugs, says, "I'm here to patch up your body after what you've done to it. That's all. What's in your head," she shakes hers, "is your problem."

She says, with the flick of a finger and a glance, "You can cover up now." And I don't know what to say for a minute, so I pull the blanket up.

I say, "I didn't do this to myself."

I say, "The guy who mugged me did it."

It's so close to the truth that I think I even believe it, until Sonja asks, "Why do you do that?"

I say, "Do what?"

And she says, "Lie so much."

I don't have an answer for her. I don't even know her, and I get mad because she's not anyone to know anything about me either, or to ask this kind of thing. I get mad because she called me a liar. Most of all, I get mad because she's right and I like her. She's been kind to me, and now I'm embarrassed from making myself something less in her eyes.

Sonja stays cold at me. She judges me so clear and quick, and before I can say anything else, she tells me that the doctor wants to keep me overnight and that I'll be released sometime tomorrow, if he thinks I'm okay by then.

"You should be well enough," she says.

And that's it, she's gone. I try to roll onto my side, back to the door, but can't because it isn't comfortable. I'm left behind listening to the little noises coming in from the hallway, the conversation noises of people passing by. I'm not tired because I've been out for so long.

I stare out the window, the wall across the street, watching for it to get darker and trying not to think of how I'm so tired of myself. I never was before, not so truly anyway. I was always so exhausted, account of not being able to sleep. Now, having seen myself reflected by Sonja, I see that it was really always me. Can everyone see me as clearly and suddenly as she did? I've become lies, and I don't want that anymore.

I lay there with the television off. The magazines on the bedside table stay closed. I wouldn't understand them anyway.

I think on how obviously I've been wrong for a lot of this, think on how I've justified it, that I've been so low for so long that I couldn't do any different. That's a lie I fed myself. I've seen a lot of those broke-down people, just never realized I was among them.

I lay there, watching for the building across the street to grow darker, and can't tell when it does because I've been staring so long, so closely that I almost miss that it's been going on the whole time. Any shift that's so gradual, and examined so intently, will always be missed. The beginning and the end are clear, compared to each other. That's the only way to really see the change.

It's close to night when a nurse comes in. I'd been so lost in running thoughts, thoughts of everything, thoughts of leaving this room and reasoning to stay on a bit longer, that I hadn't noticed how much time went by. The nurse, she's not Sonja and the uncertainty if I'll see her again makes me sad. This nurse is older and she carries a tray of food in one hand and carries a smile on her face for me. She says something, wheels a bedside table over with one hand while the other puts the tray on it.

I thank her but can't tell if she understands any English, so I smile and bob my head a few times. The nurse doesn't stay around more than to take a quick peek under my blanket at the bandages that Sonja put on me. She checks my pulse, my blood pressure with a tight band hissing down around my arm. Seeming happy with everything, she writes on my chart and leaves.

The food sits on the tray, on the bedside table, and after a few moments I push it away. I swing my feet over to the side and it's easier to get up than it was earlier. I go to the window, towing my machine.

Outside, a street, a few cars parked under street lamps, people down there. There's a park a bit away and the trees have fresh green on them, pale spring leaves that seem to glow a soft light on their own, or maybe with just a little bit of help from the twilight. It's not busy out there, not more than a few people on the sidewalk, one crosses the street.

I go to the closet to check my stuff. My jeans are stained with coffee, but it's not as noticeable on them as it is on my shirt. Socks smell. Shoes smell. The Euros in my pocket are not enough for any place to stay that has a ceiling overtop. My hotel room is probably someone else's by now and any thoughts of leaving this room that were strong in my head when I stood up, they're a whisper now. There's nowhere to go.

I close the closet door and lie back down in bed to wait out the night.

4

Sonja says, "Wake up."

I do with a start because I haven't felt safe anywhere I've slept, not since the motel in the valley and maybe not even there. It takes a moment to figure out where I am, and she's looking down at me. Her hand is light on my shoulder, warmth through the thin blanket, a gentle touch, and then gone.

She says, gentler, "You're okay."

She's not like she was yesterday, not mad anymore. I see she didn't mean to scare me and that she's sorry she did, but she's also looking at me with a question on her face. I push myself to sit up and the blanket slides to my waist and I quickly pull it back up, over my shoulder.

Sonja shakes her head, like give me a break, and she says, "I've seen it all before."

She says, "And I'll see it now. I have to change the bandages. The doctor is on his rounds soon. You'll be able to go if everything looks okay."

"Great," I say. And let her take the blanket down.

She says, "We need the bed."

She puts on rubber gloves and peels my dressings back. She looks me over and prods at me a few times before she nods and says, "Looks good."

She takes the tape off my i-vee and pulls it out of my wrist without saying any warning. I wince at it. She pushes a cotton ball on the bead of blood that leaks through and says, "Hold this a minute."

My finger replaces hers and she walks to the door. There's a folder hung on the back, a paper clipped to it. Sonja reads, makes a note on it, and then says, "Happy birthday."

She walks out and I didn't even know what day it was. I look for a clock and find one on my machine showing it's still morning.

Happy birthday, I think.

I look down at my cut. It does look better. I push up off the bed and get my clothes out of the closet and put them on. Everything smells bad, but I have nothing else and I'm not going to wear a hospital gown out of here. It takes a little time to get my socks and shoes on because I have to bend and have to be gentle about it. I take my time, and when I'm done and standing and wondering what's next, Sonja returns with the doctor.

She unhooks my folder from the door and says, "Going somewhere?"

And I say, "Getting ready to."

Sonja tells me to sit on the bed and I do. She says something to the doctor and glances at the folder, at where he points. He lifts my shirt and I wait while he looks. He tells Sonja something quick, pulls my shirt back down over me, and then leaves.

Sonja makes a few notes, and without looking up, she says, "You can go once I put new dressings on."

I sit there while she does it, embarrassed by how my clothes smell and not sure what to say, so I wait. Sonja finishes and hands me a small slip and tells me to get these pills from a pharmacy.

I say, "I'll be all right."

Sonja sighs and says, "You're a stubborn boy." She doesn't say it mean, just like she's heard the same words before. "And you smell."

I look at my lap, face hot with shame and mad about that.

I stand up and say, "I don't have any money for pills. I don't have a place to stay. I know I stink but I can't do anything about it. All I have is a place I want to go and I don't even know where that is really." I walk to the door while I'm talking. My voice shakes and I can't stop it.

I hear her say, "Meet me in front of the hospital. My shift is over in six hours."

She says, "I can get you some pills, and I can take you to Miloš Milić, if you want."

I don't know if she keeps talking because I'm in the hallway, down the stairs, out the front door and then gone.

I stand outside the automatic doors and watch people come and go for a while, thinking to go back to Hotel Moscow because it's the only place I know, but don't know where I am in the city, where anything is from here. There's quick panic that comes and goes like a snap because I've grown used to the feeling of being lost, ever since I was fourteen.

People come and go past. The door slides open and closed.

My face folds up to cry and I turn away, trying not to, and then trying to find somewhere no one will see me because I can't stop it. I wonder if I'll ever lose this ease with being lost. I think if I ever do, I'll call that place home and stay there forever.

I heard what Sonja said, that she'll bring me the pills and she knows where Milić is, but I was mad at her when I left. I think of not meeting her here in six hours, but know I have to, if she even still comes after I walked out like a little kid having a fit. I think to go back in and find her but can't bring myself to do it. It's pride that made all of this happen, I know it, but still can't get over it easy.

I sit on a bench near the entrance, wipe my face, pull a deep breath. I'm going to wait for Sonja, for my pills, for Milić. I'll sit and wait because it's the only thing left to do. Where I was headed has thinned out to this point, a wide road narrowed down to a track with barely a purpose left, one so thin that it could be gone in the time it takes Sonja's shift to end.

I think about my birthday, today, and how I've never made a big deal out of it, but I've never lost half of it before either. It doesn't matter because I can't even buy myself a shirt that doesn't stink like my armpits, that isn't stained with coffee and splotches of blood. I can't even know where I am, let alone keep a hold on where I was going.

So, I settle and wait, watching people come and go.

5

Sonja says, "I'm glad you waited."

I can tell she means it, from her voice, the look on her face. She's just come out the door, just found me still sitting on the bench. It's late afternoon and the shadows pinned under each tree have tumbled out, longer than the trunks they're rooted to. The shadows from the base of each building and each car tire stretch longer than they did before.

I stand up. It's easier to move now than even this morning. When she's beside me, I apologize for being an idiot earlier. I tell her I'm grateful for what she's done. She only nods and hands me a little plastic bottle of pills and says, "One in the morning and one before bed. Both with food."

I say, "Thank you."

I'm not sure what else to do because she's the one who's taken care of me and given me the pills I need. She's the one who can take me to see Milić. I need her and don't know how to be on my own anymore. I know I can't make that work, and looking back, I never really could. I wait for her to direct me.

She says, "My holidays start right now."

Then she says, "Not really holidays, but I have a few days off."

I don't know what to say, so I stay quiet.

She says, "You want to see Milić?" And I nod.

She says, "I'm going to Zrenjanin, to my dad's cottage just outside the city. It's on Tisa River, and he's on the way there." She takes a few steps and turns to me, "You are coming?"

I follow her, almost smiling because direction suddenly springs out of nothing. I tell her I only have about twenty Euros and she tells me a bus ticket isn't even that much.

I tell her I have nowhere to stay when we get there and she tells me there's a couch at her dad's cottage I can sleep on. She says it without thinking on it, like we already talked about me staying there. She sees me hesitate and says, "Don't worry. I'm not going to hurt you. I've got a soft heart for strays. Besides," she looks down at her feet, continues talking, "you came all this way. It'd be horrible to be stuck here when you're so close." She looks around and then smiles, and I do too because it's weird for me to assume she'd be scared of me when she's not.

I say, "A soft spot for strays."

She says, "What?" And I tell her the saying is soft spot, not soft heart. She shrugs at me like it doesn't matter and says, "Mine makes more sense." She tells me we should start walking, that the station isn't far and the bus leaves in less than an hour.

And we walk.

Sonja says, "Where did you come from?"

And I tell her.

She tells me she doesn't know the place, so I tell her about the prairie, about the little canyon town with one traffic light. We stop for cars and then cross a road, walk from side by side to single file and back beside each other again whenever we pass people. We go slow because my knee can't go fast. I tell about the rabbits hiding in the scrub brush like how they're just waiting around to bolt scared. I tell about the diner with the coffee and good chocolate chip cookies, and how the dust glows in the full grey of moonlight, details so she can picture it.

She says, "It sounds like a nice place."

A car with a loud muffler and burning oil from it passes by, so loud we have to wait to say anything else.

Then I say, "It wasn't a bad place, I guess. I hated it when I was younger because it was small and boring, but looking back, from now, it felt safe because of that."

We walk and Sonja tells me she grew up in the town we're going to, surrounded by flat fields, green crops in the summer and fallow brown in the winter, clumps of twisted old trees along skinny creeks and around shallow water holes. She tells me she was born in a different town, an even smaller one in the mountains to the west.

Sonja says, "I like to go back to my dad's cottage because that's what I remember from growing up. The cottage reminds me of summer, long days with nothing to do and tomatoes from the garden." She smiles at that. "The smells of the river remind me of its water drying on my skin and the sweet smell of the crops in the night air remind me of sleeping with the windows open."

She says, "The cottage isn't much, a few rooms, an outside bathroom and a couple acres of fruit trees, and a small garden with onions and garlic and some other things growing in it. That's it." She tells me the sky is big there in the day, and it goes out forever at night because there aren't many lights for the stars to hide behind, not so many as there are here in the city.

She says, "At night, it's so quiet you can hear the blood moving inside your body."

I say, "That sounds really nice." And she agrees with a quick nod. We walk a bit.

She says, "I came for school here in the city. I stayed because of my job, and now I share an apartment with another nurse."

The bus station is down the hill, across an intersection knotted with the old trams running through the middle. It's a few squat buildings, spray paint graffiti walls, and a jumble of chain-link fences.

It's a mess of people and cars and motorbikes and it's loud and busy and I don't know which way the traffic is coming from, so I follow Sonja close. She doesn't wait for the signal lights, just froggers the gaps between cars until we're on the other side.

Sonja knows where to go for tickets. I follow her and don't know what the lady at the counter says, so I give Sonja my Euros and she talks to the lady awhile, they laugh and talk some more, then a couple tickets are handed across. Sonja gives me mine and some money back and I take it, not sure how much it is because I don't recognize the bills. I put it in my pocket and we go to a bench on the curb, facing a huge parking lot.

Sonja leaves me sat there for a few minutes, and heads to a kiosk near the ticket building and buys a bag of chips. There's a lady with purple-red hair beside the kiosk. She has some bread and vegetables and other things spread out on a table. Sonja buys some things from her, too.

When she's back, she has a plastic bag of food and we share the chips, watching the old buses come and go, them with dents in the side, mismatched with all different colour paint jobs and black smears at the back from where badly tuned diesel engines have stained them with exhaust.

When we've shared most of the chips, she asks, "Why Miloš Milić?" And I tell her it's that I read all his books, all the ones I could find translated anyway. She licks salt from her fingertips. I tell her that he wrote most of his later stuff in English anyhow and she nods and tells me that's because he left during the civil war, taught somewhere in England.

For a moment I think that's enough an explanation, but she touches it again, says, "It's a long way to come. Even if he's your favourite."

I don't say anything, just look out at the parking lot. It is a long way, and a foolish plan, now, but one that's almost done and almost played out. I don't want to tell her about the newspaper article or the real reason I came all this way. Instead, I tell her about my dad giving me a second-hand, dog-eared and cover-creased copy of one of his books for my birthday five years ago. I don't tell her it was the beat-up copy in my backpack when it got stolen in Amsterdam, and now that it's gone, I miss it horribly. I don't tell her he's my granddad and the only family I know of that's left anywhere.

"It wasn't the first book of his I ever read," I say. "But it was the one that meant the most to me, made the most sense."

She tells me everyone had to read his books in school and I ask her which ones and she tells me.

I say, "He made me want to write. Been trying to ever since."

We don't say more and in a few minutes a bus pulls into the stall in front of us. I close my eyes because it throws a cloud of dust, riding heat from the engine. People get off, get bags from underneath, and go. Sonja and I climb on when it's empty and I try to figure out which seat is ours, looking from the number on the ticket to the ones above the seats. Sonja tells me it doesn't matter and to just sit down, so I do, near the window. She sits beside me.

We don't talk, just watch more people get on. The people putting their bags under the bus, every one of them looks worn out, their bags a bit beat up too, like with a broken handle or a frayed edge or a broken latch. I try to figure out who is going to drive us. It's not obvious until he gets on and shuts the door. After he walks up the aisle, checks tickets, talks to someone, laughs with another, after all of that's done, he gets behind the wheel and we go.

As we bump out of the station, I shift in my seat and try to get more comfortable, but can't. My whole body is dull ache, nowhere specific and no easing it with a different position. The bus stops at the gate until the boom rises, then again at some traffic lights, and then we're on a road along the river.

Sonja leans across me and points up a hill. I look and she says, "That's Kalemegdan. The fortress that was in a few of Milić's books. More than two thousand years old."

I know it from the books, and it's a lot less in real life than I pictured in my mind. It's smaller, more crumbled, and a less coherent pile of stones than I figured a fortress could be and still be called one. I don't tell Sonja this though because the real fortress works its way into my mind pretty easy and replaces the one I had always pictured.

I watch it go by the window.

The bus has speakers that crackle to life with busy, tinny music. The lady seated in front of us unwraps tinfoil from a sandwich and starts to eat it as we cross a bridge over the Danube and are into a suburb of mismatched cinderblock houses. The lady's done her sandwich by the time the city is gone from the windows and all that's left are little rundown houses dotting the brown dirt fields all around.

I tell Sonja about how I read that book my dad gave me, read it until the cover came off and the glue let go of the spine and some of the pages were loose and would fall out if I wasn't careful. I tell her how I put a rubber band around it in the end instead of finding another copy because it was the one my dad gave me, and that meant something as much as the words in the book did.

She listens, watches me, watches the farms go by on the flatland we're going over.

I tell Sonja about how, after my dad couldn't manage any longer, my mom had to be put into a care home in a bigger town a few hours away. I kept visiting her until I realized the effort didn't matter anymore. Not for her, anyhow.

I tell Sonja about how we needed money really pretty bad for her care, and my dad had to go work the rigs as much as he could, and how I would read that book, waiting for the bus to go visit Mom, and how I would come back feeling more alone than when I started out to see her. The book was like having someone with me who knew me, someone safe who was there when I needed them. It made being alone less lonely.

I tell her how I'd call Dad from a pay phone outside the Big T's grocery store, how sometimes he'd be there on the other end and sometimes he wouldn't. Whenever I talked to him, there were trucks running in the background and noise that buried his voice and he always sounded so far away. And then, after a while, he wasn't there ever again. I tell her about the trailer outside of town and how I lived there until I was taken away from it.

Sonja listens, like she knows that I'm going to tell her everything, but I stop for a bit because it's already the most I've told anyone. I look out the window and think on how it's good to tell someone, but how I feel pathetic, too, because I should be able to deal with all this without saying it out loud, without needing help. But I need help, I know it, and that makes me feel a bit better because, I reckon, we all do sometime.

The music coming through the speakers, it's barely louder than the bus engine and the rattling emergency window a few seats in front of ours. I can't take the noise and the silence buried in it, so I have to talk some more.

I take a breath.

I tell Sonja about Mr. Langman and about what I was doing in the canyon bottom, and how it all wound up in the bone dust. She nods at my arm, to show her, and I turn it to show her the purple scar there, the pinprick dots where the stitches were holding it together. She shakes her head at it, but doesn't say anything.

I tell her about hiding in the town, about going to get my money and getting out. I tell her about Evelyn watching the space station and about Cheryl and the guy from the semi-truck, about how she said he was one of my kind when I'd never thought of myself as any kind, but I guess I am, if a kind is needed. Then I stop, embarrassed. I squint outside but see nothing because I can't think. The music in the speakers. The engine noise. The emergency window rattles.

Sonja says, "I don't know what you expect."

I glance at her, not ready to look at her for longer.

She says, "From me . . . I don't know what you expect from me." And her voice and her face tell me nothing more than that.

I want to tell Sonja that it'd be great if she'd just listen, that I just have to tell someone this stuff, and can't carry it all anymore, how I can't make stuff up to people anymore. My lies have run out and I can't even think to keep the ones I've told straight, them that are so many I don't know what's true from what's not now. I want to tell her it would be great if she would forgive me everything, but I know it's not for her to do. I want her to know exactly who I am, but the problem is I don't even know. I can't ask her to know all of this and still like me after and that's what I want, the impossible.

Instead, I say, quiet and almost under the bus noises, "Can you maybe just listen?"

She says, "The bus takes another hour."

I don't say anything for a while, don't think I can. The bus stops randomly on the side of the road. There're fields out there, nothing in them yet but dark brown dirt. There's gravel and some garbage along the side of the road and an old couple gets on from there, sits near the front, talks to the driver as he gets us moving again.

It's weird that I'm not sleeping with the world going by fast outside. It's weird, my heart beating like this, fast and panicked, nervous about telling all of this to a stranger, but someone who is becoming less so by the minute. Sonja listens to me tell her about the night in Calgary and about my kiss with Mon in Amsterdam.

And she listens like she said she would, doesn't say a thing the whole time and that makes it easier. Her eyes are sometimes looking at mine, when I'm brave enough to meet them back. The rest of the time I talk to the seat-back in front of me, to the window glass beside me, to my fingers knitted like a bird's nest in my lap. It feels like I have to talk and don't want to stop.

On the bus looking out, the buildings turn from the occasional erratics out near the horizon line, to a few beside the road, to more of them as we go on. We're getting closer to a city, I guess. The sun's getting closer to the ground, and the shadows out there're so long they go out for miles. Then they're gone and there's just a glow left behind, above the horizon, no sun.

My voice says the names Sam and Maria and Eva and Gio, says stuff about them, the plan we made to steal cameras and how we played it out. Just louder than the clatter of the loose-set emergency window, the rattle of the engine, I tell her about how they felt like the family I once had, the tomato sauce in a fry pan bubbling on the small stove near the rain-streaked window, falling asleep to the sound of them talking nearby. That's what I really wanted, always wanted, people to feel safe with.

I can't read anything from Sonja's face. She listens, sure, but not much else, sometimes she nods or a frown twitches on her forehead. I talk about Sam's brother and Sam's brother on top of me in the bushes by the river, fiddling with his belt and the panic that got stuck in me there and hasn't left since, might never leave.

I look out the window, the city we're in now. It's a jumble of low and raggedy buildings, rusted metal roofs, and pitted plaster walls with the brick behind showing through some patches. Then I tell her about how Sam's brother put the same knife in me that I did him and last I tell her about how I wound up in her hospital.

I want her to look disappointed, laugh at me and shake her head, anything, but she doesn't. Her face doesn't tell on her thoughts. She looks out the window as we pass a chain-link gate and pull into another parking lot. The engine chugs before it stops running and the silence is uncommon after it being loud for so long. People stand and people struggle the bags from under their seats, from the compartments overhead.

I tell Sonja I want her to say something, and she says, "We're here."

She says, "This is where we get off."

She stands and goes and I follow her down the steps in the last of the evening light. It kills me every second, this drifting feeling, this thinking about how she must see me now, what she must think. The helplessness of that, it makes me want to run from her, but I don't because that's what I've always done and it's time to be new. She's my tether here, the only one, and even then just barely.

While I'm thinking all this, she's waiting in the back seat of a rusty little sedan that blows blue from its tailpipe. The back door's open and she's talking to the driver, so I get in beside her and close it. The driver takes us from the curb and guides the car back the way we came in on the bus. They say Miloš's name a few times and the driver laughs and Sonja doesn't, just looks out the side.

When they stop talking she sees my confusion and says, "It's okay. We'll go see Miloš now and this guy will wait for us and then he'll drive us to the cottage."

A few minutes later, twilight is gone and the air is grey and the world settles flat and quieter than it was all day. Our tires roll across gapped pavement and the bumps come straight through to us because there's not much left of the car's suspension. A few minutes gone from the bus station and on the edge of town, we pull into a cemetery parking lot. Gravel pops under tires and the potholes are worse. The driver stops beside a low stone fence and turns the engine off.

I know that I won't meet Miloš, but instead I'll meet his tombstone. I'm not mad at Sonja for not telling me this first. She may have thought I already knew, might have thought this is what I wanted to see all along. Maybe she thinks this is what I deserve after telling her everything I did, but I don't think she's like that. I think she's kind and it's who she is. I'm just sad that all's been for this, all along for me going to talk at a rock stuck upright in the ground.

The car doors creak and the cab driver lights a cigarette. His face glows quick in the match strike and then gone. The smoke is in the air. He says something, his voice rumbles as we walk away, the air sweeter as we leave the cigarette smoke. The edge of town is a checkerboard of lit windows and dusty stucco, shadows behind the glass, all of it a short way across a field from us. In that direction, the sky is still steel down low, but grades to deep blue above the rooftop strings of chimney smoke, smoke that reminds me that it's still cold in the hours between daylight. I cross my arms against a fresh chill and my fingers rub the mass of bandages on my side.

I tell Sonja that I'm sorry because I can't say it to anyone else. We pass the stone fence and walk on grass. I tell her I'm sorry for this, coming here, and if I'm trouble for her and for everything I told her about on the bus.

Sonja tells me that it's enough. She says, "It's okay." Quiet voice beside me and I don't look over at her because there's nothing to see in the dark. Her voice is an anchor because it's disorienting walking through the black, like I have to trust that each foot will land on the ground.

She says, "It's fine, you telling me. Sometimes it helps, but sometimes it only brings problems back and makes them real again. Either way, they'll always be there." She's quiet and I think she's looking around at where we are, trying to find where we're going. Then she figures it out and we walk again. "I think you have to stop it. Stop talking and stop thinking too much on everything. Everything that's done can only make how you are now. That's why every day is important because it'll become the past you will have to live with tomorrow."

We walk side by side and the air smells like wet earth, cold and heavy, like clay in the rain. Stones are set upright here and there. Crypts are peppered about, orderly blocks of shadow in the failed light. There's one tree, back beside the parking lot, and I look back but can't see the cab because there's a curve to the hill.

Sonja breaks my thoughts when she says, "He's over here somewhere."

And we find him in not much time, but have to get real close to the stone to read that it's really him. The grass is still not all grown back where he is, but it mostly is. Looking at the stone, there's no reason for me to be here now, never was in the first place I suppose. We stare for a while before Sonja touches my shoulder, like the light feet of a quick bird, and she says, "The only thing you can't change is that your last breath will be an exhalation. And the only thing you must do in life is take that breath. The rest of the time is yours, however you want."

Those words are from Milić, I know it. They were in the book, the worn out one held together by an elastic band. I recognize them, but I don't say it.

Sonja sighs and says, "Seems like a good arrangement though, doesn't it?"

And I can't think it's not.

Milić meant it to say how we can change almost everything if we try and I know now what Sonja meant earlier, to stop it, carrying too much of what's past. I don't know why, but I don't feel too sour about not getting to meet Milić, like this has saved me some trouble that I never needed, like I'm not the person now I first thought I was. And after everybody I've met to get here, the idea that this stranger is family doesn't seem as important as it once did, lying under Mr. Langman and needing someone to come looking. Like Sonja said, I don't have to be the person I was. I know it now because it's over, this trip, me and him are here together.

I tell Sonja he was my granddad, but she's gone, a shade of black in the night, not too far away, her neck bent looking close at another stone.

I kick my shoes off, and stand stork to pull my socks off, one and then the other. The ground is cold, wet. I don't know what time it is, but that doesn't matter because the part about having to say the words at eleven-eighteen was made up later. After my dad taught me to remember the words, I made up the ritual to go with them.

And I say the words. It's the ones I told the little girl on the airplane while her mother pretended not to listen, the words that are magic and that'll make things right for the year ahead, the words that have never worked yet, but I can't give up on saying them just in case they do. My voice is quiet, almost a whisper because Sonja is there. She can probably hear me anyhow because it's so quiet. I'm a bit embarrassed, but it'd be a shame to waste the hope of them for a whole year because I'm shy that Sonja might judge me a fool.

I say, "And here at the edge of this minute and in the breaking forever ahead, I'll work to forget what the past has done to me. I'll work to remember only what's to come, to remember only the future. I'll remember that the table will be topped with food and circled by friends. I'll remember the glasses will be filled and the sunlight will come green through the leaves overhead, and all around. I remember that I will never be empty."

I stutter through the next few words because Sonja joins, quiet voice, saying them with me. She knows the words like I do, by heart, and her voice is with mine saying, "I remember that there will be enough sorrow to teach me what happiness is, enough pain to teach me pleasure, and enough hate to teach love."

And then we both stop talking and the silence is absolute in our wake.

Sonja says, "That's my favourite passage."

And I just want to stand beside her in the dark for a while, and we do, because it seems like she wants that, too.

6

We go together, back toward the silhouette of the tree, nothing said between us as we follow the base of the hill to the parking lot. The taxi's there, door open. A weak light from inside outlines the driver leaning against the car, looking back at the edge of town. The ember of his cigarette floats red. He doesn't say anything when he sees us, just slumps back into the seat and rolls down the window so he can tap ashes out.

Sonja gets in and I get in. The little overhead light goes dark when the door claps closed. She tells him something and we're gone from the parking lot, popping gravel until the tires turns into the drone of the engine carrying us along pavement.

Only one headlight works and there's a crack across the windscreen that draws a line through the darkness ahead. The driver rolls up his window, mostly, and leaves a small gap at the top that lets a cool breeze in. As the road slides under, the headlight picks up the slight waver of the centreline, leading us on. It's either an unplanned back and forth as we waver in the lane or it undulates out there where it's drawn on the pavement, neither can be trusted to be a constant and the chance is that both are probably imperfect. The headlight fades quick in the straw grass off the side of the road, the flash of a white plastic bag slumped against a shrub and nothing else that I can see, out forever dark.

We could be falling through space, driving through nothing, the three of us and the sounds of the engine and the whisper of speed through the gap in the window. Maybe I'm out there walking, like in the prairie black, far away and watching us go by silently on the horizon. My eyelids close to the fantasy and I listen and I fall asleep wondering if the driver can actually see anything, or if he just moves forward with the faith that the road keeps going and everything still exists out there, ahead.

I don't dream, not that I know about when I wake up. The little car has stopped, pulled to the shoulder, still in the black, but not as absolute as it was. A moon is up now and near full, lending an edge of pale light to everything. Sonja is talking, handing some money over the seat, and she looks back at me to make sure I follow her out of the cab.

We go together to the side of the road as the car bends a hook and speeds off, back the way we came, two red taillights and one white headlight shrinking from us. We listen to the night grow quiet again. I look around at the flat and black land. A track heads off into a bunch of trees, two dirt ruts with grass grown tall on either side and between them. It seems secret, safe, like you have to know it's even there before you could ever find it.

"Come on," Sonja says, and I follow her down the track.

The trees on either side make no noise, no breeze to stir their small spring leaves, nothing to move the bushes starting to grow underneath. The only sound is the occasional rustle of the plastic bag of food Sonja bought from the lady at the bus station. As we walk, the ground rises gently, lifting us onto the whaleback of a berm by the time we're out of the trees, a short way up from the flat fields around us.

Sonja tells me this berm keeps the river under control if it rains too much. She tells me the river isn't far from here and her dad's cottage isn't far either, just a bit back from the river edge, down on the dry side of the berm.

I ask if her dad is there and she tells me he isn't, that he died a while back, that was who she stopped to see at the cemetery. Her mom rests there too, she shrugs, says, "So they're still together."

I say, "I'm sorry."

And she doesn't say anything for a while. Then, "The strangest thing about them dying is that the world went on just the same."

We walk, her in one dirt rut and me a few steps behind in the other. In the moonlight, I can see my breath and there's a cotton mist rising off the fields several feet below us. It stretches out from us, surrounding the humpback earth we traverse and fuzzing out the ground, glowing ghost-blue from the moon.

Sonja says, "It's my cabin now, but I'll always think of it as his. He built it before me and my brother were born. I remember us happy there. It makes me happy to be there."

I ask if she grew up here and she tells me no, that this was a place they always came for the summer when the state companies had vacation, when school was out, and the days were hot. And, she tells me, this is where her parents wound up for the war, and where they stayed after.

I say, "Why didn't they go home?"

And she says, "Their town isn't there anymore."

I ask, "What happened?"

In the dark, she shrugs, says, "History."

She tells me that she believes history should be left to the historians, that it should be their burden to remember it for everyone else, not to remind everyone of what's best forgotten. "It's best to move on and leave it behind."

She says, "Sometimes it's better to make the same old mistakes rather than new, worse ones. At least things can be good until then, instead of always living with the weight of mistakes made. Sometimes it's better not to learn anything."

I don't know any different, so I stay quiet and just hug myself for warmth. I have nothing more to put on than the clothes I wear, so I resign to the cold damp and just shiver. We walk like this for a while, above the mist on our earth bridge until it starts to curve a bit.

There're trees on one side and Sonja tells me the river's over there, other side of those trees. She says, "You can't see it now, but it's beautiful. The trees are tight to it, but not so tight you can't find a place to sit. The water's slow, so it's easy to swim. It's warm in the summer."

Down the opposite side from the river, there's a little house sitting with hunched shoulders in the night. A short, raw wood fence makes uneven pickets strung across the front.

Sonja says, "Here." And then she starts down, diagonal through the knee-high grass growing on the side of the berm. I follow, but slower than she goes because the slope is uneven and I don't know the ground like she does. At the bottom I'm ankle-deep in water for a moment, my foot in a puddle that Sonja somehow avoided. There's a gate that Sonja knows and I follow her through. The bulk of the berm is lost in the mist behind us and there's just a gauzy outline of the cottage in front.

The step onto a low wood porch creaks. There's the sound of keys, metal jangles against metal, and the lock tumbles and Sonja goes in. Suddenly there's light and I wince at it, my eyes grown used to the moonlight we walked under for the past hour. Sonja's inside and I wait on the porch step until she tells me to get in and she'll light a fire and get some heat for us. The cottage is an open room, a couch, a small kitchen with pale blue cabinet doors, an old wooden table with two chairs on either side. There's the same chill air inside as there is out.

She points to a door and says, "That's my room."

She says, "The couch is yours." And she pulls some twigs and yellowed newspaper from a basket and starts a fire in a barrel-belly cast iron stove. She goes outside again, to the end of the porch, to the wood stacked there, and she has an armful of it when she comes back in.

I sit at the table and soon there're logs crackling in the stove and a bit of woodsmoke in the air. The stove door squeaks closed and latches with a rasp and clang.

I ask her, "Why did you bring me here?"

She doesn't answer, looks at me and then pulls a green plastic bottle and a few small glasses from a cabinet. There's some bread and sausage she brought and she puts them on a plate with some green onions and a little hill of salt.

I lean forward and ask, "Why did you let me come with you?"

She doesn't answer for a moment, joins me at the table and puts the glasses on it. She pours each small glass half-full of clear drink and puts the plate of food between us too, taps the green onion into the salt and takes a bite.

She chews and says, "You needed some place to go."

She holds up a glass to me and I get what she wants. I lift my glass from the table and ring it against hers. She says a word I don't get then drinks a sip. I drink a sip, too, and it burns and I fight not to cough. My eyes water up. She smiles and tells me, plum brandy, and that she made it herself.

Then she says, "I've needed a place to stay before and had nobody offer one, when we had to leave our village. It was very hard, and it always seems wrong to me, to not help someone when you can. And besides, it's nicer to talk to someone here when it's dark outside. Watching the river go by in the day is nice alone, but it can be lonely." She shrugs. "These are easy things to share."

We take another sip and she tells me she was always in trouble with her mom for bringing home stray dogs and cats. She smiles while she tells me this. I get it, her joke, but there's something nice under it, that she's kind and wants to help. We drink to the bottom of our glasses and I'm warm inside after. The fire crackles and snaps, quiet noises from inside the heavy stove. Sonja refills the glasses and then leans back in her chair, stretching back to put the bottle on the kitchen counter.

She says, "Eat." She points at the plate.

I'm hungry and could eat everything. I have a piece of bread, a bit of sausage, not much. I don't know where her hospitality will end and I'm thankful for what she's already shared. She says it's easy, but it means a lot.

She smiles and says, "Okay." Her cheeks are flushed pink and her eyes are tired in the dim light.

The table and glasses between us, the silence between us, and I want to know more about her because I told her a lot about me. I ask her how long she's been working as a nurse. She tells me two years. She tells me since she graduated from school and she says, "It's mostly a good job."

She says, "Weeks can get long, but I think things could be worse. My friends are in Belgrade and I've been there almost as long as I can remember. It's a good city."

She tells me about the apartment she rents and her roommate, another nurse from the hospital. "It's a small place," she says. "But we often work different shifts, so we don't see each other much, not enough to get in each other's way."

She talks more about her parents, her dad was an engineer and her mom was a receptionist for the state power company. The drink spins my head around pleasantly and the late hour fuzzes over any leftover pain in my body. The room is warm now, and when I lean closer to the window there's a skin of cold night seeping through the glass, so I lean back away from it again.

I don't know when it is, but Sonja hasn't talked for a few minutes. The fire in the stove is quiet. Just the metal ticks occasionally, either still expanding with the heat or contracting because the fire is mostly done, I don't know.

Sonja yawns and says, "It's time to sleep."

I nod and stand up from the table when she does. She brings me a few blankets and there're already a few pillows on the couch. It sags soft in the middle, but it's long enough to stretch out on.

She says, "You left these behind at the hospital." And she holds out the notebook and pencil Gio gave me. She says, "Put it near you, for if you think of anything to write down tonight."

I start to say thank you, but she tells me something and I don't understand it.

She says, "It means good night." She says it again and when I say it back to her she says, "You have a funny accent." And she laughs, so I smile at that. She flicks the light off and goes to the bedroom. Through the closed door, through the thin walls, I hear her moving around. Then it's quiet.

The air's still warm, the silence near absolute, except for the murmur from the wood stove as the embers fade out inside it.

I'm not asleep, but dizzy with spinning thoughts about what's next, what to do with the nothing I have, and the nothing left of me. I'm thinking how the future wound up being here, at the end of a dirt track that crosses on the humped back of an earth berm into the empty midnight fields, on the bank of a river I don't even remember the name of, an hour's car ride from a town with a name I can't pronounce.

I have to smile at the sound of her snoring from the other room, starting quiet and growing louder. It's a sleep I'm envious of, one less beautiful than I expected of her, but I'm not sure what I expected because it's not for me to assume anything, just to be here for as long as she says it's okay.

Time slides, and at some point, when the dark's not as deep through the window, when I can see the outline of the two little glasses we left on the wooden table, the plate we left behind, I fall asleep.

7

Sonja moves quietly in the kitchen. The stove is crackling, fire-bellied again. I watch her through eyelashes, not sure what time it is, but happy to let these minutes pass as slow as they can. It's cold in the room, so I guess it's still early. Maybe only a couple of hours since I fell asleep, maybe minutes. Having been detached from time for a while, it's hard to know much about it anymore. Sonja spoons out dry coffee grounds into a little brass pot with a long handle and a beak in the rim. She pulls a few cups from the cupboard, white porcelain yellowed ivory. She glances at me once and I'm sure she catches me watching, but maybe she doesn't. She pours the boiling water in with the coffee and the smell of it is warm. She glances at me a second time, watches this time and doesn't turn away.

I open my eyes slow and fake waking up and Sonja quickly looks at the coffee pot, like she doesn't want me to know she was watching. I sit up, stretch, and go sit at the table. She pours coffee, places one of the cups in front of me, then sits across from me with her own cup.

"Smells good," I say.

She smiles and says, "Better than you do." But she doesn't say it mean.

A blush on my face and I lift my shirt to my nose.

I say, "These are all I have."

She says, "We can wash them in the river. There's probably something of my dad's that'll fit you. But eat first."

She leans back to the kitchen counter and there's bread, butter, and a jar of jam she puts on the table between us. We eat and I take one of my pills and set the little plastic bottle on the windowsill beside the table. I look out and eat some bread and drink the thick coffee. There are short trees growing in rows, clumps of little white blossoms on the branches, stretching back from the house to the edge of the low wooden fence. We talk easy talk, like how we slept, what clothes could fit, the food is good, and say nothing much sitting in the rising light through the dusty window glass.

After we're done, I stand, take the plates to a plastic basin on the counter to wash them with the leftover hot water from the dented pot.

Sonja tells me she'll show me the well out back after I'm done, how to work the pump to get water up from it. She takes me into the bedroom, a tiny room with a window view of more white blossom trees. The air's cooler away from the stove. She pulls some clothes from a battered dresser in the corner and says, "These should fit."

A teeshirt, white turned a bit grey from age, clean but with pale stains around the armpits. A wool sweater, worn shapeless and with a short split in the shoulder's seam, and a brown pair of corduroy pants. She puts them all on the bed and I wait for her to leave, so I can change, but she doesn't move.

She says, "Take off your shirt. I'll check your cut."

I don't do anything at first, not because of the mess I look or how I smell, but because I like Sonja and I'm embarrassed to take any of my clothes off in front of her.

She knows my hesitation and says, "I've seen you before. Let me look."

I pull my shirt off with awkward movements because everything's still sore, still stiff. I watch her face for how she judges my skin, but there's nothing bad there. Her eyes are on me, her fingers on my skin and then peeling the gauze back slowly. She looks at the cut, comes close to see in the weak light. Her breath tickles the fine hairs on me. She puts a hand flat to the side of the cut. Her palm is warm, soft, and I look at the ceiling then meet her gaze, and she smiles at my modesty, says, "There's still some infection there, but it looks better than it did."

She says, "Keep taking the pills until they're gone. You'll live."

I want to tell her I already feel better than I have in weeks, even better than before Sam's brother stuck me, but instead I say, "One with breakfast and one with supper." And she nods and tells me to get changed. Just when I think she isn't going to leave, she does. I bump my palm against the side of my head, roll my eyes at myself, at how stupid I sounded.

With my old clothes in hand, I go out and Sonja is waiting at the table. She has a plastic bag for my dirty clothes and a smaller one with powder detergent and a bar of soap inside. She has a book in her hand and I take the notebook and pencil Gio gave me. We go out front and the sun is full-on and it's warm on my face, even though the air is still cool. I see the things now that I couldn't when we came in last night. There's no mist and the berm is a grassy hill with treetops showing from the other side.

Sonja tours me around the space inside the fence, shows me the rows of plum trees, shows me the water well and how to use the hand pump. The air is dew grass and hints of plum blossoms and woodsmoke. She shows me the garden, and excited, says, "Look. Already onions coming up." And she points at the deep green sprouts poking an inch through the dirt. There's other stuff, still not grown enough to know what it is.

There're a couple of faded folding chairs we take from the porch before we go out the front gate. We climb the berm and stand at the top, the flat land stretching out to forever on the one side, brown fields of dirt and small crowds of trees dotting the space from here to there. Behind us is the river. The dark water, glimpsed between the trees, is wide and flat and smooth.

Down the riverside of the berm, Sonja finds a narrow trail I wouldn't have found and we go along it through the trees. There're faraway sounds of kids playing in the water, happy voices and splashing. The air's still and warming up quick, even in the shelter of tall, ash-grey tree trunks and their bright spring leaves. The smell of the plants, the living ground, the musty slow water and forest litter decay. The trail ends at the river's edge and there's a clearing off to one side, big enough for our two chairs, room enough for a few more if there was someone else with us.

Sonja unfolds her chair and then I do mine. She finds a plastic bucket in the bush because she knows where to look for it.

She says, "Wash your clothes in this."

With the bucket in one hand, I pull up my pant legs with the other, then wade into the water. The river bottom is soft and my feet sink into pillow silt. The water's warmer than I thought it would be and the current is almost nothing pulling past my legs. I fill the tub and go back to sit in the chair beside Sonja's, scrub my clothes while she reads her book.

I can see the kids, two little ones in their underwear, playing on the far side the river just a bit upstream from us. They're all stick legs and skinny arms splashing and laughing, birdcage ribs puffing from play. Maybe they're brother and sister, maybe just friends, but I don't know. I watch them in glances while washing my clothes. There's nothing else for that time, just them laughing and me thinking how water would feel splashed on me by someone laughing so hard, thinking on nothing at all but that.

I peek over at Sonja, book open in her hand, but she watches them too. She smiles when the little girl dunks the little boy underwater. He comes up shouting fake angry and laughing at the same time. He tries to dunk her, but she's too quick and scoots up onto the bank before he can get her.

Sonja sees me watching and says, "Their mother will be mad. It's too cold for kids to play in the river."

I say, "The water's not bad."

Sonja shakes her head and asks, "Do you have a sister or brother?" And I tell her no.

She says, "I have a brother in London. He works programming computers and comes to see me every year or two. He wants me to immigrate there, work in London. I visited him a few times. I like it better here. I have memories here." When it seems like she won't say any more, she does. "But then some memories are to push you out and others are to hold you stuck. My brother would never live here, not after he lived through the war. He's older. I don't remember as much as he does."

I nod and look back to the bucket of clothes. I go rinse them in the river and wring them out and then find some low branches to hang them over in the sun. I sit down again, watch the water go by for a while, watch the kids play until they leave, and everything after is calm. It must be midday or sometime around then because the light comes from up high.

Sonja says, "I'm going in."

She stands and right there strips down to her underwear. She's slim, but not skinny, and she's nice to look at. I don't want to get caught in a stare, don't want her to think I like her like that, so glimpses is all I do. She's not shy about it though. She steps into the water, the line her spine draws down her back. She walks up to her waist and then pushes off, treading in a deeper part not far from the shore. Under the surface, the ripples of her pale arms and legs move back and forth.

I stand up and take off my shirt, take off my pants, just wearing underwear too, and Sonja sees what I'm doing. She says, "Keep your bandages dry."

She says, "There's soap. You should wash." She splashes around a bit and says, "Like a bird." And I know it's been a while, so I wade waist deep and splash and wash my skin.

Sonja comes back to shore when I'm done and she loses her balance getting out of the water, gives a shocked shriek and then laughs at it. I laugh with her because it's the first time I've seen her surprised and the noise she made was funny. It's the first time I've heard her laugh and it's a nice sound that I want to hear more.

We sit in the sun together, don't dress and just dry off for a while, both our faces tilted toward the sky. With the kids gone and us quiet, there's only birdsongs in the trees, and water noises from the river. A loud bug flies past my ear and I open my eyes, track it zagging out to the grey specks of other bugs hovering and spinning around above the water. Sometimes one dips and taps the surface, or a fish breathes a bubble out and it breaks in rings moving slowly outward to disappear.

Sonja sits up and looks out at the water, too. After a while she says, "Me and my brother and my parents used to spend a lot of time here, just waiting together for the days to pass. We would come in the late morning and there would be food to last us from lunchtime all the way to dark. Served right here," she looks around the clearing, "on clean tea towels in the middle of a blanket laid out."

She says, "Half the time my parents would have to carry me and my brother back. Those nights I remember waking up, being hugged close to my mom or dad, barely seeing the dark forest trail and the skinny outlines of the trees before falling right back asleep again. The next morning, we'd wake up in bed, in the cottage, safe and warm like magic."

I don't say anything, cross my legs under and pull at some blades of grass in front of me. I look sideways at her and she watches the water, keeps talking. Her face is light in remembering.

She says, "We'd spend all summer out here. It's funny all the things that I think I'd miss from the city, like movies and music and restaurants and buses. I didn't miss them back then, not as long as there was my brother and my parents with me. Even when we were older and didn't play in the river as much, even then I'd still want to be here whenever I could." Sonja looks at her knees and then upstream from us. "Now I miss them very much, whenever I come here."

"Why come then?" I ask. "If this place makes you sad?"

Sonja smiles, says, "It doesn't make me sad to miss them. Remembering them isn't sad. It's the most wonderful feeling to miss something so much, a reminder that things can be that good. Missing someone is the feeling of hope that you'll get to spend some more time with them, and hope is never bad."

And I say, "I'm glad I'm here."

We both watch the bugs over the water.

Sonja says, "I am too."

There's a gap between us as we watch the river, watch the birds in the trees along the edge, and then Sonja says, "Back there, on the bus," she says, "why did you tell me all of that?"

I say, "I felt like I had to." And she asks why, again.

I say, "Because I wanted to tell you who I am."

"But it's not all of you."

I agree, then say, "It's some of it though. I'm glad I said it. I don't deserve you, you know, I mean the help you're giving me. Your kindness."

She smirks at my fumble and blush, says, "That's not a choice for you to make, what I offer to you. That's for me. You can only choose to accept it or not."

I say, "I suppose. Then I guess it's the same with what I told you on the bus, it's mine to give, yours to take or leave. I guess I wanted you to know. I wanted to say that Milić was my granddad."

And she says she's sorry.

I say, "Thank you, but I never knew him. Don't even know if he knew of me."

She says, "You misunderstand. I'm sorry for you, that you came all this way because of him and he's not here anymore. Sorry that you won't get to meet him."

I tell her that even my dad didn't know much about him. I tell her that I didn't really come all this way to see him, just that it was the last bit of family, so it felt like it might be a safe place, how having somewhere to go is better than having nowhere to go, no matter how far away it is.

I say, "Now, he's under the earth from on it. I guess that makes me the last man in the universe, as far as my family knows it."

Sonja ticks her tongue, says, "So dramatic, you. It's not like that, if you choose for it not to be."

A branch snaps in the trees across the river and we both watch to see what caused it. Time stretches and the source keeps its mystery, the quiet between us stays gentle like the river going by. It feels good, like there's comfort now where there wasn't earlier. Sometimes we say stuff, ask each other things when we think of them, but mostly we just sit in the sun, nothing is rushed, and nothing is necessary. After a while, Sonja reads her book and I close my eyes again and drift. Sometimes, Sonja translates me passages she likes. I glance at her sometimes, mostly when her eyes are on the page.

We're like this until the sun drops below the trees on the other side of the river and shadows settle in on us. We're dressed and walking the trail back to the earth berm and I smack a mosquito from my arm, from my neck. Sonja tells me she thinks there'll be a lot of them this year, because it's already rained so much since winter. There's a chill coming back, and from the top of the berm, shadows lay long across the dirt on the other side.

After we get across the berm and into the house, Sonja tells me she'll make some supper and I guess it's about that time. I go out to the end of the porch and tuck some logs into the crook of my arm, stop to watch a spider scuttle deeper into the pile. Through the window, Sonja's cutting something on the counter in the pale yellow light. She pulls a jar from the cupboard and I watch for a minute more before going back inside and putting the wood into the basket beside the stove.

She asks me to start a fire and I do, and by the time it's going, the table's set. Bread and a few sliced-up tomatoes, some pickled vegetables and some sausage on a white plate that has a soft grey crack running through it. From the cupboard, she pulls a bottle of wine that has no label.

She says, "This is the perfect wine to have with pickled salad."

She laughs and I do too. She pours us two glasses full. I taste it and she's right.

We don't turn on the lights. We play cards after dinner, with a wide candle flickering on the windowsill and another one lit on the table between us. Sonja teaches me a game with cards that're old and worn and the ten of hearts has a fuzzy patch where the backing has been torn off a corner. It takes me a while to learn the game and I'm a little drunk by the time I do. Sonja wins and probably would even if I didn't have too much to drink.

The bottle of wine finished, the conversation is quiet. It's dark black outside the window, just us reflected in the glass, just the inside of the cottage framed there, where the outside should be.

Sonja yawns, says, "I'm going to bed." And I tell her, I'll do the dishes.

She says, "Leave them for tomorrow," but after I tell her good night, after her bedroom door is closed, I quietly clean up. She's snoring when I cross the room to the couch and I smile about it, that noise she's too pretty to make. I blow out the candles, take off my pants to get comfortable, lie on the couch in the dark, and listen to her sleep through the thin wall. Everything slows down from the day, from the river going by out there in the dark, from the quiet where the kids played at nothing.

At some point in the night I wake up to Sonja whispering my name. She's standing in the dark, by the stove, with her arms wrapped around her. I don't know when I fell asleep, but I'm right awake in a hurry at the noise, my heart beating fast and ready from old habit, from sleeping in unsafe places. I lie there unmoving because I'm not sure at first what I heard, or if I really heard it.

Sonja whispers, "Are you awake?"

I say, "Yes." My voice sounds loud in the space, so I say it again, but quieter.

She's a shape, an outline with no details in the dark. She shifts and the stove door squeaks. Her legs are two orange lines in the ember glow. There's the crackle of the new wood in the stove and the door squeaks shut to dark again.

She says, "It's colder than last night."

I hear her moving, barely see her going back to her room. She leaves the door open. I lay there for a few minutes, wondering what that all meant, why she woke me to tell me that when she could have just put more wood in the stove and gone back to bed.

After a while, I hear her moving in the dark, shifting in her bed. She's still awake. I quiet my breath to listen to her breath. After a while, I swing my legs to the floor, the wood planks cold under my bare feet. I stand up and gather my blanket in arms and cross the room to her door. I stand in the doorframe for a few moments. I shouldn't be this nervous, because nothing can happen.

"I'm . . ." I say, "I can't be for you. Just can't be."

And she laughs quietly, says, "That's right. Me neither for you. But you have heat and a heartbeat, which is better than cold and alone. Friends are always better than alone."

I nod though she can't see it and go in and put my blanket over the others on the bed, before getting under them. Sonja doesn't say anything, but puts her back against my chest and I put my arm over her.

We're warm together, alone and nowhere together.

I flex my fingers and the numbness fades for feeling. Thoughts race for a while, about how this moment was built, about what this moment builds.

There's always the chance of something happy, somewhere ahead.

Because it's never really over.

What used to be and what is now are never the same thing.

All of these things are true.

And, eventually, we're asleep together.

BOOK V

1

We meet in the city often for coffee or a meal, and we've met at the cab stand near the bus station a few times, now. From there, we return to the little house by the river together. Sonja says I can come here whenever I'd like, but I think it would feel different alone. She says it does.

I like to see the changes, small ones missed between days, but easily spotted over the longer arc of time. The brown dirt fields have gone green. The flowers on the trees around have turned to fruit, and the morning mist is barely a thing anymore because the nights aren't as cold.

I hand Sonja a cup and we sip that bitter coffee. Our eyes come together and then part and she nods, I made it right, tastes good. There's a chip on the edge of the cup that's rough against my lip.

We sit at the wood table near the window, my back to the open door and her back to the cupboards. The deck of cards with the fuzzy ten of hearts is between us, still scattered from the game we played last night. I'm getting better at it, the game, even good enough to win once in a while. The little glasses we sipped her brandy from sit there, too.

The morning sun angles in low and catches the fine thread of a spiderweb on the dusty windowsill, catches a few bits of dust drifting through the air. Without those things the sunlight would be invisible, but invisible things are still always there.

It catches Sonja, too, brown hair, brown eyes, the freckles high up on her cheek, close to where it's already sloping back toward her lower eyelid. She smiles, drowsy morning eyes looking away when a cool breeze breathes through the door. The scent of black earth and the shiftless river nearby. The smell of summer plants and the start of a fresh-cut woodpile, stacked and drying in the sun at the end of the porch, these things are all invisible and all there.

I say, "What do you see when you look outside like that?" And she doesn't say anything back for a time, just watches the morning with a smile, but one that has some distance, some sadness in the line of her lips.

Months ago, when we first met, us like this would have made me nervous; these long silences between slow words would have made me chicken, but now we know each other a bit, it's comfortable.

When she does speak, she tells me, this is her favourite time of year, this, right now.

She says, "Summer is when everything's so alive again and the cool gets warm pretty quick. Good for morning swimming."

She drinks her coffee and I drink mine. I don't need to say anything. I'm happy to listen and she seems happy to talk for a bit. It doesn't need to be about anything. It doesn't always need to be about something.

Sonja tells me she likes the cool air in the dark, early morning, and the way it makes the ground smell, how it makes her blanket seem that much warmer when she's laying in when the long-sun day's already started. She tells me the garden vegetables taste so much better than the supermarket cardboard that comes in winter, and she likes the colours of the purple fruits on the plum trees, like they are getting now.

She says, "I remember swimming in the river around this time of year when I was a kid, me and my brother, and it was warmer than the air. And when we got out we'd get goosebumps all over, and we'd shiver. Our mother would scold us every time, told us we would get sick, but we would still sneak to the water anyway, when she wasn't watching. We never got sick, but she'd still scold us."

Then we're quiet together.

I watch the windowsill spider's silk billow gently with liquid ripples. Sonja watches something over my shoulder, out through the door, might be nothing, might be something only she can see, and her eyes get stuck there for a while.

It doesn't need to be about anything right now, us here.

Sonja says, "Miloš isn't why you came all this way, you know."

I smile and say, "I'd love to know why then." I yawn and stretch my back out, roll my shoulders back. "Because I don't know any more, what I thought I once did."

She says, "It's simple."

I wait and she doesn't say anything else, so I say, "It leaves me not knowing anything and ready to believe everything."

She says, "You had to leave, and you came here because you had nowhere else to go." She taps a fingertip on the tabletop.

And still smiling, I ask, "That simple?"

She says, "It doesn't need to be more. Why should it? I could say you came here by chance or by fate, but that's just as silly. You came here for me to take care of your cut." And she stops and smiles at my expression, my raised eyebrows, my surprise at her boldness. "You came here to work paperless, to live in that horrible flat with the others, washing dishes until you got your papers, then to teach English."

I regain my face and say, "Maybe that."

I say, "Maybe these are my reasons, but what are yours?"

She says, "Not sure. I'd need to see the future before I can know." There's some quiet between us before Sonja shrugs. "Finish your coffee."

I tilt my cup, careful of the thick sediment settled at the bottom. She swirls my cup and sets it upside down on the saucer, tells me she's going to read my fortune in the coffee grounds, but we have to wait for them to open up and dry out a little, which we do.

I ask, "Where did you learn to read the future?"

And she says, "Gypsies taught me."

Her face is serious and I like it when I can't tell if she's joking or not. It makes the real stuff less serious and the fake stuff she jokes about more real, like she's mixing up reality and fantasy into something better, so we can live somewhere touched by both.

This time, I guess she's joking and gamble on that and say, "When they kidnapped you from your real mother, who's a queen in a palace?"

A slow smile spreads and I still can't tell. She rights the cup and stares at the smear of coffee grounds inside, forehead creased in concentration. She gasps and brings a hand to her mouth and shakes her head with concern.

I laugh at the drama and angle to see, ask, "Is it that bad?"

"It's horrible."

Then she laughs, too.

She shrugs, says, "Who can say? I'm really no good at this. I thought I could make something up, make a joke and get you to laugh, but I couldn't think of anything fast enough. My gyspy princess mom is better. I'll get her to do it, if I ever find her."

I take the dishes to the sink. There's still enough hot water in the kettle to wash them, so I do. I peek in my cup at the grounds, swirls and twists, spots of yellowed porcelain showing through the thick lines in places. There could be shapes in there, maybe if we wanted to stare at it long enough, we could see them.

It all disappears in the suds and I stack the clean cup on a frayed tea towel with the other dishes. I take the basin outside and throw an arc of wash water over the grass, dusty diamonds through the sunlight.

ACKNOWLEDGEMENTS

A nod thanks to these fine people . . .

It's crazy, this writing thing, this making stories and this living things out in my head for a bit. I'm not all that able to do it on my own, even though I try. There's always lots of people to thank, lots of people who helped a bit, and a bit of people who helped a whole lot.

This one is for Nenad and the language we share right now and all the words that have been and all them that'll come. I want it to keep being good, so it will be. I know it.

It's people like Ali and Judith and Leanne and Nancy and Chase. It's people like Amanda and Sandra and Andrea, and a whole bunch of others that make this pile of words even better than it was at first. They make it go and they make it get onto paper and they get it onto shelves and in front of you. They are so good and challenging and giving that I'm lucky they're here in my life. These words don't seem like enough, but it's all there is.

There's a lot of mighty people at Freehand Books, itself a mighty press hoisting up amazing books. Can't thank enough: Kelsey for putting it all together and Debbie for lending such a fine tuning to this work, that it's so much better than it was before. Thanks Natalie who makes some right-stunning covers and the rest of the crew there for getting this done.

And finally, it's such a weird thing that you read this. It's such a trick that you can make pictures of it in your head and feel it, too, like you can live through it with only a little bit of trying. That's the magic of readers and it's always been, you making this book go. Thanks for being that person because without you to do it, this wouldn't even be a thing.

— Bradley Somer

ACKNOWLEDGMENTS

BRADLEY SOMER's novels have been published in over twenty countries, translated into several languages, and produced in many print, digital, and audio formats. A few have even been optioned for screen.

He is the author of three previous novels: *Extinction* (Blackstone Publishing & HarperCollins UK, 2022), *Fishbowl* (St. Martin's Press & Penguin Random House UK, 2015), and *Imperfections* (Nightwood Editions, 2012). He has also written a ton of short fiction, which has appeared in literary journals, reviews, and anthologies over the past twenty years.

Bradley holds degrees in Archaeology and Anthropology, where his studies focused on paleoenvironments and human prehistory in North America. He lives with his husband at the foot of the Rockies and has worked in cultural resource management, real estate, landscaping, and has also slung dough in late night pizza joints, all the while writing and editing and writing some more.